I0565632

Darke Paranormal
Investigations

DARKE HOMECOMING

ROSANNA LEO

Darke Homecoming
ISBN # 978-1-80250-768-3
©Copyright Rosanna Leo 2024
Cover Art by Kelly Martin ©Copyright March 2024
Interior text design by Claire Siemaszkiewicz
Totally Bound Publishing

DARKE
HOMECOMING

Dedication

For all my beautiful freaks and weirdos.
You are loved.

Acknowledgements

I'd like to extend a hearty thanks to the team at Totally Bound Publishing for publishing this series and allowing me to bring my love of weirdness to my readers. Thank you so much to my editor Rebecca Baker. Rebecca, you have been wonderful and patient and I appreciate you letting me know when I've used certain words far too much!

Thank you to author Anise Eden, my friend and beta reader. I can't even tell you how much I cherish our friendship and the support you've given me over the years.

Thank you to the awesome Kelly Martin, for creating such stunning covers for this series. You brought my weird girls to life!

Thank you to Jacqueline Lee for all the support during this series and my previous series. Jacqueline, I appreciate you being there when I needed an extra pair of eyes, and for always sharing your love of the series with such enthusiasm.

When not writing, I work at my local public library. Two of my colleagues were instrumental in helping me access the materials I needed to research old Cabbagetown. Thank you to Bandy Dodhi and Elise Cole for your expertise and assistance. You are both incredible at your jobs and I'm so fortunate that I get to sit near you and soak it all up.

As we all know, libraries are under tremendous pressure right now. It is imperative that customers be able to access a wealth of materials. Book bans have no place in our society. We all need to support our local libraries. Donate, volunteer and check out items regularly. Support your favorite authors by suggesting their books for purchase. Every time you check out a book, that stat is recorded and it shows the library is a necessity in your community.

Finally, thank you to all my readers. Your love for this series and your reviews have meant so much to me.

Author's Note

My husband and I were on holiday in the Hudson Valley last year. Being a taphophile, much like Adelaide and Will, I wanted to visit the creepy Sleepy Hollow Cemetery. While there, I noticed a plain headstone, set amongst the more elaborate mausoleums and monuments. It was for a woman named Sarah Beckinsale, who died in 1894 at the age of twenty-eight. On her headstone was written, "Sheltered and safe from sorrow."

I was extremely moved by the emotion behind that statement. Frankly, I couldn't stop thinking about it and knew it had to be an element in Adelaide's story. I can only assume Sarah's life was a difficult one and I sincerely hope she rests easily now.

Of course, I had to give this story a Canadian connection and I immediately began researching the historic neighborhood of Cabbagetown. It's one of my favorite places to visit in downtown Toronto because of its picturesque homes and gardens. However, anyone who has lived in Cabbagetown for many years will know that its origins were a lot less picturesque. While there was wealth in the area, there was also extreme poverty. In the mid-1800s, more than 38,000 Irish Famine refugees arrived and they quickly formed the bulk of the urban poor, serving as workers in the many factories along the Don River. Their lives were harsh and they lived on the periphery of society. Infant and child mortality was high and malnutrition was a fact of life.

One of the factories near the Don River was the P.R. Lamb Glue and Blacking Manufactory. Peter Lamb was a successful businessman and his family were part of the Toronto elite. His factory operated for almost forty years, until it was destroyed by fire. Although it provided employment to many, it had a negative effect on the neighborhood, emitting foul odors and spilling noxious waste into the local waterways. In reading about it, I found myself wondering if such a place could leave a spiritual stain on that location.

Another early Cabbagetown landmark was the Don Vale House, which sat below the Toronto Necropolis from the late 1840s to about 1875. This public house was a place where poor workers could go after their shifts at the factories for drinking, cockfighting, gambling and boxing contests. After spying an image of the Don Vale House in John Ross Robertson's *Landmarks of Canada*, one in which the Necropolis headstones stood ominously in the background, I knew I had to make it part of my story.

A final note: if you travel to Cabbagetown, you may walk by the beautiful home that neighborhood children call the "Witch House." Like the home in my story, there is no history of witchcraft associated with it and it was given that name because a former owner hung a witch ornament near the front door.

I hope you love this homage to Cabbagetown history and that you've enjoyed living in the world of the Darke sisters!

Prologue

Toronto, August 2001

Adelaide Darke hated funerals, but probably not for the same reason other people did. For most, it was because of the grief, raw and twisting in their bellies. For others, it was the fact that attending one was a stark reminder of one's own unpredictable mortality.

In Adelaide's case, it was much simpler. She disliked funerals because they made her see things no one was supposed to see. Dead people, specifically.

Of course, she always saw dead people and it didn't matter where she went. She saw them in the cereal aisle at the grocery store, in her favorite nook at the public library's children's department and even in the lonely corners of her school. The dead lingered everywhere there had once been life, and when they saw Adelaide, they followed her and tried to talk to her. Sometimes she thought she talked to more dead people than living people. It wasn't even that she minded. It was more that the constant barrage of otherworldly communication left her zapped.

Funerals were the worst, though, in her experience, because spirit people saw them as a final opportunity to communicate with their loved ones. And as Adelaide had already learned in her ten short years of life, unfinished spirit business could cause a lot of unrest for the living.

She fidgeted in her place and glanced at her older sisters. Edwina, the eldest, didn't like funerals either. They always made her cry, which smudged her makeup. At sixteen years of age, Edwina spent a lot of time perfecting her look every morning, and she had a healthy disdain for anything that might cause mascara tracks.

Their other sister, Susannah, was just as uneasy at funerals, but it was because she said they made her feel sick. Even now, Susannah stood around the coffin with the rest of their family, chewing on her lip. She discreetly pushed her fist into her stomach, trying to force her feelings deep into that pit. Adelaide shook her head. Even as the youngest sister, she knew Susannah couldn't keep her feelings down forever.

Despite being young, the girls had been to several funerals, due to their grandparents having had several elderly brothers and sisters. So, Adelaide had had lots of chances to study her sisters' reactions, and those of the adults in their family.

Today's funeral was being held at the Necropolis, the old cemetery in downtown Toronto. It was for her great-uncle John, her grandmother's youngest brother. Uncle John hadn't been a churchgoer, so it was just a small service at the burial site. Everyone stood around the coffin as it was lowered into the big hole in the ground, while the priest said some prayers.

Adelaide was fairly sure the priest had been someone else's idea. She'd once overheard Uncle John talking to her mom about the church, and he'd called it "a corrupt collection of reprobates." She wasn't sure what "reprobate" meant but had a feeling it wasn't good.

Everyone looked so sad, which was kind of funny because Uncle John was standing a few feet away. A new spirit person, he watched his family with an amused expression on his face. He didn't look sick anymore at all and even had the roses back in his cheeks. With his hands on his hips, he seemed surprised to see everyone making such a fuss.

As the priest started yet another prayer, Uncle John waved at Adelaide. He pointed at the priest and made a goofy face.

She bit the inside of her cheek so she wouldn't laugh.

"I wondered if you'd see me today, Addy. I'm glad you can."

"*I see everyone*," she mouthed.

"Yup. Your granny told me that about you. You're just like she was when she was little."

Adelaide didn't remember her maternal grandmother. She'd died when Adelaide was a baby, but Mom always said Grandma knew her littlest granddaughter was "gifted." In fact, she'd passed on a necklace to her, one that Adelaide now wore every single day. Whenever she got scared, she touched it and remembered her grandma was always around her.

"I gotta get going, Addy," said Uncle John. "You be a good girl now, you hear?"

"I will, Uncle John," she said, forgetting to whisper.

"Don't get into too much trouble, but if you do, make it good!"

Adelaide giggled.

Her mother grabbed her hand and gave her 'the look.' "Addy, please."

"But it's just Uncle John. He wanted to say goodbye."

Mom frowned. She knew the dead talked to Adelaide, and she understood Addy couldn't help talking back to them, but it didn't mean she was comfortable with it.

Adelaide looked back over to Uncle John. He winked, danced a little jig and vanished. She couldn't be sad to see him go, not when he seemed so happy.

As the funeral ended and the adults chatted, Adelaide and her sisters walked around the graveyard, checking out some of the old headstones.

"I hope they don't take long," complained Susannah. She was twelve and Daddy always said that was the age for complaining. "I'm hungry and I don't feel good here."

"Cemeteries are cool places. They're full of history. You love history, Suz." Edwina ran over to one of the monuments. "Check it out. This guy died in 1870! That's like, ancient. I bet he haunts this place. Do you think so, Addy?"

Adelaide shrugged. "Nah, not that guy. He's long gone. Most of them don't stick around cemeteries, but some do." She turned to Susannah. "There's a dead lady standing next to you. That's why you don't feel good. But she doesn't want to scare you. You just remind her of her daughter."

Susannah bristled, glancing over her shoulder, and grabbed Edwina's arm.

"Ooh! Talking about ghosts in the spooky cemetery, are we?" Someone rushed up behind them, his laughter harsh and cutting. "There's no such thing as ghosts, you know. Addy, you're such a little weirdo."

Adelaide sighed. It was their cousin Geoffrey. Mom called him "a challenge." Dad called him "a pest."

Edwina whipped around first, her fists clenched. "Weirdo, huh? You say that like it's a bad thing. Wanna say it again, to our faces this time, Geoffrey?"

Although Geoffrey was the same age as Edwina, he hadn't reached the same maturity level. They went to the same high school but he still hung out around the elementary school so he could pick on younger kids and try to look like a big shot. He was always calling Adelaide names, but he was sneaky about it and never did it in front of the adults.

Susannah moved in front of Adelaide. "Yeah. Say it again, Geoffrey."

Adelaide stepped around her older sister and faced her bully. Her sisters always tried to protect her, but she wasn't afraid of him. "You should be nicer to people."

His lip curled. "Says who?"

"My spirit guide, Maria."

He laughed out loud. "Oh, well. If Maria says so."

Adelaide peered at him. "Maria said you're going to have a lot of bad relationships in your life. She said you're going to get married four times and divorced four times, and none of your wives are going to stick around because none of them will actually like you very much because you only care about yourself. Your kids won't want anything to do with you and it's possible you'll die alone one day. But you could change all that if you started being nice to others now."

He backed up a couple of paces, his nose wrinkled in horror. "Shut up. You're all a bunch of freaks." He shoved his hands in his dress pant pockets and headed back to where his parents were standing.

Edwina patted Adelaide's shoulder. "Are you okay?"

"Yeah, he doesn't bother me. Maria says he only bullies me because he has no friends. I think that's sad, but it doesn't mean I have to be nice to him. Maria said so."

Edwina and Susannah's eyes widened. That happened whenever Adelaide mentioned Maria.

Maria had first appeared to Adelaide when she was a baby, but no one else saw her. She gave her all kinds of good advice, like when to avoid a certain part of the schoolyard because the mean kids were gathered there. Maria also helped her talk to some of the dead people, but she also taught her how to be brave and to politely let the dead know when she wasn't in the mood to communicate. You had to be clear and firm with them, Maria said.

Adelaide liked Maria a lot, but her mom warned her it wasn't always a good thing to talk about her in public because she made people uncomfortable. Adelaide couldn't help it, though. Sometimes, Maria just sort of popped out! Whenever Addy was near something bad, dead or alive, Maria made noise. Lots of noise. That usually scared living people.

Adelaide and her sisters wandered around the Necropolis for a few more minutes, reading some of the headstones. They walked over to the iron fence at the edge of the cemetery and stared at the pretty houses across the street. Dad said their neighborhood, Cabbagetown, had so many pretty houses because it was so old and they didn't build homes like that anymore. Adelaide loved the houses, especially the big one right across the street. Mom said it was garish because it had so many colors, but Addy loved that. The bottom half was made out of red brick and there were blue tiles on the top half. The roof had a lot of swirly designs that Dad called "gingerbread."

Adelaide wanted to live in the gingerbread house someday, even though the neighborhood kids called it the Witch House. She knew a witch didn't really live there. It was just a nice old lady who had a cute witch ornament hanging by her front door. Still, some of the neighborhood kids avoided the place on Halloween night. She definitely didn't understand that. The lady gave out full-sized chocolate bars! Last year, she put two of them in Addy's bag.

As she licked her lips, remembering those chocolate bars, someone appeared at the top front window. It was a girl. She had blonde hair and she looked like she was about Adelaide's age. She waved at Addy.

So, Addy waved back.

Their parents came to collect them. "Who are you waving at, Addy?" asked Mom.

"The girl in the window of the Witch House."

"I don't see anyone."

"She's on the top floor."

"There's no one in that window, sweetheart."

Adelaide looked again. Sure enough, the girl was still there.

Her heart beat the way it always did when anyone doubted her. "She's there. I see her. She has blonde hair with a white ribbon in it, and she looks really friendly. I promise, she's there." She understood that she saw things others couldn't see, but sometimes it upset her when they acted like she was lying. Her throat hurt and she wanted to cry, but she squeezed the hurt down into her tummy, like Susannah always did.

"It's okay, love," said her mother. "I believe that you see her and I'm sure she's happy you can see her. I'm sorry I doubted you. I sometimes forget you have a different sort of sight. Time to head home, girls."

Their parents led them to the cemetery entrance and onto Winchester Street. Adelaide kicked the dirt as she trudged behind the others. When they got to the corner, she looked back toward the house's window.

The girl was still there, waving, but she looked unhappy now that they were leaving. She leaned on the windowsill, slouching.

Maria told her that spirit people sometimes got lonely. It was one of the reasons they tried talking to living people. That, and sometimes they had unfinished business. This girl looked lonely too and Adelaide wished they could be friends. She waited until her family members weren't looking, then waved back, keeping her hand close to her body.

"How about we all stop for a cone at the ice cream parlor across the street?" asked Dad.

Edwina and Susannah started talking about what flavors of ice cream they were going to get, but Adelaide didn't say anything.

She didn't feel like having ice cream. She just wanted to go home and read her new book about Yoda.

Like the girl in the window, she felt alone sometimes too.

Chapter One

Toronto, present day

It wasn't unusual for Adelaide Darke to encounter handsome men in the cemetery, but nine times out of ten, those men were dead.

This handsome dude, on the other hand, was definitely alive.

She sat on her favorite bench in the Necropolis, the one that perched in the shade of an overgrown willow tree, and tried not to appear too obvious as she ogled him. She held up her book, a dog-eared and worn copy of a behind-the-scenes guide to the making of *Star Wars*, and discreetly cast her eye toward him.

The man led a small group of people toward one of the graves, about twenty feet away from where Adelaide sat. He was tall, white and slim, with angular features, ones that were somewhat softened by his tousled sandy hair. It was a warm summer's day and he was dressed in shorts, sneakers and a gray T-shirt.

Adelaide peered at the familiar logo on the shirt, an illustration of Edward Gorey's *The Gashlycrumb Tinies*.

She had the same shirt. They clearly shared the same dark sense of humor.

The view just got better and better.

The man gestured toward the grave, a red stone obelisk, and spoke to the people in his group. "This is the monument for Thornton and Lucie Blackburn. Enslaved in Kentucky, the Blackburns managed several daring escapes over the years. At one point, when Thornton was imprisoned, the Black community rose up in protest, an event now known as the Blackburn Riots. Eventually, the couple escaped for good and settled in Toronto in 1834. Thornton established the city's first taxi business in 1837. Known as 'The City,' it consisted of a horse and carriage. The business grew over the years, giving the Blackburns resources to assist other enslaved people with their escapes. They remained active in the community and with anti-slavery activities, and helped to build Little Trinity Church. When Thornton died in 1890, his estate encompassed eighteen-thousand dollars and six properties in Toronto. Lucie passed away five years later. In 1985, the remains of their home were discovered under a local school. After an archaeological dig, a plaque was erected to commemorate this amazing couple. They were deemed 'Persons of National Historic Significance' in 1999."

He gestured for the group to follow him. "Now, let's head over to the grave of Ned Hanlan, Canada's famed professional rower."

He must be the new tour guide at the Necropolis. The previous tour guide, Nancy, had told Adelaide someone would be replacing her.

Because Adelaide hung out at the cemetery a lot, probably more than her sisters thought was healthy, she'd gotten to know Nancy. When the guide had mentioned she was retiring, Adelaide had assumed her replacement would be...similar.

"Another old lady, you mean?"

"Ssh, Maria. Not now."

She must have said the words louder than she thought because the hot tour guide glanced in her direction, a curious expression on his face. He led his group toward the Hanlan grave.

Great. Yet another person who thought she was a weirdo for talking to herself when she wasn't actually talking to herself.

Maria had been with Adelaide for as long as she could remember. Adelaide's recollection of her early years was remarkably vivid, including the first time Maria had materialized. Addy had been in her crib, happily gurgling away, when all of a sudden, a little girl had entered the room. She'd smiled at Addy and held out her hand, saying they would be best friends forever, that she would take care of her. Even at such a tender age, Adelaide had experienced a surreal calmness and a sense that everything was right.

They'd been inseparable ever since. Maria's outward form had changed over the years, growing along with Adelaide. When she saw her now, she presented as an adult. Maria had guided her through tough situations and had helped her through her most difficult paranormal investigations. With her sisters Edwina and Susannah, Adelaide ran Darke Paranormal Investigations, and they'd made a name for themselves by clearing their clients' homes and businesses of unwanted spirit people.

So, basically, she and Maria were a package deal. As much as she was at peace with her strange reality, she still couldn't help feeling like an outsider sometimes.

"He's attractive. Definitely has that 'I-was-a-goth-in-high-school' vibe," Maria teased. *"Just your type."*

Adelaide frowned and shoved her book back into her tote bag. She pulled out a green apple and angrily nibbled it.

"What? You know I'm right. Don't you have that exact same shirt?"

"Irrelevant," Adelaide mumbled behind her apple.

Curious about the new guide, she got up from the bench and followed his group discreetly, pretending to read a couple of the headstones. Of course, she didn't really need to read any of them to learn about the occupants of the graves. All she needed to do was close her eyes and concentrate on the person, or touch the monuments, and images would flood her brain.

It was a lot to take at times, but Adelaide had learned how to filter the information and the messages from the dead.

It didn't mean they didn't sneak up on her sometimes.

The tour guide hit a few of the other graves that Nancy had included on her tour. George Brown, a Father of Confederation. William Lyon Mackenzie, rebel and Toronto's first mayor. Kay Christie, one of only two Canadian nurses to have been taken prisoner in World War II.

Every so often, the guide's gaze strayed toward Adelaide.

She hung back, conscious of the fact that she wasn't a paying customer. She didn't want him to think she was trying to get the tour for free.

He approached another grave and turned to it, a wistful expression on his face. "I think, of all the monuments here at the Necropolis, this one means the most to me. It's not flashy, like some of the others. It's not dedicated to a famous person. The headstone is simple plain gray marble. What fascinates me most is the inscription. 'Sarah Byrne, died Nov. 24, 1860. Aged 28 years. Sheltered and safe from sorrow.'"

He paused, never lifting his gaze from the headstone. "Sarah Byrne was an Irish immigrant, one of many who escaped Ireland during the Great Famine. Although she didn't have to deal with famine here in Toronto, her life would not have been an easy one. Sarah's family lived in a worker's cottage at the north end of the cemetery, on Amelia Street. For people like the Byrnes, there was plenty of hardship, poverty and loss. In fact, Sarah lost all her children. During the time Sarah was alive, Irish Catholic immigrants lived on the edge of society and formed the greater part of the urban poor. My own ancestors came here on the 'coffin ships' from Ireland, ships that were so rife with overcrowding and sickness that many of those passengers never made it."

His voice cracked. "'Sheltered and safe from sorrow.' And she was only twenty-eight years old. Well, we've got a couple more stops. Watch your step on the tree root as you follow me around the bend."

Moved by the guy's words and the emotion in his voice, Adelaide approached Sarah Byrne's burial place. She'd never really noticed this grave before on her previous cemetery jaunts. It looked like so many of the other headstones. Still, the poignant inscription made her pause.

Out of habit, she touched the marble stone, curious to learn something more about the woman resting under it. A terrible wave of sadness washed over Adelaide, distressing her to her core. It was an overwhelming, clawing sensation and it dug its nails into her being.

"Be careful," warned Maria.

All at once, Adelaide's gaze was drawn to some movement at the far end of the cemetery. A spirit woman glided between the monuments, her face turned toward the tour group. Her Victorian garb was torn and dirty and her brown hair hung loose around her shoulders. She was pale in the face, paler than anyone ever should be. Her dead eyes were lit with a frightening sort of focus. She walked right in front of Adelaide without sparing her even a glance.

Strange. They always come right to me.

Instead, she headed toward the tour guide. All her attention was concentrated on him.

As the man continued his talk, leading his group to several other graves, the spirit woman followed. She snaked between the tourists, even passing through a few of them, her unsettling gaze never faltering. At one point, she extended a hand toward the guide, as if trying to latch onto him.

"*That might be a problem,*" Maria said.

Immediately on edge, Adelaide put up her mental wards. Over the years, she'd learned how to protect herself from invasive spirits. In general, they swarmed her once they sensed her light, but she was able to erect a sort of barrier when the attention from the dead became a bit too much.

But this woman didn't even seem interested in her.

Without trying to connect directly with the dead woman, Adelaide tried to glean as much information as she could about her.

All she saw was harrowing anguish.

"Who is she, Maria?"

"*She is darkness.*"

Maria could be cryptic sometimes.

The guy finished up his tour and thanked the others for joining him. A few people lingered to ask him questions, but most of them scattered quickly, obviously having had enough of cemeteries. Adelaide understood. Places like the Necropolis oozed creepy, gothic atmosphere.

As it happened, Adelaide was quite comfortable among creepy, gothic things. She understood dead people.

Living people, though? Not so much.

"You have to tell him," Maria urged.

"And say what, exactly? 'A dead woman has the hots for you?'" Normally, Adelaide didn't have an issue with approaching strangers with messages from the dead, but this guy intimidated her with his tousled hair, chiseled jaw and superior taste in T-shirts.

"Tell him. If she lingers, he's not safe."

"Okay, okay. Just let me do it in my own way. No outbursts, please."

The guy said goodbye to the last tourist and headed over. His generous mouth curled with what looked like a shy sort of interest. He was completely oblivious to the gruesome specter following him.

Adelaide's face heated.

"Sorry to bother you," he said. "I couldn't help but notice that you seemed interested in the tour. We run them every couple of weeks."

"Oh, I know. I knew Nancy, the previous guide."

"So, you're a…regular, here at the cemetery?"

And here we go. Cue judgment in three…two…

"Because I love it here," he interjected. "So much history in one place and it's really beautiful. You can see why Victorian people made coming to the Necropolis a bit of an event. They'd come to pay their respects to dead loved ones and hang out for a few hours, having picnics and catching up with family."

Hmm. He really is a nerd, just like me. "Yeah, right. And, um, yes. I guess you could say I'm a regular." As a psychic medium, Adelaide needed lots of time in the fresh air, to break up the moments spent in the presence of the deceased. Aside from her work with Darke Paranormal Investigations, she was a professional medium and did a lot of readings. All that spiritual energy could be draining. "I live nearby and I come for a lot of walks here."

The whole time they spoke, the spirit woman hovered near him, drinking him in.

As much as it put Adelaide on guard, she could understand the fascination. Up close, he was super cute. He had amber brown eyes and the cheekbones of a soap opera actor. There was something lovely about the way he was smiling at her, but Adelaide knew that smile would disappear the moment he figured out she was a weird girl with an interest in dead things.

She was definitely interested in the dead thing clinging to him.

He held out his hand. "I'm Will Moran."

"Adelaide Darke." She waited a nanosecond before grasping his hand. Touching others could sometimes be problematic for people like her because it tended to release the hounds, so to speak. Sure enough, as she slid her fingers against his, a barrage of other spirits appeared behind him, wanting to pass on messages. Adelaide tuned in for a few seconds, in case anyone had pressing concerns, but they were mostly just trying to share their love. She released his hand and silently held his dead relatives at bay. She couldn't afford to become invested in his family backstory, not while he had another, darker entity hovering around him.

The spirit woman gazed at him like she wanted to make him her next meal.

Somewhere in the background, Maria began to cough. That was her way of warning the living that shit was about to go down. Adelaide quickly covered her mouth and pretended to be the one coughing.

"You okay?" asked Will.

Begging Maria to settle down, Adelaide held up a finger. "Sorry about that. Seasonal allergies." Once she was convinced Maria would behave, she resumed the conversation. "So, are you a full-time tour guide?"

"No, that's just a fun side hustle." He rolled his eyes, obviously aware that not everyone would consider that fun. "I work for the City of Toronto Museums. We're opening a new location right here in Cabbagetown, in one of the old workers' cottages on Amelia Street. I'm the lucky guy who gets to curate it."

"Amelia Street. Where Sarah Byrne lived."

"You really were listening." His voice rose in delight. "And yeah. Believe it or not, that's exactly where I'm working. The City was able to acquire the Byrne house when it went up for sale a while back, so that'll be the museum's home."

"Interesting." Adelaide tried once again to extract information from the dead woman, but she refused to engage. "It must be fascinating to be a curator."

He leaned in conspiratorially. "Well, I think so, but I'm kind of geeky that way. How about you, Adelaide?"

Gosh, her name sounded nice in his mouth. *Hello*, she reminded herself. *There's a dead woman hanging off his every word, just as much as you are.* "Addy's fine."

"Addy, then." He grinned, nibbling his bottom lip.

Is he flirting? I think he's flirting. It hadn't happened in a while, so she wasn't sure.

"*He's totally flirting*," added Maria.

"So, what do you do, Addy?"

She hesitated with how much to reveal. After a number of tragically bad dates recently, she'd grown hesitant talking about her career. Hell, her vocation.

On one date, when she'd mentioned she was a medium and paranormal investigator, the dude had accused her of flat-out lying. Another date had teased her to the point of annoyance. A third one had actually tried to argue that there was no such thing as ghosts. She had no time for those people. Besides, he'd shut up pretty quickly when Adelaide listed off by name all the spirits flitting around him.

Of course, it wasn't as if Will Moran had asked her out on a date. "You wouldn't believe me if I told you what I do."

"Try me."

She'd likely never see him again. For that reason, she decided to put it all out there and amuse herself with his reaction. "Okay. I'm a psychic medium. I do readings and I investigate haunted locations."

Wait for it....

In a second, he'd avert his gaze. He'd make some limp excuse about needing to be somewhere, anywhere but there. He'd head for the freaking hills.

Only he didn't. Will angled his head and narrowed his eyes, without even a twitch in his smile. "And you called *my* work interesting?"

"I run a paranormal investigation group with my sisters. I literally see the dead all around us."

"Wow. Look, I don't want to take advantage, but do you mind me asking if you see any dead around me?"

For the first time since she'd appeared, the spirit woman looked directly at Adelaide, her cloudy eyes full of a cold awareness. She brought a finger to her lips and said, "*Sshhh.*" She then drifted away. Immediately, the atmosphere around them lightened.

Thank goodness. She was gone.

"Nope, no dead around you." Adelaide cleared her throat. "Sorry. That's not quite accurate. When we shook hands, I saw your grandmother, an uncle and a great-grandfather. They all want you to know they're proud of you."

"Really?"

"Yeah. Their names were Nell, Jake and Francis."

Will's mouth popped open.

"You did ask. I'm just passing it on."

"No, that's fine. It's awesome, actually. Thank you."

Her own lips parted on a surprised breath. She was unaccustomed to responses that weren't dripping in skepticism and disdain.

"I was really close to my grandmother. You've made my day, Addy Darke." Will chuckled. It was a deep and heady sound, one that sent pleasant shivers up and down her arms. "You know, my colleagues insist that the museum site is haunted."

"I wouldn't be surprised. An old worker's cottage would be full of history. Have you had any experiences there?"

"There's an energy about the place, but that's about it." His cell phone buzzed. "I have to leave for an appointment, but could I...call you some time?"

"Sure. Just be aware we already have a few people waiting for our services."

"Ah. I'm sure you do." He dragged a hand through his hair. "But I wasn't actually thinking of that. I was hoping maybe we could grab a coffee sometime because I think you're really interesting and I like talking to you." His voice rose at the end of the statement, as if he wasn't sure he should have admitted it.

"Oh." It didn't even occur to her that he was asking her out. "Yeah, coffee's cool."

"Great." Will asked her to put her number in his phone, then gave her his. "I'll be in touch."

Adelaide stared at the new number in her contacts. Will Moran would never call, not after he'd had a chance to reconsider it. "Looking forward to it."

"All right. Talk to you soon, Addy." He waved and walked away, looking once over his shoulder to give her another cheeky grin.

Her knees wobbled a little.

That smile should come with a warning.

Adelaide waited a few minutes then followed Will out of the cemetery, passing under the decorative Gothic Revival entryway. When she got to the intersection of Winchester and Sumach Streets, she glanced out of habit toward the Witch House, the property that had so fascinated her as a child.

Just like all those years ago, the little blonde girl waved at her from the top window, unravaged by time.

"Oh my stars. She's still there."

Adelaide had passed the house often in her travels over the years but hadn't seen the child since she was one herself. Back then, the girl would appear every time Adelaide walked past the house, but over time she'd faded, even for Addy. She moved closer, hoping it was some other blonde girl, but it wasn't. Everything was the same. Her smile, her outfit, even the ribbon in her hair. There was a gauziness about her, another clear indication she no longer belonged on this plane.

Her heart tugging, Adelaide waved back. Was she stuck there or, like some spirit people, did she just pop in every so often to visit her old home?

Something told Adelaide the girl was unable to leave. That, or she refused to leave.

A sign in the front yard of the house caught her attention. She drew nearer. It was a real estate sign.

The Witch House was for sale, and there was an open house coming up soon.

Still waving at Adelaide, the girl faded away.

Her skin tingling, Addy pulled out her cell phone and messaged her sisters.

Chapter Two

Will Moran approached the Amelia Street house, balancing a box of donuts in his hands and a sense of wonder in his heart. He'd wanted to get an early start today and had left his place on Salisbury Avenue as the sun was still rising. Now, as he reached his workplace, the pink tinge in the sky cast a rosy aura over the house, infusing it with warmth.

For the hundredth time, Will uttered a thanks that he'd snagged this job and got to work in this amazing place. Every time he passed the sign in the front yard, his heart began to pound. *The Cabbagetown Museum...opening this fall!*

Will Moran, Curator.

He'd never felt such a curious sense of destiny in applying for a role before. Yes, part of it was because he'd finally made the leap from assistant curator to curator, but it wasn't just that.

Will had grown up in Cabbagetown, just a few streets away, and had lived in the vibrant neighborhood his entire thirty-four years of life. His ancestors had lived in a simple worker's cottage, much like the Amelia Street house, although that dwelling had since been torn down to make way for a modern home. He'd spent his career and had tailored his education around learning about the struggles of early Cabbagetown residents, and to be put in charge of such an important project filled him with awe.

Plus, his home on Salisbury Avenue was just a couple of streets away, so the commute to work was pretty sweet.

All in all, walking to his job site every morning felt more like coming home.

He took a moment in the quiet of early morning, as he often did, to stand outside the house and luxuriate in its vibe. The rest of the team wouldn't be there for at least another hour and he loved being alone on the property, pretending it was all his.

There was nothing grand about the old Byrne house, but like the other historic properties in the Toronto History Museums department, it was a snapshot from another era. Over the past few years, he'd had the opportunity to work on projects at Mackenzie House, the home of Toronto's first mayor, William Lyon Mackenzie. He'd assisted at Montgomery's Inn in the west end, a Georgian-style inn built in 1830. And he'd done some work at Spadina House, a dazzling uptown mansion.

But none of those properties excited Will the way this one did. Maybe it was the romantic Irishman in him—having learned a bit about the Byrnes, the original inhabitants, he felt a sort of kinship to them. He was over the moon at the prospect of sharing their story and others with visitors, but the sense of responsibility and the need to get it right kept him up at night too.

At least, the place now looked ready, although there was a lot more to be done. The preservation work was complete, thank God. The team had put in long hours to restore the house, everything from its distinctive finial and bargeboard to the white stucco cladding, to the gable over the centered door. The house itself was tiny by modern standards. Originally, it would have consisted of only a kitchen and a family room on the main floor and two small bedrooms upstairs. An outhouse would have served as the original plumbing. However, one of the previous owners had updated it to include a couple of extra rooms in the back and modern washrooms.

Because of these additions, they had enough space for plenty of displays, as well as a museum office and a gift shop. A portion of the interior had been designed to look as it would have in the mid-nineteenth century. The idea behind the design was to sweep visitors into the past, to give them a glimpse of a working family's lifestyle.

Will unlocked the front door and entered, disarming the security system. A cool blast of air hit his cheek, making him shiver. That happened a lot. He'd have to get someone to check the vents.

"I'm home, Sarah," he called into the empty house, bringing the donut box into the office for his colleagues. He wasn't sure why he addressed Sarah Byrne every time he walked into the building, but of all the Byrnes, hers was the story that touched him most. There was a part of him that wanted her to be proud of what they'd done here.

Maybe he was more like Grandma Nell than he'd thought. His grandmother had always said that old houses had personalities, that one should be respectful of their quirks. That was his grandmother. She'd attributed her fanciful temperament to her Irish blood. When Will was little, she would tell him all sorts of stories, ones peopled with fairies, changelings and banshees.

Grandma Nell.

Adelaide Darke had mentioned her, claiming she was around Will, that she was proud of him. What Adelaide might not have gleaned was the fact that his grandmother had passed away only a month ago. Even though she'd been ailing for some time, her death had still come as a shock.

Even now, when Will thought about the loving woman who'd helped to raise him, his throat scratched and his eyes stung. Nell Moran had been a shell of herself before her death — the dementia had annihilated her personality. She hadn't recognized any of the family at the end, and Will still felt as if he hadn't really had a chance to say a proper goodbye.

Had Adelaide Darke seen that too?

Sighing, he relegated Grandma Nell to the painful pocket in his chest where her memory now resided and thought of nicer things.

Like Adelaide. The cute medium had thrown him for a loop, and in more ways than one.

It had only been a couple of days since he'd met her in the Necropolis, and while his finger had hovered over her contact information on his phone several times already, he'd resisted texting her. He was so bad at dating etiquette. Was it too soon to call? Was it better to text? Would he look like an overeager creep?

Some guys might choose to wait, to string her along, but that wasn't his style. He wanted to see her again. There was something so intriguing about her.

Will tapped his cell phone, impatient. "I mean, it's been almost forty-eight hours." Besides, once he got started at work, he'd be busy all day long and probably into the evening as well. "Shoot your shot, dude."

Will: Hi Addy. I enjoyed meeting you the other day. Feel like grabbing that coffee some time this week?

"There. Done." Coffee was casual enough so there wouldn't be any pressure. *Geez.* For some reason, he was more nervous than the day he'd applied for his job, and he wasn't sure why. Perhaps it was because there had been a curious feeling of destiny in meeting Addy as well.

She'd seemed interested. When she'd handed over her phone for him to enter his details, a smile had tickled her sensual mouth. She'd tucked her bobbed chestnut-brown hair behind her ear and her dark eyes had flashed.

At the same time, there had also been a wariness about her. When she'd told him about being a medium, there had been a slight tone in her voice, as if she'd been testing him. Whatever yardstick she'd been using to take his measure, he hoped he hadn't fallen short.

Will pulled up the blinds on the front windows of the museum to let some light in. The building faced the north end of the Necropolis, Section "T," in particular. He doubted most people would choose to live across the street from a cemetery, as the former residents of the Amelia Street house had. However, death had played a big part in the lives of poor Cabbagetown residents, especially those from Sarah Byrne's time.

For neighborhood kids, himself included, the cemetery had always been a great, big playground. How many times had he careened down its hills with his pals, dodging headstones, or played hide-and-seek amongst the larger monuments? Too many times to count.

His phone pinged, arousing him from his nostalgic daydreams.

Adelaide: Hi Will. I enjoyed meeting you too. I'd love to grab coffee with you...on one condition. Please answer the following question honestly. How do you feel about Star Wars?

Will laughed out loud. He had a feeling he was going to like this woman.

Will: You mean my favorite fictional universe of all time?

Adelaide: Excellent answer. How does Saturday sound? Beans at 7?

Will: I will be there, Ms. Darke. I'm excited to hear your thoughts on who shot first, Han or Greedo.

Adelaide: Oh, it's on. She ended her text with a gif of Han Solo winking.

Will: Out of curiosity, what would have happened if I'd told you I hate Star Wars?

Adelaide: We would still have had coffee, but I would have judged you.

Will shot her another smiley face and put his phone down. "Adelaide Darke, I might already be in love with you."

Icy fingers danced across the back of his neck.

Will whipped around, but there was no one there.

The sound of footsteps racing upstairs chilled him to the bone. Even as Will turned toward the stairs, the mysterious footsteps hit the upper landing. They echoed above him, slow and deliberate.

He froze. As he expelled a long breath, it appeared before him, a wispy plume of air more suited to the dead of winter than to high summer.

A woman's voice sounded over his shoulder, charming with its Irish lilt. *"Hello, my darlin'."*

"What the hell?" Will did another spin.

Laughter erupted in the room.

There was something about the laugh that was so familiar, and the accent had sounded so much like his grandmother's.

He took a step. "Grandma Nell? Are you here?"

There was no response.

His brain went through the motions of piecing out some kind of explanation, but nothing made sense. He was clearly alone in the house. If anyone had broken in before he got there, it would have set off the alarm.

"It's okay if you want to talk to me, Grandma. You're welcome here. I hope you know that."

Was she trying to communicate beyond what she had relayed to Addy? Will was open to it. Frankly, he'd been hoping for some sort of sign that Gran was okay, that she hadn't forgotten him after all.

Even though his feet didn't want to cooperate, he managed to move to the bottom of the stairs. He slowly looked up, expecting to see someone standing at the top. Of course, that wasn't the case.

Then why did he feel another presence? It vibrated all around him, filling the space with its energy. Cloying and thick, it hampered his breathing.

Not really his grandmother's style.

"Sarah? Is that you?"

As soon as the words were out of his mouth, he felt silly. What was he even doing, talking to a dead woman as if she were capable of hearing him?

More out of instinct than anything else, Will looked about for a weapon of some sort. He grabbed a pewter candleholder from one of the tables, brandishing it at his side. His throat constricting with a sense of foreboding, he ascended the stairs. He inspected both bedrooms and the small washroom, but found no one, and no evidence of a break-in.

Once again, a cool breeze passed over his shoulders. He braced himself, expecting those icy fingers to stroke the bare skin of his neck. Stricken with a sense he was being watched, Will clutched the pewter candleholder and did a slow circle of the room.

When the front door opened downstairs, he almost jumped out of his skin.

"You here, Will?" Miguel Ruiz, the head of their programming team, called up to him.

Will responded, as his pulse started to regulate. "Yeah. Just upstairs, scaring myself."

Miguel bounded up the stairs and stopped short outside the bedroom door Will was in. "Whoa. What happened?"

"I, uh, heard a voice."

"Is that why you're holding onto that candlestick like it's a baseball bat?"

"Yeah. I thought I heard footsteps but…"

"I'm telling you, something's not right in this building." He looked over his shoulder, clearly expecting to see some Cabbagetown equivalent of Jacob Marley. "As soon as we started this gig, I got a bad vibe."

Will understood, but what was he supposed to do about a vibe? Yes, he'd had some off-putting moments too, mostly the sensation that he was never truly alone, even when he was clearly alone. But he'd also had times when he'd been convinced he was seeing a shadow figure out of the corner of his eye, and it turned out to be a coatrack. "It's just a vibe. My imagination got carried away."

Miguel raised an eyebrow. "Okay. So, there's no need for you to be wielding a candlestick, huh?"

Will lowered his arm.

"Look, Will. You and I have worked in a bunch of old properties, but none of them has felt like this one. Even Terri came to me the other day because she swore she heard footsteps in an empty room. Alison has heard it too. Neither of them gets spooked easily. Maybe we need to call in a priest or something. A medium, even."

"I don't know. It seems a bit much." Will hesitated. "Actually, I met a medium the other day."

"Wait, what? How did you meet a medium?"

"We ran into each other at the Necropolis and just started talking."

"Of course, you did, Cemetery Boy."

He ignored the dig. "She's cute. I'm having coffee with her this weekend."

Miguel's expression changed from one of consternation to mirth. "Coffee? Like, a date? I thought you didn't have time for dating."

Will had indeed said that several times. He'd been working with Miguel for years and they'd grown tight, so Miguel knew all his excuses. His friend had encouraged him to get out there a bit more, but Will freely admitted he could become obsessive with his work. He might look good on paper to a potential date, but most of the women he'd socialized with had learned it was hard to pry him away from his projects. It was a problem, he acknowledged that, but this gig was the most important one yet and he couldn't screw it up.

That being said, there was no way he was canceling his coffee with Addy. He'd make time for that.

"So, when do I get to meet your cute medium friend? You should swing by the museum with her after your coffee, maybe ask her if she'd be so kind as to remove the scary-ass dead people from the building."

"Miguel."

"Okay, okay. We're all imagining things, I guess."

"I think we all just need to take a breath. As for Addy, we've barely even said two words to each other. Let me get to know her a bit before I ask her to whip out her candles and holy water."

"Addy, eh?" Miguel chuckled darkly. "Ooh, the way you said her name, all breathy-like. You must really have the hots for her."

Will headed downstairs. "I'm shutting this conversation down." He called over his shoulder. "Feel free to keep the ghost company, though!"

Miguel tore after him.

Chapter Three

On Saturday morning, when Adelaide and her sisters arrived for the open house, they weren't alone. A small crowd had gathered on the sidewalk and the lawn. There was considerable interest in the Witch House.

Adelaide's attention was drawn toward the upper window, where the blonde girl waved.

"Still there?" Susannah asked.

"Yeah. I can't even tell you how surprised I was to see her again. I knew she was a ghost, way back when, but I'd always figured she'd moved on."

Edwina, who was also able to see the dead, squinted toward the window. "Well, she's not showing herself to me. She must want your attention, Addy."

Adelaide wasn't surprised. She'd always gotten the impression the little girl didn't appear to everyone. "Okay, here's the deal. Considering there's lots of interest in the house, I'm guessing the agent will be kept busy. If things slow down, I'll need you guys to run interference for me so I can get upstairs and make a connection. If you get a chance, see if you can dig up any dirt on the history of the house."

The front door opened and the real estate agent appeared. She was as polished as any other real estate agent, her brown hair expertly coiffed and her pantsuit pristine, but Adelaide spied an inner dishevelment. The woman's eye twitched as she greeted the guests and her voice quavered. "Welcome, everyone. I'm Cindy Lawrence, a broker with the Bond Team. Sorry for the, uh, slight delay. Just making sure everything was perfect. Please come in and jot your names and email addresses on the contact sheet by the door."

As the others filed in, Adelaide made eye contact with her sisters. "That woman has seen a ghost."

Susannah and Edwina both nodded. They knew the look as well, that distracted expression that said, *I just saw something that wasn't supposed to be there and I'm not sure how to react.*

Adelaide rubbed her palms together as she entered the infamous Witch House, the colorful home that had captivated her imagination all those years ago. Unfortunately, as soon as she crossed the threshold into the expansive foyer, she was disappointed.

"Wow." Edwina's voice was flat. "It's so…white."

Everything was alabaster, the walls, the draperies and even the furniture. The elegant Victorian home had been transformed into something uber-modern. It looked more like an industrial condo than a well-loved home. There was a cool sophistication about the design scheme, but it was completely wrong for this house.

Adelaide certainly couldn't live in a place like that. She'd spill red wine or pasta sauce within a week of moving in.

"As you can see," Cindy Lawrence said to the group in the foyer, "this grand old property has been fully renovated from top to bottom. What was once a dark and dreary interior is now flooded with light. The airy open plan makes living ideal, and is perfect for busy families. Please have a look at the custom-designed kitchen while you're here. With top-of-the-line appliances and finishes, it belongs on the pages of a style magazine." She smiled, but there was still a tic about her eye.

"It feels sterile," Adelaide said.

Susannah scratched her head of blonde waves. "They've removed all the interesting period features. A house like this wouldn't have had an *open plan*. It would have had rooms, proper rooms. Where are the carved moldings and high skirting boards? And look what they did to the fireplace. What was probably once an ornate wood burner is now that gas monstrosity. I bet the Cabbagetown historical society would be up in arms."

Edwina grumbled. "No self-respecting witch would ever live in this place. It's so shiny it makes my head hurt."

Just then, a foul odor reached Adelaide's nostrils. Thick and acrid, the smell was unmistakable.

Something was on fire.

But that wasn't just it. The stench was layered, as if something else was woven into it, and it was unlike anything Addy had ever smelled. She clapped a hand over her mouth and nose.

On instinct, she checked the gas fireplace, but there was no way it could have produced that funk. No one else seemed to be aware of it. The visitors to the house continued to wander through the space, unbothered. Not a single person grimaced or gagged.

And yet, to Adelaide, it was everywhere. It oozed from the walls, from the fabric of the furniture, even from the paintings on the wall. When she realized she didn't have the urge to cough, she understood the origin of the smell was preternatural.

"Do you smell that?" she whispered to her sisters.

Edwina wrinkled her nose. "The man with the heavy cologne?"

"No." Once again, the ghosts of the Witch House were speaking directly to Adelaide. "There's a terrible burning smell here, some sort of residual energy." Most of the time when a spirit person chose to manifest for Adelaide, it was as a full-body apparition or a voice. She didn't often experience smells, so this had to be an important detail. "I'm going upstairs."

Bypassing the designer kitchen, she headed toward the wide staircase. As she moved, the stench of burning began to fade. She silently called out to any spirit inhabitants of the house. *My name's Addy and I come here with respect. I'd like to talk to the little blonde girl who sits in the upper window. I don't mean you any harm. I just want to meet you and find out if I can help you in any way.*

A couple passed her, already on their way down. "Let's go, Tyler," the woman said to her companion. "I don't like this place. Something feels off about it."

"What did I tell you about watching all those horror movies, babe?"

Adelaide shot the woman a sympathetic glance, recognizing a fellow sensitive. Once she was upstairs, she did a quick tour of the upper floor. There were three spacious bedrooms, all just as white as the rooms below. A few other open house guests wandered about this floor but no one paid her any heed as she completed her circuit.

At the end of the hall, there was a door. She almost missed it because it was painted white like everything else. Even the doorknob was a clear crystal that faded into the background.

Feeling a sizzle of energy, she walked down the hallway. When she turned the doorknob, she found it locked.

Looking around to make sure no one was in earshot, Adelaide called out in a quiet voice. "I'm here, and I'd really like to talk to you. Could you come to the door, please?"

She closed her eyes and opened herself up to any and all impressions from the other side. At first, she was hit with a sense of fear, then a tingle of dread. Even more alarming, she got another whiff of burning. With each breath, it coated her lungs, restricting her airways. This time, she did want to cough, ached to cough.

Maria, take it off me, please. I can't breathe.

As always, Maria came through, clearing Adelaide's passages. Sucking in clean air, Adelaide once again addressed the spirit. "Hello? Are you there?"

From the other side of the door came a quiet, trembling voice. "Daddy? Where are you?"

Adelaide's eyes shot open. She rested her palm on the door. "Can you tell me your name, sweetie?"

The girl hiccuped. "Why won't you come, Daddy?" She began to cry. The soft noises, so laden with confusion and forlornness, broke Adelaide's heart. She was obviously all alone in her realm.

"Don't cry, honey. It's me, Addy, the one you waved to from the window. I'm going to help you, okay? Can you tell me your name?"

But as the cries faded, Adelaide knew the girl was retreating.

She knocked on the door. "Sweetie, talk to me."

A young couple had just arrived on the upper landing. When they noticed Adelaide speaking to a closed door, they paused, and hurried back down.

Unconcerned, Adelaide recited a prayer of progression, meant to usher spirits toward the light. However, even though it had worked with numerous stuck entities, it didn't work with the girl. Even now, she heard soft creaks above as the girl returned to her room.

"Maria," Adelaide whispered, "what's her story? Can you get through to her?"

"The little one has learned how to create walls of protection around herself. She won't let me in, but she likes you."

"How do I help her?"

"She won't leave until she's been reunited with her father."

"Okay. Is he still here, somewhere in the house?"

"No, and he isn't at peace. I see him wandering by the river, where he used to work, punished by his own memories."

By the river. She must mean the Don River, the body of water that snaked through Toronto's east side. "Do you have a name for me?"

"All he shows me is pain and remorse. That's all that's left of him."

"Okay." Adelaide understood that even Maria's special sight had its limitations. They could only see what the spirits chose to reveal. "If I could get into that room to talk to her, I might be able to help her find her father. I could help them both cross over." Adelaide went downstairs in search of the estate agent. She found her in the kitchen, being bombarded by questions from her sisters.

"Do you know the year the house was built?" Edwina asked. "And the original owners. It would be helpful if we could find out who was here first."

Susannah had her notebook out, pen poised above it. "Also, could you tell us whether or not anyone has ever died in the house? Natural or unnatural causes. Were there ever any fires on the property?"

Poor Cindy. Her eye was really twitching now.

Adelaide interrupted them. "Excuse me. There's a door upstairs leading to an upper floor, but it's locked."

Cindy's cheeks became as pale as the ivory backsplash behind her. "Ah, the loft room. That area's off limits. I can give you the specs and email you some pics, though."

"I really need to get in there," Adelaide said.

"It's not fit for viewing."

"I don't care if it's unstaged. I'd still like to see it."

Cindy shook her head. "I won't unlock it. I'm sorry."

"Come on, Addy." Susannah touched her elbow. "I think we should go."

Adelaide stood her ground. "I know you've seen her, the little girl."

"I-I don't know what you're talking about," Cindy babbled. "There's no little girl here. Who *are* you people? Are you actually looking to buy a house at all?"

"She's asking for her father and I think she's in distress because she doesn't realize she's dead."

Cindy covered her mouth in horror but quickly composed herself when a couple of potential buyers passed through the room.

Addy waited a moment and chose her words. "I'm sure that seeing her must have scared you, but I'm used to seeing things like that. I'm a medium. My sisters and I could help her move on, but in order to do that, I need to get into that room to talk to her. We're not trying to make trouble. We just want to help her."

Cindy took a deep breath. "Look, we can talk, but I won't jeopardize my sale. Let me make my rounds, then I'll come find you."

"Fair enough." Adelaide and her sisters moved into the living room and hung out there for a while, keeping an eye on the steady flow of potential buyers heading for the door.

"See that?" Edwina elbowed Adelaide. "No one's sticking around for very long."

"I can sense a lot of discomfort," Susannah said. "People don't like the energy in the house."

"Something happened around here, something tragic." Adelaide cast her gaze around the pristine room. "All this white paint feels like a false cover. It's like putting makeup on a bruise. You can pretty it up but the sore remains."

Despite the clear interest in the home, it didn't take long for the last person to file out. Sighing, Cindy joined them in the living room. "Well, that was a bust. A stunning period home like this should sell itself." She dropped onto one of the sofas. "Are you sure I can't interest you in a house?"

"People can feel when something's off," explained Adelaide.

"You're really a medium?"

"Yeah. When did you have your encounter with the little girl?"

"As soon as I got the listing. The current owners wanted to get out as quickly as possible. They weren't here long and they moved out before the renovation was even done. They warned me that the house had 'character.'"

Cindy huffed, blowing up her expertly trimmed bangs. "Character, right. I've been here a few times on my own, and each time I walked in, I heard crying. A little girl crying. The first time I heard it, I thought it was a neighborhood kid's voice coming through a window, but the sound was too close. It was *inside* the house."

"So, you've actually seen her?" Susannah asked.

"Yes. I followed the crying to the room on the upper floor. The last owners said that room's been unoccupied for years, since even before their time, and they kept it shut. There's no furniture in there, no storage boxes, nothing. So, when I went in the first time, there was no mistaking what I saw. She was sitting on the floor by the window, her arms wrapped around her knees. It was a little blonde girl, maybe eight years old. She looked at me and said, 'Where's my Daddy? I can't find him.' I started to panic, thinking the kid had been abducted or something, but she disappeared, right in front of my eyes."

A shiver passed through her body. "I've kept that room locked ever since, but I still hear her when I'm alone in the house. Luckily, not everyone seems to."

Edwina cast her gaze around the room. "Do you know anything about the history of the place?"

"It was built in 1858. That's all I know, and it's all I want to know." Cindy turned to Adelaide. "Can you really remove her?"

"I believe so, but I'd need some time here."

The door opened and a few new people filed through.

Cindy jumped to her feet. "Today won't work. I'll have to check my schedule, but if you promise you can get rid of her, I'll find some time for you."

Adelaide bristled. "My aim is not to just *get rid of her*. It's to help her find peace. You can't rush that." She reached into her handbag for a business card and handed it to Cindy. "Give me a shout as soon as you can, please."

Cindy nodded and headed off to greet the others.

"*Get rid of her*," Adelaide grumbled, as the Darke sisters exited the house. "God forbid the fate of a little girl should mess up a sale."

"Not everyone gets it, Addy. You know that. We'll find a way to help her." Edwina patted her back as they filed onto the sidewalk. "Listen, the house has recently been renovated from top to bottom. Maybe the kid's unhappy because she doesn't recognize her old home anymore."

Adelaide shook her head. "No, there's more to it than that. She cried out for her father. Maria said his spirit is stuck down by the river, where he used to work. She said he's overwhelmed by remorse."

"Where he used to work." Susannah's eyebrows knit together, an indication her wheels were turning. "The Don River was the site of numerous industries over the years. It shouldn't be hard to find someone connected to this house who worked near there. Leave it to me."

"The girl's been dead a long time, if that helps. She doesn't reveal much, but she's definitely not from this century. Also, let me know if you turn up any details about a fire. Whatever happened around here, it was really bad." Adelaide put a hand to her brow, to shield her eyes from the bright sun. She glanced toward the top window.

The girl didn't appear.

We're going to help you. Adelaide sent the message out to the child, not even sure she would hear her. *I promise. You won't be lonely for much longer.*

Chapter Four

Will was at Beans on Saturday night much earlier than seven o'clock, not that he would admit that to Adelaide. However, the eclectic coffee shop was a Cabbagetown hotspot. Occupying the bottom floor of one of the historic retail blocks, it featured brightly colored tables and chairs, and the walls were hung with prints by local painters. Luckily, he found a table for two in the back, where it wasn't too loud.

He planted himself there and tried not to stare at the door. Then, he began to sweat. Perspiration gathered in his armpits so he rested his elbows on the table in an attempt to air them out.

Little by little, his nerves began to play up. When a lone bead of sweat crawled down his spine, the anxiety monster who squatted at the back of his brain howled in mirth.

What was he doing here? It had been ages since he'd met a woman for coffee, or anything that didn't involve work. Most of his recent social life had revolved around keeping his dementia-ridden grandmother comfortable and content. He was so out of practice.

Nevertheless, there had been something about Adelaide Darke that had made the words pop out of his mouth. *Could I call you some time?* What had he been thinking? She seemed so interesting and he…well, he read a lot of books.

Not that there was anything wrong with that, but right now, he felt like a teen on his first date. He should have scrawled a list of conversation topics on his palm.

This is what you get for isolating yourself.

In his singlemindedness to advance in his career, he'd neglected his social life. In addition, when his grandmother got sick a couple of years ago, he'd been the one who'd stepped up and found her a long-term care home. Frankly, his parents had needed the support. After dealing with so much red tape and care home administrators who simply didn't have his grandmother's best interests at heart, his dad had checked out mentally. Will had taken over the endless phone calls and the filling out of forms and had eventually found her a lovely home with staff members who could handle her unique needs.

Unfortunately, when his dad checked out, he'd stayed out. His visits to his mother had become less frequent. Will had once again picked up the slack, continuing to visit her at the home a couple of times a week because she'd been lonely. The adjustment had been hard on her. Her dementia had made her suspicious of her fellow residents, so it had been difficult for her to make friends. The weeks during that period had been long and busy, and by the time each weekend had come around, Will hadn't been in the mood to chat anyone up. He'd found himself withdrawing.

Eventually, several of his friends had withdrawn from him. They hadn't understood.

Now, he wondered whether or not he had anything to offer in the way of stimulating conversation. Not ideal, considering Adelaide had just entered the coffee shop and had him in her sights.

Whoa.

She'd looked adorable in her casual outfit in the Necropolis, but tonight, she'd pulled out some stops. She wore a green summer dress, one with little white polka dots all over it, and it emphasized her curvy figure. It dropped to around mid-calf, where the light fabric floated around her legs. On her feet were flat gladiator sandals, the kind that wrapped around the ankles. Her very pretty ankles.

A vision of him slowly unwrapping those sandals disrupted his field of vision.

Damn. Things had escalated quickly in his imagination.

She was early too. Was she excited to see him, or was she just as nervous as he was? Her skin glowed, but it didn't appear to be from sweat. It was the kind of glow that reminded him he wasn't dealing with a mere mortal here. Adelaide Darke definitely fell into goddess territory. She might fool others into thinking she was the girl next door, but Will recognized her for what she was.

She maneuvered her way toward where Will was seated and he stood, sweating even harder because he wasn't sure how to greet her. He wouldn't dare kiss this goddess on the cheek. She might smite him or something.

Maybe Miguel was right, and it had been too long since he'd done this. *Pull yourself together, Will.* He was too young to be going through such a dry spell.

Adelaide's hands were both wrapped around the handle of a small bag, but as she moved closer, she raised one and waved.

Will waved back, as the pressure to make a good impression mounted. He checked his outfit one last time in case he'd missed any stains, but his gray chinos and white button-down shirt were both clean and luckily, he still smelled fresh. He must not have sweated through his shirt. In an abundance of caution, he rolled up his sleeves for extra ventilation.

She smiled as she closed the distance between them. Her dark bobbed hair was caught up in a sparkly comb on one side and she wore a pale pink lipstick. It was sparkly too. Was it a gloss? Would it have a flavor? Cherry, maybe. No, strawberry?

Yeah. If he was obsessing over her lip gloss flavor, it had definitely been too long since he'd done this.

"Addy, hi." He stuck out his hand and pumped hers, like he was on a job interview. *Doofus*. He'd never been the definition of smooth.

"Hi, Will."

"You are stunning and that is a spectacular dress." *Calm down.*

Thankfully, she smiled. "Thanks." Her gaze drifted toward his rolled-up sleeves and her eyebrows delicately raised. Did she somehow know he was sweating? "You look nice too."

"Thank you." He should have gotten a haircut. Why hadn't he gotten a haircut? They stared at each other for a few seconds until he finally recovered himself. "Have a seat, please. I guess you've been here before?"

"Oh, yeah. I'm an old Cabbagetown girl. I've lived here all my life."

"I grew up here too. How have we never crossed paths in all this time?"

As they traded some of the basic details of their lives, comparing favorite haunts, Will began to relax. Adelaide was easy to talk to, as it turned out. Funnily enough, they'd been raised just a few streets away from each other. However, they'd gone to different schools. She'd attended one of the local public schools and he'd been raised in the Catholic system. He learned she was a couple of years younger than he was, putting her at thirty-two, so they hadn't run with the same crowd.

"And you still live in the neighborhood?" he asked.

"Yup. Just on Carlton, a block south of the Necropolis."

"I live on Salisbury. We're practically neighbors."

Her dark brown eyes shone, warming him to his core. "Small world, huh?"

"Very." *Stop staring at her or else she'll think you're a serial killer.* "What can I get you? If you're a regular here, you must have a favorite drink."

"The hazelnut lattes are incredible."

"That sounds perfect. I'll grab a couple." Will hopped up from his chair and headed to the counter to place the order. While he was there, he ordered up a selection of mini pastries as well, in case she was hungry.

As he waited for the order, he glanced back at Adelaide, unable to tear his gaze away for very long. She had her eye on a piece of artwork on the wall, which gave him the chance to admire her profile. Her lips were moving, as if she was talking to someone.

Probably just singing along to the music coming over the speakers.

He paid for the items and made his way back to the table. As he approached, he heard her say, "Maria, stop it."

"Who's Maria?"

She jumped. "Oh."

He sat down, handing her one of the lattes. "Sorry. Didn't mean to startle you."

"You didn't. I was just in my own little world, replaying a conversation with a…friend." Her cheeks a deep pink, she eyed the plate of pastries. "Sugary things. Excellent."

"Did I choose well?"

"You chose very well, thank you." She selected a Nanaimo bar from the plate and took a bite. As she bit down, the chocolate ganache top layer separated from the custard icing filling, leaving little crumbs about her lips. She laughed quietly and brought a napkin to her mouth. "There's no dainty way to eat these things."

Seeing her momentary awkwardness, he was able to shed some of his nerves and smiled. "Dainty's overrated." In all honesty, he would pay good money to watch her eat Nanaimo bars for an extended period of time. He reached for a tiny cheesecake slice. "So, should we get the most controversial topic out of the way first?"

"Ooh. Politics? Religion?"

"Han or Greedo?"

She laughed. It was an extraordinary sound. Even though her voice was light and soft, her laughter was anything but. It was more suited to a weathered sailor, one who'd just come ashore after a long spell at sea. It was husky and full of mischief. Upon hearing it once, Will knew he needed to hear it again.

"Of course," Adelaide said. "How could I forget? By the way, it was totally Han, and I don't hate him for it."

"Yes! Greedo had it coming." He leaned on the table, finally feeling capable of flirting. "I think we'll get along just fine. Have you always loved *Star Wars*?"

"Yeah. It's kind of my happy place. Yoda's my favorite character. Don't laugh, but when I was little, I saw him as a role model, even more than teachers and real-world adults. I must have watched the movies at least a hundred times because of him."

"Wow. You're a superfan. What is it about Yoda that you love?"

"He's cute and wise, but I think it's mostly because the whole Force thing spoke to me when I was a kid. The world can be a dark place. When I was little, it gave me comfort to believe we had something like the Force, guiding us. It helped me feel less alone." The light in her eyes dimmed, giving Will the impression that young Adelaide had seen too much of the world's darkness.

"Kind of like a higher power?"

"You could call it that. Anyway, like I said, it's my happy place."

"We all need one of those."

"What's yours?" she asked.

"It might sound weird, and possibly alarming, but I love wandering around old cemeteries. You've seen the proof of that. I'm a history geek, after all, and graveyards are full of history. When I travel, the local cemetery's usually the first place I hit up."

"You're a taphophile."

"Yeah."

"I don't think it's weird or alarming. I'm a taphophile too." She had an air of contemplation about her, like she was sizing him up, and he suddenly found himself eager to win her approval. He sensed she didn't just hand out gold stars to anyone. She was too discriminating for that.

One had to earn Adelaide Darke's respect.

"You must be excited about the museum opening," she said. "It's coming up soon, isn't it?"

"Yup. Just a couple of months away, actually. Mid-September, just after school starts. We're putting the finishing touches on everything now, finalizing our programming, that sort of thing."

"Sounds exciting."

"It really is. I'm fortunate I get paid to explore my passion. I'm aware that not everyone does so I appreciate each opportunity that comes my way."

"How do you even begin to curate a museum?"

"By starting at the beginning. For us, that meant a long discussion and partnership with the local First Nations communities. After all, Toronto may have been founded as the Town of York in 1793, but it was home to various Indigenous groups for about nine thousand years before that."

"Of course. What kinds of exhibits do you have planned?"

"There's naturally a focus on industrialization because the museum is situated in a former worker's cottage," he explained. "During the nineteenth century, the areas around the Don River were a perfect location for mills and distilleries, so a lot of them popped up. Of course, all those industries needed workers. The area became a home to numerous poor and working-class people. The museum is devoted to those people."

There was a reason why famed Canadian author Hugh Garner, who had grown up in the neighborhood during the Great Depression, had labeled it 'the largest Anglo-Saxon slum in North America.' Nowadays, however, Cabbagetown was an eclectic and artistic community set among green spaces, one that had been reinvented many times over.

"I want our visitors to understand that the neighborhood isn't just a collection of pretty old houses," Will continued. "It's a testament to the underdog. It exemplifies the strength and the resilience of the working class. And even though many people suffered here during those difficult days, there was a lot of joy too. People raised their families here, although it wasn't always easy. Immigrants had it hard and were often an object of derision by the upper classes. I mean, look at the name of the place. Even though the area wasn't called Cabbagetown until the 1880s, the name wasn't exactly complimentary."

"Because the poor Irish immigrants grew cabbages and other vegetables in their front yards."

"Yes. These were folks who'd fled the Famine. They had to be resourceful, but others looked down their noses at them. Now, homeowners fly the Cabbagetown flag proudly. I'm glad the neighborhood reclaimed that heritage, and not just for the Irish. It ended up being home to immigrants from all over the world."

Adelaide put her latte down and gazed at him, seemingly absorbed in what he was saying.

"Sorry about that. I don't mean to monopolize the conversation. Like I said, it's my passion."

"No, it's good. I admire that. You remind me of my sister, Susannah. She's a historian. She's been known to get lost down the odd rabbit hole."

"Right. You mentioned you had sisters. There are three of you?"

"Yeah. Edwina's the eldest. She works at the Shaw Festival as a theater tech."

"Interesting. Tell me more about your readings and your paranormal investigations."

She paused. Although she'd shown a lot of animation while listening to him talking about his work, something in her now shuttered. "You honestly want to know more?"

"Yeah, I mean, unless you can't talk about it."

"I have no problem discussing what I do, but for some reason, it's been problematic for others."

"Really? What's wrong with people?" Will ran a hand through his hair. When it fell back into his eyes, he pushed it off his face. "I mean, you already told me you saw my dead relatives, mentioning them by name, so I'm prepared to believe whatever you say."

"You're open-minded. That's not something I see a lot."

Will was starting to get a sense about Adelaide. She'd experienced the world's darkness, even as a little girl, and had looked to a fictional character for guidance and comfort. Now, as an adult, she seemed to expect distrust and disbelief from others.

It made him want to be nothing but genuine with her. "I'd love to hear about your work. How do your clients find you?"

"Word of mouth, mostly, but a lot of new clients come to me after seeing our stuff online. My sisters and I have a YouTube channel. We share our findings there. We call ourselves Darke Paranormal Investigations."

"I like that." Will pulled out his cell phone. "Mind if I have a look?"

"Go ahead."

He quickly searched the name and discovered numerous episodes that Adelaide had recorded with her sisters. They were the real deal. They traveled to haunted locations and seemed to clear properties of unwanted spirits. Even without doing a deep dive, he could tell the women of Darke Paranormal Investigations had come up against some scary shit.

He glanced up at the beautiful woman in polka dots before him and had trouble reconciling the two images.

He clicked on one of the thumbnails, in which Adelaide was standing in what appeared to be a dark basement, and turned on the audio. Her tinny voice came through his phone speaker. *"I can see the spirit of a young man in the corner but he's afraid to come forward. He died on this property a long time ago and is confused because he doesn't recognize the people who live here now. I need to make him understand we're here to help."* The Adelaide onscreen closed her eyes. *"I'm going to reach out to my spirit guide, Maria. Maria, can you help me make contact with this young man?"*

The Adelaide sitting across from Will held her breath.

He turned his phone volume down and put it away. "The Maria you mentioned earlier…she's your spirit guide?"

She sat up straight and looked him right in the eye. "Yes."

"And you talk to her?"

Adelaide waited a beat before once again answering in the affirmative. "All the time." She crossed her arms over her chest. Her eyes narrowed a little.

She was expecting a fight. How many times had she had them in the course of getting to know others?

He wasn't about to give her one.

"Cool." Will polished off his cheesecake slice and reached for a shortbread cookie. "I've never known anyone who had a spirit guide. It must be helpful in your work. So, was Maria able to help you identify the guy in that basement?"

Adelaide blinked several times. "That's...not the reaction Maria normally gets. Most people gawk at me like they're sizing me up for a straitjacket. Others think I'm sad and delusional, which I'm not. Hell, even my sisters used to look at me funny, and they grew up with me talking about Maria." She waved her hand in front of his body. "I'm not sure what to make of this. Most people would get up and walk away. Or laugh. A lot of them just laugh."

That pissed the hell out of him. "Those people are full of shit."

Another throaty chuckle burst from her. "They really are."

"Look, I don't profess to understand what you do, but I can appreciate that it's something that means a lot to you. So, no, I wouldn't laugh at you."

She nodded.

"Of course, if you want a reason to laugh, I can give you one." He chuckled. "You should have seen how nervous I was before you got here. It was not pretty and I'm lucky to not be sitting in a pool of my own sweat right now."

Adelaide had been rigid for the last few minutes, but she relaxed into her chair. "I was nervous too."

"Oh, yeah?"

"Yeah. My track record on first dates hasn't been great. To be honest, it's been a while since anyone's made it past the first date with me. I haven't met anyone who can handle my eccentricities."

"Now, that just feels like a dare."

And there it was. A smile. Maybe not the big, toothy variety, but it was soft and sexy and it was aimed in his direction. Incredible.

They continued chatting. At his urging, she told him more about some of the other cases Darke Paranormal Investigations had tackled. The more questions Will asked, the more she seemed to lose some of her wariness. Before long, she had detailed some intriguing encounters with ghosts, or spirit people, as she called them. Given the level of detail she was able to provide, he didn't understand how she met with such skepticism all the time. She struck him as completely reliable.

Of course, maybe that was because he was completely attracted to her.

Will listened in wonder. "You know, you blew me away when you mentioned my grandmother."

"I'm sorry for your loss." She inclined her head. "It's a recent one, isn't it? Just a few weeks?" Even though she phrased it as a question, her flat tone indicated she already knew the truth.

"Yeah. You can see that?"

She didn't answer him. Knowledge was written in the depths of her gaze.

"We were close," he said. "My grandmother lived with us for most of my childhood. She was like a second mom. It's been harder than I would have expected to see her pass, but your words helped me feel better. You have a real gift, Addy."

"Thanks. That's what I choose to believe, but it hasn't always felt that way. I've been an outsider most of my life." She wore a necklace that had a gold heart pendant on it, one with different colored stones. She touched it now, gently tugging.

"I'm sorry you were made to feel that way."

She shrugged. "I understand that most people can't process what I do. I mean, if you told me there was a gorilla sitting at this table with us, I wouldn't believe it. And yet I see things that aren't supposed to be there. I see them right now, here in this coffee shop. I don't know why the universe decided I should be the one to see them, but I do, and they're real and I don't have a lot of time for people who want to argue that fact."

"Are you and your sisters working on a case now?"

"Yeah, actually. We're about to start an investigation right here in Cabbagetown. The Witch House."

"You're kidding. The old Taylor place?"

"You know it?" She shook her head. "Of course, you do. You know all about the neighborhood."

"It's definitely come up in my research. If I can help you in any way, let me know."

She leaned in, seemingly eager to have his input, but retreated again. "Thanks, but we have a system in place. My sister Susannah does our research and she doesn't share those details with me until after I've made contact with the other side. That way, my findings are validated for our audience. But I appreciate your offer."

"No sweat. Let me know if you change your mind."

One of the coffee shop employees approached their table. "Sorry, guys. We close at ten tonight."

Adelaide glanced at her cell phone. "Oh my goodness. I didn't even realize the time."

Neither did Will. He'd been too absorbed in their conversation. Hopefully that was the reason Adelaide had lost track of time too.

"I guess we'd better let them close." He racked his brain, trying to find a way to extend their evening. "It's nice out. Want to go for a walk?" He gnawed his bottom lip, hoping she wouldn't want to cut their time short.

But Adelaide offered him the shy smile that had already captivated him. "Sure. I'll walk with you."

* * * *

As they strolled through Cabbagetown, Adelaide considered Will's offer of help. He probably knew everything about the Witch House, or as he'd called it, the old Taylor house.

Taylor. It was a common enough name, not one she immediately associated with early Toronto historical figures, but her knowledge of local history was sketchy anyway. That was Susannah's forte. Adelaide was tempted to ask Will for a few details, but she didn't want to step on her sister's toes.

In addition, she was wary of involving Will in their investigation, even in a small capacity. As a history geek, he'd likely be all over it. If, by chance, their relationship soured, that would make things awkward.

She couldn't stop sneaking looks at the curator. Granted, he was easy on the eyes. On the slimmer side, he had lean muscles, ones that filled out his jeans and shirt nicely. He had rolled up his shirtsleeves right before shaking her hand at the start of their date. The handshake had been adorable, but what really got her juices flowing were his bare forearms.

It was possible she had a thing for nice forearms and rolled-up sleeves. Okay, she definitely had a thing for nice forearms and rolled-up sleeves, so much so that she'd fantasized about stroking the soft hairs on his arms a couple of times in the coffee shop.

Another adorable item? He'd been pushing his overgrown hair out of his eyes a lot. His gorgeous mop of sandy waves drew her attention just as much as his arm muscles. She longed to comb her fingers through his hair. Add to all that the sharp lines of his face, his amber eyes and an endearing geekiness, and he was a package she couldn't resist.

They turned down Winchester Street but Adelaide wasn't really paying attention to where they were headed. All she knew was that she didn't want the evening to end. As they strolled, their arms grazed a couple of times, giving her a thrill.

"*I told you he was your type,*" Maria whispered in that voice that only Adelaide could hear.

"*I appreciate your insight,*" Adelaide responded silently, "*but it's too early to be making any calls.*"

"*But you told him about me and he didn't laugh. That's a good sign.*"

"*Trust me, there's still plenty of time for Will to decide I'm too weird to be worth the effort. Now, I'm going to politely ask you to take a step back so I can concentrate on other things.*"

"*Like those forearms?*"

"*Maria.*"

With an otherworldly laugh, Maria retreated, giving Adelaide space.

Even though Maria was a constant presence in her life, she always respected Adelaide's wishes for privacy. Edwina and Susannah used to joke that Maria was the fourth Darke sister, and in many ways, she was. Addy appreciated always having that friendly and supportive voice in her ear, and as protective as Maria was of her, she was equally protective of Maria.

Maria hadn't always been of the world of spirit. In fact, she'd lived right here in Toronto, although not for very long. She'd died of whooping cough as a toddler, many years ago, which was why she manifested with a terrible cough at times. She had shown Adelaide those heartbreaking images and Addy had never forgotten them. Since then, Maria had become a being of energy, one whose mission was to provide Addy with insight and knowledge. Others might not understand their strange bond, and might even judge her for it, but Adelaide didn't care. She would always choose Maria over some ignorant living person.

She'd realized early on that her unique situation could make relationships tricky. Most people weren't into sharing their girlfriends...well, not like that, anyway. There had been one guy a couple of years ago who had seemed compassionate and broad-minded. After a fun, marathon date, during which he'd said all the right things, Adelaide had confessed the truth about her gifts and her spirit guide. At that point, everything had changed. The guy's eyes had lit up with lascivious glee as he'd asked, "So, what are the chances I'll be able to bang your dead friend?"

Weary, Adelaide had gotten up and walked right out.

Once more, she glanced at Will. He seemed cool, but did he have a similar endgame? Now that he knew the truth, was he just hoping to get his rocks off with a dead chick, instead of appreciating Addy for who she was? It wasn't so much that Adelaide had anything against threesomes, supernatural or not, but it went deeper than that. She'd learned the hard way that most people weren't truly interested in her. They were only interested in what she could do, or in what she could give them. Ninety-nine percent of the time, she was happy to help, but a small part of her had become jaded.

Sometimes, she didn't want to be Adelaide Darke, the medium. Sometimes, she just wanted to be Addy, the woman who loved curling up on a cozy couch in her pajamas to watch sci-fi movies.

Lately, as her sisters had found love, she found herself wanting someone to curl up on that couch with her. She'd never had problems being alone. Considering the fact that the dead liked to pop in regularly, she never really was alone. But that wasn't the same as having an affectionate, living person at her side. Every time she saw how Simon doted on Edwina, or how Noah gazed at Susannah in adoration, she wondered if that kind of connection was even in the cards for her.

Plus, there was the whole sex issue. She'd had a couple of cold hookups along the way, but that wasn't really her style. She yearned for something deeper, for someone who cared about her soul as well as her body.

Adelaide had grown up convinced that kind of love would never be possible for her. Most days, she still believed it. The knowledge had begun to wear on her, especially every time it was reinforced by some dude who didn't give a shit about who she was as a person, and only wanted to know which lottery numbers he should play.

Lost in her thoughts, she glanced at Will, only to find him gazing at her. Illuminated by the streetlight, he blushed.

Adelaide gulped, but she reminded herself not to pin her hopes on one little look of longing.

They reached the corner of Winchester and Sumach, across the street from the Necropolis. The Taylor house was just to Adelaide's left. Drawn by a force she didn't understand, not even after all these years, she turned toward the window.

The haunted child waved.

Adelaide must have let out a sigh because Will touched her arm. "Are you okay? You had the weight of the world in that sigh."

"Oh, it's just sometimes I wish I could take a day off."

"I had a feeling you were seeing something."

"How could you tell?"

His eyes narrowed in fascination. "The day I met you in the cemetery, when you told me you'd seen my dead relatives? You had the same mysterious quality in your eyes. They became darker, deeper somehow, like they contained whole galaxies."

"Oh." Her sisters had always been a little freaked out at Adelaide's ability to 'see into their souls' as they put it, but neither had ever described it in such poetic terms.

"It must be hard for you to carry that burden."

Adelaide was taken aback. In all her days, she'd rarely heard that sentiment. Most people judged her, but Will's hushed tone spoke only of empathy. He seemed concerned about the emotional toll of her gift, and she was tempted to believe a part of him wanted to understand.

Only, no one understood, not really.

"I manage," she replied, shutting down that line of discussion.

"Of course." They crossed the street and ventured farther down Winchester. He gestured around the dark street, probably eager to change the subject. "I'm always amazed at how much this area has changed, and how much it's stayed the same."

"I guess you'd be in a good position to know."

"Sorry. I'm geeking out again, aren't I? My dad always says I live more in the past than in the present." There was an undercurrent of disappointment in his flat tone. She couldn't blame him. It was a weird thing for a parent to say.

"Well, I'm curious to know more. Tell me what's changed."

"Yeah? Okay. Take Winchester Street, for example. Right now it ends a few feet away, at Riverdale Farm." He indicated the large green space that operated as a working farm attraction for urban families, complete with animals. "In the 1840s, however, Winchester was considered the outskirts of Toronto. The only thing beyond the cemetery, right on the riverbank, was a place called the Don Vale House."

She quirked her head to the side, unfamiliar with the name.

"Back in the day, it was a tavern. Working men would go there in the evenings after their shifts for cheap liquor, boxing contests, cockfighting, that sort of thing. It was demolished in 1875. Not a trace of it remains."

Don Vale House.

The three words triggered a commotion in her core, a surge of dread. Accustomed to listening when her instincts flared, she concentrated on the historic tavern and tried to picture what it must have looked like.

An image illuminated in her brain, one of a basic wooden structure, sitting at the edge of the Don River. The only roadway leading toward it consisted of rough planks. Up the hill from the tavern, the Necropolis headstones dotted the landscape, an ominous reminder of what might happen to anyone who drank too much and wandered near the river. It would have been an isolated location then, a rough sort of sanctuary for the working man, but a dangerous place to be caught alone or unawares.

Another image appeared, one from long ago. She witnessed a young woman marching through the dark Necropolis and down the hill toward the Don Vale House. It was a cold, breezy night, and the wind caused her brown hair to escape its bun and drift around her face. Her cheeks were stained with tears. She fisted her hands at her sides. With each furious step, her heart pounded and her lips were open with desperate sobs.

Damn you, Aiden. God damn you, she cried.

Adelaide's pulse raced as if she was the one charging down that hill. She was seized with a terrible knowledge, one that chilled her to the bone.

That would be the last night of the young woman's life.

At the bottom of the hill, the woman met a man. They talked for a short time. He put his hands on her and there was a brief struggle. With no warning, he pushed her into the river. She flailed but the churning, wintery waters dragged her down.

Death had found her next to the Don Vale House.

Someone touched Adelaide's elbow. She jerked away. "Don't touch me!"

A warm, familiar voice landed on her ear. "Addy, are you all right?"

It was Will. His mouth tightened with concern. He'd removed his hand from her elbow and held both of them up in an attitude of surrender.

The vivid images, still so fresh, robbed her of words.

"It's just me. I won't touch you. What happened? You're shaking."

Seeing someone in their last moments on earth would do that. And it had happened right there near where the infamous tavern used to stand. Addy had so many questions. What was the woman's name, and who was the man who'd pushed her? She tried to insert herself back into the displaced memory but couldn't. It was all fading away.

Not a trace of it remains.

She wasn't so sure about that.

"I saw something from long ago. A woman...she died near the Don Vale House. I think she was murdered."

Will gawked.

"When you mentioned the Don Vale House, she appeared to me. Her heart was broken, utterly broken. There was nothing left in her but pain. It was powerful enough to almost crack her ribs open. There was a man there too. He pushed her into the river."

"Oh my God. That sounds upsetting."

"Um, yeah. It was." She was really trying not to read into his tone, but she'd been on the receiving end of so many patronizing comments and it was hard to recognize sincerity.

"I wonder who she could have been."

"I wasn't able to get a name. All I know is she was desperate to get to the Don Vale House."

"Interesting. It wasn't exactly the sort of tavern where women would have hung out. I doubt they would have felt comfortable there."

Okay. Was he actually arguing with her now?

Calm down. You're upset and you're getting defensive. "I know what I saw."

Her tone must have been sharp because he was quick to clarify. "Of course. I don't doubt it. I'm just trying to figure out what might have led her there." He scratched his head. "There's this historian, John Ross Robertson. He specifically said the Don Vale House was a hotbed for illegal activity. Not exactly a cozy, local pub."

"She must have had a reason for taking that risk."

"I'm sure she did." There was nothing in Will's attitude to suggest he was mansplaining the situation to her. If anything, Adelaide got the sense he was just trying to make sense of it all by talking it through.

Unfortunately, the knowledge did nothing to soothe her temper. Once it flared, it was hard to bring it back under control. The vision, combined with her interpretation of the conversation, left her feeling wounded and raw, and angry for what that woman would have experienced. It soured the moment for her.

"Do you want to talk about it some more?"

"No. I need to clear my head."

"Sure. Let me walk you home."

She focused on his kind face and tried to forget the disturbing vision and the premonition that had come with it, but it didn't work. The woman had died long ago and there was nothing Adelaide could do to help her.

Death had claimed her in the end. There was no way to change that.

Why would the universe make Adelaide witness another person's misery, if she couldn't do anything about it? Internally, she let out a scream of frustration.

Okay, you've officially spiraled.

She stepped away from Will. "Um, you know what? I'm just going to go home on my own."

"It's dark. Are you sure I can't walk you to your door?"

"I'm just a block away. I'll be fine." She turned and walked away.

"Addy, please wait."

She stopped in her spot. Her eyes burned and she didn't trust herself not to fall apart, so she kept her back to him.

"Did I do something wrong?" His gentle tone only added to her anguish. "Please tell me. I want to fix it."

"You didn't…" She let out a sigh. "Look, I'm sorry I ruined everything."

"You haven't ruined anything." His footsteps came closer. "I'm sorry if it sounded like I was doubting you. That wasn't my intention."

"I get it. It's fine."

"Can I call you tomorrow?"

What for? So she could freak him out all over again? She knew she was overreacting, but the vision had been so distressing. She turned around. Will's entire body was tense, as if he were about to jump in front of her to battle her demons. Good luck to him. "I don't think that's a good idea."

"But…"

"Will, you seem nice so I'm going to spare you a lot of trouble. If you become involved with me, this is going to happen a lot, and I have no way of controlling it. You might think it's interesting now, that it might even be a fun way to indulge your taphophilia, but it'll grate on you eventually. So, why don't we call it a day, huh?"

"Addy—"

"Goodbye, Will." Before he could respond, she turned on her heel and marched home.

Chapter Five

Will stared at his laptop screen as his list of unopened emails grew before his eyes. Just in the last two minutes, another seven emails appeared in his inbox.

Focus.

He was falling behind. For some reason, every time he sat down to craft a response, he just couldn't find the words. His head was pounding. It had been pounding ever since he got to the museum that morning. In addition, he was distracted, moody and tired. He was dead tired.

Of course, he hadn't slept well at all. In fact, he'd tossed and turned all night long. When he had managed a few minutes of sleep last night, they'd been punctuated by a weird recurring nightmare, one into which he kept slipping. Adelaide Darke had been there. In the dreams, someone had been chasing her through the Necropolis at night. She'd veered around the various headstones, trying to get away. Eventually, she'd made her way along the old plank road to the Don Vale House. At the dream's conclusion, Addy had plunged into the frigid Don River and had drowned.

He knew the nightmares were some sort of mashup of Addy's vision of the young woman and his own stress at work. But every time he had closed his eyes, the scene had unfolded again, leaving him in a frantic, exhausted state upon awakening.

Adelaide was fine, he knew that. He needed to put her out of his mind, at least for now. Unfortunately, his brain insisted on recreating the disturbing image.

Shaking his head in pursuit of some sort of clarity, he turned to his screen again. Another new email appeared and this one grabbed his attention right away. It was from their volunteer coordinator, Terri Longo.

Subject: Resignation.

"What the...?" Will opened the email. "Shit."

Their curatorial assistant, Alison Chen, was working in the office as well. She looked up from where she was labeling a donated hatbox. "What's up?"

"Terri just resigned. Effectively immediately. She said this wasn't the right fit for her." Terri had been hired as the person who would be in charge of wrangling docents and gift shop attendants, and she'd been doing an amazing job, getting their training plans together.

"Oh." Alison went back to applying Paraloid B-72 lacquer, the nail-polish-like solution that they used for artifact labeling, to the hatbox.

Will couldn't help noticing that she avoided his gaze. "Alison, did she ever say anything to you about being unhappy here? I don't understand. She seemed thrilled to get the job."

Alison put her labeling tools down. "She did mention one thing a while ago. She told me she wasn't comfortable being in the museum."

"But—"

"Will, come on." Alison, who had been working with Will and Miguel for about five years, wasn't concerned about mincing words. "This place has all the charm of an amusement park fun house."

"That's a bit much."

"Really? I told Miguel a while back that I won't hang out here on my own. No more late nights by myself. It feels like there's always someone watching." Alison frowned and looked over her shoulder.

"Miguel said it has a vibe."

"Ha! That's generous."

"Damn. Terri was getting ready to do volunteer orientations." It was too late to hire a new coordinator. Will would have to take over the onboarding of the volunteers himself, something he literally had no time to do. The ache in his temple flared, blackening his vision for a second. Terri had only been with them for a few months, but she'd become an invaluable member of the team. She'd been excited to take part in a museum opening. Why hadn't she come to him on this?

Or had she?

There had been a meeting a couple of weeks ago, during which she'd let it slip that she'd seen something like a shadow figure. He'd brushed that off as an issue of "vibes" too.

Had he completely disregarded the wellbeing of his team members, just because he was fond of an old house? It was starting to look that way.

Alison pushed away from her corner of the large desk that they all used as a workspace. "I'm just going to go grab some lunch and get some air. Maybe you should too."

This was all his fault.

"Will?"

"Uh, right. I will in a bit. Thanks." Right now, he felt more like throwing up than eating.

"Okay." Alison gave him a funny look and headed outside for her break.

The pain in Will's head took on the force of an earth-boring machine, tearing through his brain. They were about to open a goddamn museum. Invitations had been sent. Hell, the mayor had RSVP'd that she would attend. They couldn't afford to be losing staff members now.

He stood and paced in front of the desk. As he began to move, his heartbeat sped up. His breaths grew shallow. *I can't believe this is happening.*

Will had the sudden sensation of floating out of his body. Up, up, up—he imagined himself drifting, to a place where the air was cold and thin. He clenched his fists, a feeble attempt at grounding himself, only to realize his palms were sweaty and slippery.

I'm losing control. I'm going to fail.

He put a clammy hand to his chest. *Christ.* Even through the fabric of his shirt, he could feel the mad pumping of his heart.

Could this actually be a heart attack? He was too young for that shit.

Panicked, desperate for fresh air, he tore outside and across the street to the Necropolis. For some reason, the mature trees and greenery called to him. *Yes. I'll be able to breathe there.*

That, or he'd keel over. If he did, they wouldn't have to work hard to find a spot to bury him. There were plenty right here.

He ran to the nearest bench, threw himself down on it and bent over at the waist. He rested his elbows on his knees and sucked in sweet air. He closed his eyes and focused on taking deep, regular breaths. This was just stress and he was only having a panic attack, not cardiac arrest.

A couple of minutes later, a pair of green Converse shoes appeared before him. "Will?"

He looked up into a beautiful but concerned face. "Addy, hey." *Oh God, perfect.* Now she could witness him at his worst.

Aside from her green sneakers, she wore a black shirt that said *Goth girl*. It had a V-neck and emphasized her full breasts. Her heart pendant necklace drew his eye to the same area, making him even shorter of breath than he had been a second ago. Her round hips and thighs were accentuated by slim jeans. She looked fucking gorgeous, a vision sent to taunt him in his moment of need.

She crouched before him and was about to touch his knee but pulled her hand back. "Are you okay? You're really pale." She pulled her cell phone out from her bag. "Should I call nine-one-one?"

"No, please." *Been there, done that. No need to bother emergency services personnel.* It would pass. It always passed. Only every time he looked at Adelaide, his pulse hitched again. Maybe he did need an ambulance. "I'll be fine. I promise."

She didn't look convinced.

Only then did the folly of his actions occur to him. Maybe, going forward, he shouldn't run off into cemeteries while having panic attacks. He was lucky Adelaide had been around, but what if he'd tripped and fallen and bashed his brains on a headstone? Not a dignified way to go. The thought struck him as so ludicrous that he started cackling.

Adelaide gave him a side eye. "Are you sure you're okay?"

"I'm fucking fantastic. Couldn't be any better. How's your day going?" *For fuck's sake.* If he hadn't already turned her off, he would now by acting like a total weirdo.

Only, Adelaide didn't scoff or scold. She regarded him for a long moment. "Panic attacks are awful, aren't they?"

"How did you know I was having a panic attack? Was it the medium thing?"

"No." She grinned. "My powers are mighty but they're not that good. I knew because I've had a few panic attacks in my time."

"Really?"

"It's been a while, but yeah. Can I call someone for you?" She opened her handbag and pulled out a bottle of water. "Or would you like a drink?"

"No, I'm better now, but thanks." His pulse was already regulating. "Sorry about that."

"There's no need to apologize."

"I swear I don't often go on mad runs around the cemetery."

"No? I do. I highly recommend it."

She said it with such a straight face he had to laugh, even though he felt more like crawling into a sad little ball. "I, uh, thought I had the panic attacks under control, but lately, they've been creeping back into my life."

"Oh, yeah?"

"Yeah." For a wild second, he was tempted to tell her about Joe Harris, his old boss. The man who'd undermined Will's work to such an extent that he had started having attacks at work.

But Joe Harris was history, as far as Will's life was concerned, and there was no reason for him to be freaking out now. Yes, this issue with Terri was bad, but it wasn't insurmountable. Maybe he could talk to her and convince her to come back. If not, Will and his team knew plenty of people in the museum community and they could put out some feelers. Hell, he could call back some of the other applicants. Some of them had been very keen on the job and might still be available. At the end of the day, they'd fill the vacancy. The museum would open. It would be fine.

It just didn't feel fine.

For a while now, a creeping feeling had insinuated itself into his core, causing him to doubt his own strengths. Causing him to lie awake at night, thinking strange thoughts.

He was fairly sure Addy didn't want to hear any of that. She was just being nice.

"Are you sure I can't get anything for you?" Adelaide asked.

"I'm sure." Why *was* she being so nice to him? After the way their date had ended, he wouldn't have been surprised if she'd walked on past, letting him gasp his last breath in the bosom of the Necropolis.

"I should let you go." He stood, secretly triumphing when he didn't topple back down. "Duty calls."

"Of course. I'm sure you want to get back to work." She stood and fumbled with the handle of her bag. "I have an appointment anyway."

"Right. Thanks for checking on me. I mean that."

"You're welcome." She began to walk away but quickly turned back. "Will, I'm not trying to minimize your problems, but whatever is causing you stress at work, I'm sure you'll find a way to move past it."

Would he? "Yeah, thanks."

She gave him a salute. "I'll see you around, I guess."

He nodded, unsure of how to respond. Would he see her around? He hoped so.

Adelaide took a few steps, looked over her shoulder and smiled.

Something jumped in his chest. Why did it feel so good to have her look back at him like that?

Doofus. Just go back to work.

He waited around the Necropolis for a bit, bathing in a patch of sunlight that streamed through the mature trees, then headed back to the office. Before going in to ensconce himself in his mountain of emails, he took a few seconds to send a text to Addy.

Will: Thank you.

Her response, a gif of Yoda nodding sagely, put a smile on his face for the rest of the day.

Chapter Six

It had surprised Will to learn that although he and Addy Darke had both grown up in Cabbagetown, they'd never seen each other around over the years. Now, since making it clear at the end of their coffee date that she didn't want to see him, they were running into each other everywhere.

There was that one day at the neighborhood convenience store when he'd turned around in line only to see her entering the shop. Then, there was that time a few days ago when they'd bumped into one another at the local library. Each time, they'd stopped and had pleasant yet awkward conversations about things like the weather, their reading habits and the price of eggs. After those encounters, he'd begun to wonder if the Fates were conspiring to throw them together.

He supposed it shouldn't have come as a total shock to run into her at the Organic Market on a Saturday morning, but when they almost plowed into each other at the door, he couldn't help but laugh at the absurdity of the situation. He'd been going in and she'd been coming out, a grocery bag slung over her arm. As they approached the sliding doors of the market, they both slowed their paces.

Chuckling, they stepped aside on the sidewalk so other shoppers could get into the market. "Wow," Will said. "If I didn't know any better, I'd think you were stalking me."

Addy didn't bother to hide her grin. "Don't be silly. It's clear you're the one stalking me."

"Busted." He held up his hands. "Granted, I don't have much of a social life, so this is as exciting as it gets."

"Oh, come on. You're not out partying every night?"

He clicked his tongue and winked like a player. "Partying at the library, baby. You saw me in the local history section. That place is wild and I know all the librarians by name."

Addy laughed and held his gaze. She looked just as pretty as any of the other times he'd seen her. No *Goth girl* T-shirts today, but the slash of black eyeliner around her dark eyes hinted at her mysterious personality. Today, she wore a plain gray T-shirt and shorts combo that was anything but plain. There was no way it could be boring on her gorgeous body. Every time Will saw her, his hands itched from wanting to caress her curves.

He cleared his throat. "So, what brings you to the Organic Market today? You know, aside from the obvious stalking."

"Falafel salad, actually. It's really good here so I picked some up for lunch. It's nice out. I figured I'd find a park bench somewhere and have it there."

"That sounds awesome. I've never had their falafel salad."

"You have to try it. It'll change your life. I'm not even kidding."

"Whoa. How could I say no, then? Of course, if it doesn't change my life, I might have to register a complaint with you. I write strongly worded emails, so you should be concerned."

She paused and seemed to be choosing her words. "Well, if it helps, I could wait around while you buy some and we could find that park bench together. If you don't feel your life has been altered enough, you can save yourself an email, and complain to me face-to-face." Her voice petered out at the end.

Will studied her. He drummed his fingers against his thigh in excitement.

Was Adelaide Darke asking him out? Or was she merely on some bizarre quest to make everyone eat falafel salad?

From somewhere deep inside him, a woman's voice rang out. *Don't go with her.*

Taken aback, Will took a bit longer to answer Addy. In that few seconds, she gnawed on her lip. He was making her nervous.

He recognized the strange voice for what it was, his wounded heart trying to protect him. Addy had already turned him down. Did he really want to chance another rejection?

At the same time, he really wanted to explore whatever was happening here. "I would love to have life-changing falafel salad with you on a park bench."

It may have been his imagination, but she sighed in apparent relief. "Great. I'll wait for you out here while you grab your lunch."

Will headed inside and tried his hardest not to career around the store, collecting his lunch items. He wanted to pay and get back out there quickly so she didn't change her mind and desert him on the steps of the Organic Market. He was grateful to see her still standing there when he exited the shop. "All right. Do you have a favorite bench?"

"I was just going to head to the Necropolis." She turned a deep red. "Cemeteries tend to be quieter than other places for me, if you catch my drift."

"Oh. But you saw my relatives there."

"Yeah, but by and large, most spirit people don't tend to hang out in cemeteries. They usually stick around the places where they lived or died. It's just a bit more peaceful for me in graveyards."

"I hear you. Lead the way."

She was quiet as they walked along Parliament Street, probably reconsidering her decision to have lunch with him. Will tried to think of something to say that would keep her engaged. Of course, the only thing that popped into his head was history. The area where they were walking was a retail district, one that had been there since the days of early Toronto. As they walked by a sushi restaurant, he was reminded of some random tidbits of information. "Did you know that this sushi place used to be a soap factory and candle business back in the mid-eighteen hundreds?" *Aw, man. You couldn't think of anything more scintillating than that?*

But Adelaide responded with interest. "Really? No, I had no idea."

"Yeah. Most of these little storefronts have been here for generations." He rattled off quick descriptions of some others as they made their way to the intersection.

"The stationery shop was once a milliner's. The pub on the corner has always been a tavern. Toronto has never had a shortage of those. In fact, by 1856, there were over five hundred taverns in town. Early Torontonians never had a shortage of options for booze."

Back in the day, the Don Vale House was a tavern. Working men would go there in the evenings after their shifts for cheap liquor, boxing contests, cockfighting, that sort of thing. It was demolished in 1875. Not a trace of it remains. His historical tidbit from the night of their date came back to haunt him.

Maybe he should have left out the history factoids. Maybe his dad was right, and he did live in the past. Of course, that was rich coming from a man who had trouble dealing with the present.

However, once again, Adelaide made her interest clear. "That's fascinating." She fiddled with the handle of her takeout bag. "Honestly, I appreciate you sharing that kind of info with me. Sometimes, when I see spirit people, they say things that I don't understand, details about their professions, for example. It helps to know what used to be in the area. About six months ago, I walked by the stationery shop and ran into a spirit woman who was talking about hats. Now I understand why."

"Huh. I'm glad I could give you some clarity."

They made small talk as they headed toward the Necropolis. Once there, they found a bench in the area known as the Resting Place of Pioneers, an older section that contained the remains of settlers from when Toronto was still known as York. The graves in this spot had been re-interred after having been moved from Potter's Field in 1855, when the town was being developed.

They tucked into their lunch salads. Will took his first bite. "Oh my God, you weren't kidding. This is the best thing ever."

"Right? It's the tzatziki." She picked at a piece of lettuce with her fork. "So, how are things at the museum?"

"Um." He hesitated over how much to share with her. "Not great, to be honest. The day you saw me having the panic attack was the day our volunteer coordinator resigned. It's left us in a bit of a lurch. I've been checking in with other applicants who wanted the job but they've all moved on, of course. Terri was the best candidate anyway. I'm really hoping she'll change her mind and come back. I may have left a couple of voicemails for her already. I mean, I don't blame her," he babbled. "It's not her fault she's uncomfortable there."

Adelaide frowned, trying to follow. "Uncomfortable... at the museum?"

"Yeah." He chuckled nervously. "Remember how I said my colleagues thought the place was haunted? Well, she was one of them."

"And now, she's resigned."

He nodded, more sheepish than newly shorn sheep at a sheep festival.

"Okay. Want to tell me what's been going on there?"

Will was on the verge of spilling the dirt, all the experiences that had set him on edge. The sensation of being watched, the voices and footsteps, the cold touches. But once again, from within his core, a voice emerged. Sweet and whispery, it lulled him into a sense of security. "*Sshhh. Don't tell her. It's our little secret.*"

"Will?"

"Hey, it's nothing. Really." He stabbed a chunk of falafel and shoved it in his mouth. As he chewed and swallowed, he buried his concerns. "People are stressed at work. It's made us a bit jumpy, that's all."

"Right." Even though she wasn't finished with her salad, she wrapped it back up again and put it in the bag. "And how have you been feeling? Any more panic attacks?"

He got his back up. Why did he feel like he was being diagnosed here? Sure, there had been a couple of little attacks recently. Namely, the one that he'd had upon awakening yesterday morning and an embarrassing moment at work the other day, when he'd had to run out of the museum in the middle of a meeting because he couldn't breathe. But he didn't exactly feel like laying his soul bare to Adelaide right now.

What was the point?

She was just being sympathetic. There was nothing wrong with that. Frankly, it was nice to have someone care, but why was she bothering? At the end of the day, she would walk away again and so would he.

Damn. If only he could go back in time to the night of their date, to redo their conversation at the end. He wasn't sure why it had gone so wrong so quickly, but he wished he could fix it. Whether he understood her abilities or not, Addy had seen something on their date that had upset her and he'd only made it worse. Rather than spouting crap about the theories of dead historians, he should have just listened. He should have found a way to make things better for her that night.

How the fuck was he supposed to do that, though? The woman not only saw dead people, she clearly had visions of how they died as well. It wasn't exactly a situation where he could slap on a bandage and tell her it would be all right.

She certainly hadn't needed someone like him swooping in and mansplaining her own visions to her and he wished he could take it back. It had to be so hard to experience that shit.

And now, here she was, trying to make him feel better. Instead of being grateful, it just pissed him off, but he was only angry at himself.

The world can be a dark place. When I was little, it gave me comfort to believe we had something like the Force, guiding us. It helped me feel less alone.

What the hell had she seen during the course of her life?

Maybe she was right to nip it in the bud. What could he possibly offer a woman like Adelaide Darke? She was fascinating and mysterious and beautiful, and he was just some guy who couldn't get his shit together.

"It's okay," she said. "We don't have to talk about panic attacks. I just can't help noticing that you're paler than the last time I saw you."

Will had noticed it too. This morning, he'd been startled by his own reflection. He'd had dark circles under his eyes, and he'd even been able to make out one of the tiny veins that snaked beneath his right eye. Blue under his skin, it had almost looked like the beginnings of a bruise. "Too many late nights, I guess."

"Of course." Her eyes were dark and fathomless. "Not sleeping well?"

"Me? No." He scoffed. "I'll sleep when I'm dead, right?"

She quietly reached for her necklace, fingering the stones that were set in the gold heart pendant. It didn't seem to match her aesthetic. Maybe it was a sentimental piece.

He seized on a way to change the topic and keep her from leaving. "You wear that necklace a lot. Is there a story behind it?"

Patently aware of what he was doing, she peered at him and hummed. "It was my grandmother's. She had the same abilities I do. She died when I was a baby, so I never got to know her. She left pieces of jewelry for my sisters and me. This was the necklace she left me and it helps me feel connected to her."

Grief, the old bastard, came out of nowhere and put a squeeze on his ribs. "I'm sorry you never got to know your grandmother. Even though Grandma Nell has been gone for weeks now, the loss still feels fresh. It seems like I was just talking to her the other day." Suddenly, he was prattling on again. "When I visited her, I'd always bring her a cup of coffee and a treat. Something warm and comforting, you know? In those last few months, she didn't know who I was but she always lit up at the sight of those coffees and she made sure to tell me if I didn't put enough sugar in them."

"It sounds like you were a good grandson."

"I had to be. My dad...he has a hard time dealing with emotional situations. When my grandmother, his mom, became less lucid, he didn't know what to say to her anymore. When she got confused, he thought the best way to help her was to argue, to remind her of what was accurate. If she said, 'The Queen of Denmark came to visit me today,' he'd correct her and she'd get upset. You can't argue with someone who has dementia. Just let them have their visits with the Queen." He shoved his hair out of his face. "Anyway, I just tried to keep her company, to bring a little happiness to her day."

"Your grandmother knows you were there, I promise."

"You see that?"

"Yeah." She smiled through misty eyes. "I think my grandmother and I would have been really close too. Sometimes I wonder if it's better that I never got to know her at all, because I never had the pain of losing her. I mean, there's this void inside me because I missed out, but it's not the same as watching someone exit this life. There's something really hard about losing a grandparent. They're special."

Will's throat was rough when he answered. He swallowed to dislodge the itchy ball of melancholy. "Yeah. It's a whole other level of fucked up and I don't think it's hit me yet." He'd managed to bury his feelings, which he knew was unhealthy but he'd kept persuading himself that he was just delaying his grief a little bit. It would probably wallop him at the worst possible moment, like maybe the museum opening day. He could see it now. The doors to the museum would open. The visitors would pile in for their first programs and he would have a spectacular panic attack right there in the gift shop.

Adelaide was quiet, her eyes downcast.

"I'm making you sad."

"No, you're not. I know it can be hard to share things like that, so I appreciate you sharing them with me."

There was such warmth in her gaze, flickers of softness around her eyes every time she blinked. Will was ready to swear he saw something there that was more than kindness, more than basic sympathy. Seized by hope, he touched her hand. "Addy…"

She slipped her hand away and smiled. "I should go. I have…a thing."

"Yeah. Of course. I probably have a few things as well."

She stood. "Thanks for the lunch company, Will. Take care of yourself."

"You too." Before he got the second word out, she'd turned and started walking away. Will sat there for a few minutes, watching her retreating figure, picking at his salad.

When it dawned on him that his appetite had disappeared with Addy, he collected the remains of his lunch and tossed them in a garbage can.

Chapter Seven

On Friday evening, three weeks after first visiting the Taylor house, Adelaide stood once more in its foyer, her sisters in tow. They'd had some trouble pinning the real estate agent down but Cindy had just handed over the keys so that they could do a vigil. Now, as the sun began to set, the agent shuffled in her spot.

"You've got it for the night." Cindy looked over her shoulder at the staircase. "Will that be enough time? I've got another open house tomorrow."

Edwina popped some fresh batteries into her headlamp. "That's not exactly a lot of time but we'll do our best."

One night. Adelaide did her best not to produce an actual growl. What did Cindy honestly think would happen in the course of one evening? That the little spirit girl would skip up to them, surrender herself and prance off into the fucking light?

"*Addy, take a breath.*" Maria's soothing voice interrupted her string of silent curses.

Adelaide did take a breath but ended up holding it in frustration.

There was an old source of anger, one lying dormant deep in her core. She called it Vesuvius. It had been there for decades, appearing right around the time she started having her troubles at school. Thanks to a lot of therapy, she'd managed to mostly contain it.

Every so often, though, it bubbled and rumbled. Like the original Vesuvius of Pompeii, it threatened to obliterate everything in its path, leaving a wake of ash and smoke.

"*It's okay. You're okay,*" Maria reminded her. "*Cindy doesn't understand.*"

Adelaide swallowed hard, trying to stem the flow of lava. "*I don't like her.*"

"*I know but it's not really her you dislike. It's the situation.*"

"*You're right.*" Adelaide forced a measure of calm into her being. She would think of things that gave her joy. Things like fluffy kittens and greenhouses full of plants and that new set of bath bombs that she'd recently purchased, the ones shaped like little skulls. When she submerged them in the bath water, glittery fake blood oozed from their eyes. *Super cool.*

"All right. Well, lock up after you're done." Cindy gave them all a once-over. "Boy, outfits and everything. You girls are…fun."

Because they planned to film the proceedings, they'd worn their DPI uniforms, black cargo pants, a black shirt with their logo and Doc Martens. Normally, Adelaide dressed it up with some of her personal flair. A lover of all things sparkly, she often added a bedazzled hair comb or barrettes, but she hadn't bothered this evening. She didn't feel particularly sparkly right now.

A couple of times during the week, she'd stood in front of the Taylor house, begging the girl to appear and communicate. However, she hadn't even appeared in her window. Now, Adelaide was concerned all the commotion at the house had scared her off.

Although, in truth, it wasn't the only reason she felt off her game. She couldn't stop thinking of Will. By her calculations, she was due to run into him again at any time.

Ever since she'd witnessed his panic attack, her emotions had been in a state of all-out anarchy. She couldn't seem to control them. It had only gotten worse after their last chat over falafel salad. Even though he'd opened up a bit about his grandmother, he'd made it clear he wasn't cool discussing everything with her.

Who could blame him? She hadn't exactly been Miss Approachable herself.

She still wasn't sure what she'd been thinking when she'd asked him to have lunch with her. First, she'd shown interest, then she'd turned him away. At some point, she'd thought it was a good idea to try to seduce him with falafel, clearly an indication she had no idea what she was doing. Will must have whiplash from all the back and forth.

She was starting to think that maybe she'd made a mistake in shooing him away after their date, and she wasn't sure how to come back from that.

Plus, she was worried about him. It was clear he was suffering on a couple of levels and there seemed to be a situation at his work. She wasn't sure if it was actually paranormal in nature or not, but if employees were leaving because they were scared there, or "uncomfortable" as he preferred to think of it, that was a bad sign.

Mainly, she was concerned for him, though. The last couple of times she'd seen him, his skin hadn't been the right color. Maybe he was simply fighting off a bug, but she'd seen that kind of paleness before and it generally had nothing to do with the common cold.

She still couldn't shake the image of him hyperventilating during his panic attack. Seeing him like that had also brought back some painful memories of her own panic attacks. It had been years since she'd had one, but she remembered them well, along with the trauma that inspired them. They'd begun in high school, when she was already a target for bullies. The attacks had just given those kids something else to talk about.

Adelaide the freak.

She'd been called every name in the book as a result of her unusual talents. Aberration, weirdo, loser, mutant, demon and her personal favorite, "handmaiden of Satan." That one had been muttered by a youth pastor when she was a teenager, and it had been the last time she'd ever attended a church function of any sort.

Perhaps the most cutting epithet, however, was the one people had spoken with good intentions. *Special.*

One of her aunts used to say that one a lot. *Addy can't help that she's special.* Aunt Deborah used to pat Addy's head and repeat the phrase, as if it made everything better. At least, she did so until Addy's mom put her in her place. Aunt Deborah didn't come around the house much after that.

Did Will think she was *special* or a handmaiden of Satan?

Considering he'd reached for her hand at the end of their falafel lunch, probably not. He was still interested, it was clear.

She was too. It was the reason she'd invited him to join her on that park bench. It had taken all her courage to even ask him to join her, especially after turning him down so spectacularly before. What must he think? She was all over the place.

He tempted her, like no one ever had. He was sweet and funny and his grief made her want to gather him to her bosom and whisper words of love into his ear.

Love. What a laugh. This was lust, plain and simple.

She had a hard-on for a guy with problems. The nurturer in her wanted to bring him home and take care of him, while the neglected sex kitten in her wanted to bring him home and *really* take care of him.

But she was afraid to lay it all on the line. That was why she'd run away from him. Again.

Stop it. They had no relationship and never would. At best, Will was an acquaintance.

An acquaintance she really wanted to bone.

She'd been right to walk away. It was better that way. He could find some other person to spend his time with, one who didn't have regular conversations with the dearly departed. One who wasn't *special*. He didn't need that shit in his life, on top of his other issues.

Get it together. You might not get another chance to help the spirit girl after tonight. This thing with Will was history before it even got started.

Maria rattled her insides with indignation. *"Why are you being so defeatist? He likes you, I can tell. Talk to him."*

Maria had been hollering at her for a while now. Adelaide hadn't even told Edwina and Susannah about Will and their failed attempts at dating yet, but she suspected their reactions would be similar. *"Leave it alone, Maria. It's for the best."*

"I know what you're thinking," Maria persisted. *"You think you've saved Will from having to deal with your gift. I hadn't pegged you as a martyr, Adelaide Genevieve Darke."*

It was possible she had indulged in some martyr-worthy theatrics this past week, while on her own. Lots of dramatic sighs, even the odd bit of hand-wringing, and she knew it wasn't like her.

Will had done something to her, the adorable bastard. He had no idea what he'd unleashed when he'd rolled up his sleeves that night and showed her his sexy forearms.

"Listen," she said to Maria, *"we have more important things to discuss. I need you to be on guard tonight. The Taylor house is our priority right now."*

Maria sniffed. *"I am capable of multitasking, and you haven't heard the last of this."*

"When do you plan to post your video?" asked Cindy, as they hauled in the rest of their equipment.

"Don't worry." Susannah's smile was tight. "As we discussed, we won't post anything until after you get a sale. Just keep us in the loop, please."

"I know they say any publicity is good, but I don't want anything to jeopardize this sale. I stand to make a good commission on this place. Once that goes through, you can post to your heart's content." Cindy grimaced as Edwina and Adelaide hefted one of the larger tech cases through the front door. "You won't scratch or break anything, will you? Are objects going to be flying around in here?"

Adelaide huffed. Vesuvius spewed a teeny bit of poison gas.

Susannah, ever the diplomatic empath, touched Adelaide's elbow to let her know she would handle the agent. "I promise you, Cindy, we will take good care of the house. If anything should get damaged during the course of the investigation, we'll take full responsibility and have it repaired immediately." She smiled and ushered Cindy to the door. "Have a lovely evening and thanks for allowing us to do this. I'll make sure you get your keys back."

"Fine. You have my number if you need anything." Cindy raced down the front steps of the porch and hurried to her parked car.

Adelaide glared. "I don't like that woman."

"We've dealt with worse." Edwina shrugged as she set up a motion detector in the front hallway.

"She doesn't give a crap about the actual people who lived here." Adelaide ran her finger along the edge of the decorative hall table. "All she cares about is her precious commission."

"That's because the economy is shit," Edwina said. "It's her livelihood. Don't be too hard on her."

Susannah stood in front of Adelaide and fixed one of her stray hairs, tucking it behind Addy's ear. "Are you okay? I'm getting a lot of anger coming off you."

Edwina and Susannah both had their own abilities, but her sisters hadn't been aware of them until a short time ago. During their investigation in Niagara-on-the-Lake a while back, Edwina had realized she was a medium. Susannah, on the other hand, was an empath and had the ability to feel the emotions of others. Adelaide was pleased to see her sisters embracing their unique talents.

Until they turned them on her. "I'm fine."

Edwina cackled. "Dude, you're so not fine. You've been grumpy every single time I've spoken with you this week."

"Grumpy? When exactly was I grumpy?"

"Let's see," teased Edwina. "Morning, noon and night."

"That's ridiculous. I'm nothing but...but sweetness and light." Adelaide sputtered so much that they all burst out laughing.

The momentary hilarity turned out to be cathartic. It calmed old Vesuvius right down.

"What's wrong, Addy?" asked Edwina.

"It's really nothing."

Susannah grabbed Addy's hands. "Hey, I know how much this investigation means to you and we only have one night. You won't be able to focus on what needs to be done here if you're worried about something else. So, spill."

Dammit, she was right. Adelaide had taught her about how important it was to embrace emotion and all that shit. How could she possibly argue with them when they threw her own words back at her? "I met a guy."

Both Edwina and Susannah paused.

"A living guy, not a dead one."

They let out happy exclamations.

"Don't get too excited. I made a mess of it."

Susannah tipped her head to the side. "I'm sure you didn't."

"Trust me, I did." As much as they loved her, her sisters couldn't relate, not completely. "You can't tell me you're surprised. Look at my track record. No one sticks around. They're all afraid of me, and of what I see." She sighed. "And on the night of our date, I did see something. I had a vision of a woman dying. I think she was murdered."

"Oh my God," Susannah said. "A recent death?"

"No, it was from a long time ago, but it managed to upset me."

"Of course it would." Edwina crossed her arms, in defense mode, as she had been for most of Addy's life. "So, was this guy an asshole to you? And do you have his address?"

"Calm down, tiger. It was the opposite, actually. He was cool. He even offered to help us on this investigation. He's a historian," she explained. "He's the curator for the new Cabbagetown Museum."

Susannah's jaw dropped. "You're dating Will Moran?"

"You know him?"

"I know of him," Susannah said. "I've read several of his papers. He's *the* expert on Cabbagetown history."

"Yeah, I gathered that. You know, before I sent him packing."

"Do you like him?" asked Edwina.

Adelaide nodded.

"Then you should call him." Edwina rubbed her arm. "Listen, I know you've had some shitty experiences in the dating world. People can be awful, and you know that better than most, so no one would blame you for wanting to protect yourself."

"I thought I'd handled it, but we keep running into each other all over the place. I tried to put myself back out there, I really did, but then I got nervous. What if I freak out on him again? What if, the next time, he rejects me?" She groaned. "Why do I keep putting myself through this? I would retire to a nunnery if I didn't think the nuns might try to burn me at the stake."

Edwina smiled in encouragement. "Addy, it sounds like Will's into you. Talk to him. Give him a chance to understand your world. It's not as scary as some would think. You're a medium, not a gorgon."

"Some days, I wish I were a gorgon."

"Don't we all?" Edwina's evil grin made it clear she had a few people in mind who would look good as statues. "My point is you don't have to save him from yourself."

"Don't I? I should have tried harder to save you guys from my *special* gift." Her sisters had been plagued by intolerant bullies just as much as Addy had.

"Hey," Susannah said, "we didn't need saving either, not then, and not now."

"And maybe you should let Will make that decision for himself. Look at Simon," Edwina said. "He hasn't been scarred from being with me. Well, he'll tell you he is, but that's his sad sense of humor and we should indulge him."

"And the last time I checked, Noah wasn't suffering either," Susannah added. "Does he worry about us heading into potentially dangerous situations? Of course, but we're experts and he knows that. Plus, I give him a lot of blowjobs, so he'd be a fool to let me go." She smiled sweetly.

"Ew. Thank you for that picture." Adelaide gave Susannah the side eye. Her sister was far too comfortable talking about sex. Addy couldn't understand why she was even having this discussion.

"To be honest, it would be great to have our very own Cabbagetown expert on call." Susannah tugged at one of her blonde waves. "I'm kind of slammed at work right now and I haven't been able to do as much research for this case as I would have liked. I'm on deadline for a couple of articles and those deadlines are coming up." Susannah was a regular contributor for a local history periodical. Since DPI had earned a measure of fame in the ghost hunting community, she'd been approached by a couple of other publications as well. Now, she was busier than ever. "Personally, I'd love to bring Will on board. He has such an intimate knowledge of the area."

"I didn't want to step on your toes."

"You wouldn't be, I swear. But it has to be what you want."

Was it what Addy wanted? She wanted to see Will again, and it was getting hard to convince herself otherwise.

"In all seriousness, there's a very good chance Will's ready knowledge could enable us to help the spirit girl sooner." Susannah's eyebrows arched as she left that little tidbit floating in the air.

Adelaide hadn't considered that point.

Goddammit, her sisters were too smart for their own good.

"Well, he's not here right now. We have a job to do and only one night to do it. Let's concentrate on connecting with the spirit girl." Adelaide reached for one of the equipment cases. "What else can I do?"

Susannah ushered her away. "Ed and I can set up the rest of the tech. You have your own prep to do. Go get some fresh air."

Adelaide nodded, grateful. She headed out to the deck and checked out the back garden. The sun was just setting so she could still appreciate the various flowers. There was a pretty seating area under a pergola in the far corner. It nestled between some mature azalea shrubs. The fuchsia pink blooms were a riot of color amongst the greenery, a jolt of pure happiness. Surrounded by her beloved nature, she began to calm down.

Adelaide made her way over to the bench and sat. The garden was an oasis in a busy city. Even the street traffic from Sumach Street seemed to fade into the distance. After a few cleansing breaths, she closed her eyes.

This was how she started all her investigations. Although messages from the world of the dead could often surprise her, like walking into a room full of Jack-in-the-boxes, she had learned how to quietly absorb and funnel those messages. Before a reading or an investigation, she found it helpful to meditate on a person's spirit or on a particular location, as a sort of warm-up. If she opened herself up to communication while emptying her mind as much as possible of other concerns, she tended to have success.

She called out to the spirit girl. *I'm here for you. I want to help. Please let me.*

Adelaide opened her eyes. The Taylor house loomed before her, just as colorful as the azaleas in the garden. Aside from the red brick and blue tiles that dominated the design, there was some yellow brickwork atop each window. She took in the other quirky details, from the intricate white bargeboard under its roof peaks to the delicate railings on the wraparound porch.

How could it look like such a happy place, and yet be filled with such sorrow?

Her hands shaking in anticipation, Adelaide stood and walked back to the front of the house. Even as she re-entered, waves of energy hit her. When she touched the doorknob, a terrible smell filled her nostrils, coating her throat.

Rather than trying to choke it back this time, Adelaide summoned all her strength and breathed it in. Redolent of chemicals, carcasses and charred things, it was the most disgusting thing she'd ever smelled.

She opened the door and went inside. Edwina and Susannah emerged from where they had been setting up.

"Why are you making that face?" asked Edwina.

"The smell's back."

Even though she was a medium as well, Edwina shook her head. "I'm still not getting anything."

"Someone's definitely trying to tell me something. Let's find out what it is."

The women each put on headlamps and Susannah turned out the lights. Although the setting sun illuminated a few of the windows, there were still plenty of shadowy corners. It wouldn't be long before the house was robed in darkness.

Susannah held a camera. She nodded, giving them the signal, and spoke into it. "This is Darke Paranormal Investigations and we're here in Cabbagetown, a neighborhood in downtown Toronto. My sisters and I grew up in this area and we all heard stories about a home that local kids called the 'Witch House.' Despite the colorful nickname, there's no history of witchcraft associated with this property. But something lingers here, and we're going to see if Addy can make contact tonight."

As they headed upstairs, Edwina took over the commentary. "On our visits, Addy has smelled something burning. She also heard the disembodied voice of a little girl. She is known to haunt the room at the top of the house, so that's where we're headed. The house has a reputation for being active, and it's already living up to its reputation tonight. Buckle up, people." She paused and shivered. "I'm feeling a chill in here right now, even though my thermometer is registering a comfortable twenty-one degrees." She turned her camera toward Adelaide. "Addy, you getting anything?"

Adelaide slowly climbed the stairs, absorbing the energy of the old house. "My skin is prickling. We're being watched."

They reached the upper floor and Adelaide led them to the door where she'd heard the little girl before. She pulled out the set of keys that Cindy had given them and unlocked the door, struggling a little because of her clammy hands. She tucked the keys into her cargo pants pocket. "We're coming in. We mean you no harm and we just want to talk to you."

Behind the door was a small set of stairs, ones that creaked underfoot. They led to a loft space under one of the roof peaks. The slanted roof would have made it a difficult room for an adult to enjoy but it was perfect for a child. It was completely empty. The only indication it had once been a bedroom was the fact that faded lace draperies still hung on the two windows. One window looked out over the front yard and there was another that looked out back.

She walked over to the front window and sat on the built-in seat. It would have been a cozy space all decorated. She imagined soft pillows on the window seat, a small bed with a handmade quilt and drawers full of fussy clothing from the Victorian era. She turned to Susannah. "Do you have the bear?"

Susannah reached for the backpack that was slung over her shoulder. She opened it up and pulled out an antique teddy bear. Before handing it to Adelaide, she explained their process to their viewers. "If you've watched us before, you'll know we sometimes use trigger objects. In the cases of child spirits, we often bring teddy bears or antique dolls, whatever we think might get a reaction. We're hoping that this child will appreciate the stuffed animal."

Adelaide set the bear down on the window seat next to her and addressed the spirit. "I've seen you sitting here as I've walked in front of the house. I'd like to think this room was your happy place but I think it might have been one of loneliness too." She waited a moment, listening for a voice. "Can you tell me your name?"

Edwina held out the device in her hand. "My EMF meter's all over the place."

Suddenly, there was a voice. There was no mistaking it. It was clear and bright and it seemed to be coming from the window seat area. "Lottie."

Judging from their wide-eyed expressions, Edwina and Susannah had heard the voice too.

Adelaide nodded. "That's excellent. Thank you, Lottie. Is that a nickname for Charlotte?"

The spirit made an affirmative noise.

Susannah spoke into the camera. "I can confirm that there was someone who lived here who was named Charlotte. She was the daughter of Robert Samuel Taylor, a local businessman. He built the house in 1858 and is known for being the owner of the R. S. Taylor Glue and Blacking Manufactory."

Edwina made a rolling motion with her hand, an indication for Adelaide to keep the spirit talking.

"Lottie," asked Adelaide, "how old are you?"

"Eight."

"A big girl, then." Adelaide smiled. "Do you have any family here with you? Any friends?"

"Can't find th—" Lottie's voice cut out, much like a staticky radio signal. "Want to play with someone. Will you play with me?"

"Of course, honey. I'll play with you," Adelaide said. She moved the teddy bear closer to where she imagined Lottie was sitting. "Should we give the bear a name? What would you like to call it?"

Lottie didn't respond, but the bear shifted on the window seat, moved by unseen hands.

"I'm seeing pictures of your life here, Lottie," Adelaide said to the girl. "You had a big family, with several brothers and sisters, but you were the youngest, weren't you? I'm getting an image of you with a lot of adults. That's one of the reasons you were so lonely. By the time you came around, your siblings had grown. You felt left out a lot."

Again, Lottie remained silent.

"Then you got sick. I see you in a bed, hugging a toy bear, much like the one we brought you today. You felt very hot and very sore, but it didn't last long, did it? I'm very sorry that happened to you, Lottie." She turned to her sisters. "Typhoid."

"Horrible," whispered Edwina.

Adelaide noticed some movement out of the corner of her eye. It was Susannah, rubbing her stomach. "You feel something, Suz?"

"My stomach hurts." Her mouth twisted.

"Lottie, is that how you felt? Did your stomach hurt too?" Adelaide asked. "My sister Susannah is able to feel what others feel. Are you trying to make her understand how it was for you?"

The door leading to the loft slammed shut.

"Shit." Edwina was the first to move, racing down the steps. She pulled on the door, then rattled the knob. "It's locked."

On the other side, a child laughed.

"Okay, that's not very nice, kid. I'm sorry for how you died, but we don't like those kinds of games." Edwina yanked on the door again, to no avail.

Adelaide knew all the yanking in the world wouldn't make a difference. They wouldn't be allowed out until Lottie wanted to let them out.

Edwina took a deep breath, rested her hand on the door and schooled her voice. "Lottie, *sweetheart*? Would you please open the door? Be a good girl now." She waited, tried it again, and grunted out another curse.

Once again, the child laughed.

Edwina's nostrils flared. "This is why I'll never have children."

"Let me try." Adelaide stepped in front of Edwina and touched the doorknob. "Lottie, I know you're excited to have visitors and you don't really want to scare us. You're just having some fun now. Open the door, so we can all play together."

Adelaide tried the door, but it remained shut.

Behind them, Susannah let out a soft moan. "It's getting worse."

They turned to her. Even in the darkness of the room, the whiteness of Susannah's face was evident. Abandoning the door for the time being, Addy returned to her ailing sister. She led Susannah over to the window seat and made her sit down. "Take a minute. Breathe." Addy sat next to her.

She held Susannah's hand, but with each labored breath, her sister's face went from white to green. Susannah held a hand to her mouth.

"We need to get her outside," Adelaide said. "This place is making her sick."

"I don't think it's the house. It's your pal, Lottie. The kid has powers." Edwina huffed and put down her camera. "Why is it that the ghosts of children are always the creepiest? I'm going to try the door again."

Adelaide and Edwina helped Susannah to her feet and guided her toward the loft room door. This time, thank the universe, Lottie decided to let them out.

The Darke sisters headed downstairs and outside for a breather. About fifteen minutes later, the color returned to Susannah's face and she insisted on going back inside. Although Edwina and Adelaide suggested their sister sit this one out, Susannah was determined, so they tried to connect with Lottie again.

By that time, Lottie no longer wanted to play. They continued their vigil for another couple of hours, investigating other rooms, to no avail. At that point, they decided to call it a night. Susannah still wasn't feeling one hundred percent and was growing tired.

Outside, Edwina handed Susannah a bottle of cold water. "What's Charlotte Taylor's story? Did she really die of typhoid?"

Leaning against the Jeep, Susannah took a sip. "Yeah, and in that room." Her cell phone vibrated in her hand. "Noah's worried. I texted him that I wasn't feeling well."

As Susannah reached out to Noah to let him know she was on the way home, Adelaide took a moment to consider their situation. She didn't like seeing the effect that the house, or its former occupant, had on Susannah. They'd have to be careful if she came back to the house for another vigil.

"Gee," teased Edwina, "if only we knew of another historian who might be familiar with the Taylor family. Know anyone, Addy?"

"Fine. I'll talk to Will."

She had no choice. If the dead weren't forthcoming, she had to resort to interacting with the living. Even the hot ones with the compelling back stories, amber eyes and sinewy forearms.

She would do it for the case. She would do it for Lottie.

She certainly wouldn't be doing it for her peace of mind.

Chapter Eight

"And here, we have Ned Hanlan." Will rested his hand on the gray monument that bore the name *Hanlan*. "Ned was born in 1855. Some of you may have visited the Toronto Islands in our harbor. Well, Ned and his family lived there. His father built a hotel there, in the area now known as Hanlan's Point. Ned used to row across the harbor every day to go to school and became a professional sculler. A champion here in Canada, the United States and the winner of the World Championship, he only lost six of his three hundred races during his rowing career. In fact, he was Canada's first world champion in an individual sporting event. Later on, he became a hotelier like his father, a politician and was the first head coach of the University of Toronto's rowing club. He was one of Canada's most revered sports heroes and is now a member of Canada's Sports Hall of Fame. Unfortunately, this great athlete was felled by pneumonia in 1908, when he was only fifty-two years old. Any questions?"

"I've seen his picture," one woman called out. "He was a hottie."

Will laughed. "He definitely had that beefcake factor. Ned Hanlan had swagger and that sexy, bushy mustache. A winning combination, I guess." He looked around to see if there were any other questions.

That was when he saw Adelaide. She stood about fifty feet away, in the shade of a mature oak tree.

Will swallowed hard, his throat suddenly dry. Clearly, this was not a case of simply bumping into her. From her determined posture, he could tell she'd come here looking for him. Why?

Still bashful about their last conversation, he began to sweat. He had no idea where he stood with her and every time he saw her, it chipped away at his soul a little.

A couple of the straggler tourists hung around and, frankly, he was relieved to have a few extra minutes' reprieve. He had no idea what to say to Addy, or what she wanted to say to him. He answered their questions and eventually the tourists wandered away. As the last one departed, Will walked over to greet her.

"Hey, Will."

"Addy. If we keep meeting in cemeteries like this, people are going to talk."

"Yeah." She shifted her balance from one foot to the other. "Good tour?"

"No one yawned. Always a good sign."

For a few seconds, they just stared at each other. Her mouth opened and closed a couple of times, but nothing came out.

He took the opportunity to check her out. She wore shorts that came to the midway point of her plush thighs, her green Chucks and a shirt that brought a smile to his face. "*The Gashlycrumb Tinies*. We have—"

"The same shirt. I know." She laughed and the tension broke a little.

"That is seriously awesome."

"It's seriously unnerving that we both have such a dark sense of humor. Should I be worried?"

"Nah. Edward Gorey was a genius. And who doesn't love tales of untimely death?""

"Right." Although she was smiling, her face was pinched. Something was bothering her, and he guessed it was more than just their awkward tension. "How've you been?"

So they were back to small talk. Okay. He'd play along. "Oh, you know. Keeping busy."

She took another step toward him. "Could I, um, steal you away for a minute?"

He should say no. Adelaide Darke was bad news — not literally, of course. She was just bad news for his defenseless heart. Even though he totally understood she wasn't stringing him along, toying with him, he couldn't help feeling a little played.

But she looked so pretty, with her bobbed hair tucked behind her ear on one side. Her soft perfume wafted toward him on a breeze. He'd been wondering what that scent was. For some reason, it made him think of his grandmother. Lilacs, yes! There had been huge lilac bushes in Grandma Nell's old backyard. Grandma used to ask him to cut down bouquets of the flowers for her.

The poignant memory, combined with the air of vulnerability surrounding Adelaide, destroyed any semblance of self-preservation Will might have had. "You can steal me for as long as you want." *Dude, you sound desperate.*

Roses appeared on Adelaide's cheeks. "How've you been?"

"I think you already asked that."

"You're right, sorry."

"No, it's fine. I'm good. Same old, same old. Work's just been challenging, that's all. It's nice being able to do these tours, so I can forget about it for a while."

Concern knitted her eyebrows. "I was going to ask you a favor, but on second thought, maybe it was a bad idea. I don't want to dump more on your plate and I'm not sure I have the right to ask you for anything."

He didn't like hearing that. "No, it's fine. What's up?"

She indicated a nearby bench, and they sat down. "You mentioned you might be interested in helping my sisters and I with our case."

"The Taylor house?" His voice rose in pitch as the words tumbled out of his mouth.

"Yeah. My sister Susannah is on deadline and she's finding it hard to squeeze in time to do more research. You're the expert on all things Cabbagetown. We could use your help. You know, if that's not asking too much."

He had a million items on his own to-do list. If he wanted an out, he had one. But he didn't want an out. He'd been trying to wrangle an invitation to see inside the Taylor house for years, but the previous owners hadn't much cared about its history. Besides, if it gave him more time with Adelaide, in any capacity, he was all for it. He was, after all, a glutton for punishment. "It's not too much. I'd love to help."

"Really?"

"Yeah. What's been happening at the house?"

"I made contact with a girl there. Charlotte Taylor."

"For real?"

"I've seen her in one of the bedroom windows. The first time I saw her I was just a kid myself, and now after all these years, she's reappeared." She bit her bottom lip. "I was actually hoping you could share your knowledge of the family dynamic with us. I saw that Charlotte died of typhoid."

"You did? I'm sorry you had to see that. It must have been horrible." Without thinking, he reached for her hand, only meaning to console her. He tensed, waiting for a rejection.

But it didn't come.

Addy glanced at their linked hands and the hint of a smile danced across her lips. She didn't pull away. "It's never nice to see those things, but I think Charlotte passed quickly after contracting the disease. I didn't see her suffering for long."

"I'm not surprised. Typhoid was a serious threat. There was no water filtration back in her day. Private citizens and industries were still dumping all their crap into the local waterways, including her own father at his factory. By the 1860s, Toronto was considered to be one of the unhealthiest cities on the continent."

"Well, I can tell her apparition has nothing to do with the manner of her death. It has everything to do with her father."

Will absorbed the implications of her statement. "You're saying old man Taylor is out there somewhere?" He waved his free hand and moaned like a cheesy TV ghost.

She nodded. "Would you be interested in coming with us the next time we go to the house?"

"Hell, yeah. I've always wanted to look inside that place."

Adelaide curled her lip. "Don't get too excited. It's been renovated from top to bottom. It doesn't even look like a period house on the inside anymore."

"Figures. That happens a lot. I'd still like to join you."

"That's…great." Only then, did she slip her hand out of his. "We'd pay you for your time and expertise, of course."

"Addy, don't worry about that. Being able to finally explore that house is payment enough."

"That's kind of you." Her eyes darkened with curiosity and her tongue slipped out to wet her plump lips.

He followed the path of her tongue, unable to drag his gaze from that delectable piece of flesh. "Thanks for asking."

"Okay. I'll be in touch and we'll set it up. We're at the mercy of the real estate agent's schedule, so I'm not sure when it'll be." She was rising from her seat on the bench when a bird trilled in the tree right over their heads. Smiling, she looked up into the canopy of leaves.

"Black-capped chickadee," he said.

"Come again?"

"The bird call. It's a black-capped chickadee."

"You know it from its song?"

"Yeah. My mom taught me about birds when I was a kid. She used to bring me to the Necropolis and we'd sit for an hour or two, trying to identify them by ear. They've always fascinated me. When I have the time, I still enjoy birding. Sometimes, after my tours, I bring out some birdseed and they eat right out of my hand."

"They do?" Her face was awash in wonder.

"Yeah." He reached for his backpack and rummaged around inside it. "Here. I always keep a little bag of seeds with me. Hold open your hand."

They stood close together and he poured a small amount of shelled sunflower seeds into her palm. She looked up at him from under her eyelashes, her very long eyelashes. Her dark eyes and those lashes were a killer combination. If she could literally annihilate him with a glance, he'd go to his death willingly. He cleared his throat. "That's it. Now, just hold your arm out and keep still."

It only took a few seconds for the clever birds to notice Adelaide was holding out some seed. The birds were accustomed to Will feeding them, so they'd likely had them in their sights already.

When one of the little black-and-white creatures alighted on Adelaide's palm, gently pecking at the seed, she stifled a happy squeal. "Oh my gosh. I'm feeding a chickadee!" As it flew off, she watched it go. Another soon took its place.

"They're curious birds and they're super smart. They know people like to feed them so they'll often follow you around the park." He poured some seed into his palm and held it out, and another bird landed there to partake.

Adelaide gazed at him in pure joy.

It was the most incredible thing he'd ever seen, so beautiful it made his heart ache. Right then and there, Will knew he had to see that look again, and often. "Want to know how to recognize their call? It's one of the easier ones to learn because it sounds like their name. *Chicka-dee-dee*. They also use it when predators are near. The more "dees" they add to the call, the higher the threat level. *Chicka-dee-dee-dee-dee-dee*."

She gazed lovingly at the tiny bird on her hand. "Who would hurt you? You're the sweetest little thing." As she turned to him, there was a shine in her eyes that wasn't there a minute ago. "This is amazing. Thanks, Will."

His throat tightened at her lovely display of emotion. "You're welcome. You can come birding with me anytime you want."

"I would love that." She gazed at him for a long minute, but her happy expression crumpled and she let out a sigh.

"Addy, talk to me. I won't judge you. Hell, you've seen me at my worst. Go on." He softened his voice. "I've got you."

She held back a breath and Will got the impression she was also holding back a flood of past hurts and painful moments. But, to his great relief, she nodded.

They both dumped their remaining seeds on one of the nearby headstones, and the chickadees continued their meal there. "Here." Will pulled out the small package of sanitizing wipes that he kept in his backpack, along with the bag of seeds, and grabbed a couple of wipes. "Let me wipe your hand first. Our bird friends are cute, but one of them peed on you a little bit."

She held out her hand to him this time and he handled it as if it were a Faberge egg, gently smoothing the wipe all over her palm. Addy watched, seemingly rapt, as he slowly wiped each of her fingers, dipping between them. Once again, her gaze met his, so full of curiosity and a long-withheld anguish.

The desire to make everything better for her was fierce and biting. He knew that it would give him no rest. "There," he murmured, when he was done with the wipe. "All better."

As he pulled out a fresh wipe and cleaned his own hands, she was quiet and seemed to be choosing her words. He didn't want her to feel awkward, but at the same time, he welcomed this chance to peel back one of her layers. He wanted her to feel good about confiding in him. God only knew he'd been thinking of ways to prove to her that he could be what she needed.

Here was his chance.

He wasn't sure why he'd become so attached to Adelaide in the short time he'd known her. She put him completely off his game...as if he ever had game to begin with. He felt this overriding need to get it right, to not screw up with her. He'd come close to screwing up already, so this moment felt significant.

He disposed of the wipes in a nearby trash can and sat back down.

She collected herself and looked him in the eye, in that forthright manner that intrigued him so much. "Firstly, I should apologize."

"No, it's not necessary."

"Please. I know I've been hot and cold, and I swear I'm not playing games with you. Here's the deal. I have trust issues, bad ones. And I know what you must be thinking. Everyone has trust issues. Everyone's been hurt on some level, right? I'm not saying I have it any worse than anyone else, but sometimes it feels like my problems are...different."

He was reminded of their conversation at Beans. *The world can be a dark place. When I was little, it gave me comfort to believe we had something like the Force, guiding us.* After seeing what Addy could do, what she could see, he was starting to understand why she shut him down so quickly.

"I know we haven't spent a lot of time together, but I like you. I have no expectations about where you and I are headed, if we're even headed anywhere, but I feel a need to explain. When I was young, I was bullied because of my abilities."

Will's heart sank. It fucking plummeted. At the same time, he was furious at himself for not having anticipated that this could be the cause of her hesitation to get involved. She'd been traumatized. How did he not figure that out?

"I was an object of ridicule by numerous people for years, and the hardest part was that it didn't just affect me. It affected my sisters too, my whole family, really. Because my sisters always came to my rescue at school, they were painted with the same 'freak' brush. As much as I understand that was ancient history, and even though our parents made sure we all got help, those feelings have bled into my relationships and my social life. There's a side of me that not everyone gets to see and it's not pleasant. I hide it from my clients, from acquaintances, even some friends. But it's there, and even though I've learned how to manage it, it never quite goes away."

Will leaned in, completely focused on her. He clenched his hands into fists.

"I'm going to lay it all out for you. I can be defensive, I'm quick to judge, and even though I may not show it on the outside, I get angry. Really angry."

It was hard for him to picture Adelaide Darke transforming into a ball of fury, but given everything she'd had to contend with, she'd probably earned the right to lash out every so often. If people had picked on him his whole life, he probably would have done the same. Worse, even.

What had they done to her? He wanted to ask all the terrible details so he could support her, but he understood she might not want to discuss it.

He also knew the information would change him. It would turn him into a creature of rage. Even now, he could hear his heartbeat in his ears.

But he would willingly carry that burden if it meant lessening hers.

She played with a chunky ring on her middle finger. "Then there's the matter of the dead. They're always with me, in one way or another. It's who I am, but I realize it makes other people uneasy, to put it mildly." She laughed but the sound held no hilarity. "I think some people look at me and they see Death. I know that's ironic coming from a woman who's wearing a *Gashlycrumb Tinies* T-shirt. In some ways, I love being the freak. I play it up, but it also catches up to me every so often."

"Addy, when I look at you, I don't see a freak and I definitely don't see Death."

"Do you see a handmaiden of Satan?"

"*What?*"

She grinned. "Never mind. It's just one of the loving nicknames I've been given over the years."

What the actual fuck? He wanted to punch a goddamn wall. Still, her grin was a ray of sunshine in the darkness.

"Anyway, this is my longwinded way of warning you that I have baggage, like, so much baggage the airlines would charge me extra to fly." A blush of sweet vulnerability spread across her cheeks. "I'm sure you already figured that out. That being said, I enjoy being with you. You've been nothing but kind and considerate, and I think you're interesting and easy to talk to. The thing is, when the shit hits the fan, a part of me still expects to be bullied and ostracized, so it's easier to walk away than to be rejected. That's all." She stopped fiddling with her ring and rested her hands in her lap.

"I hate that you were bullied. I'm so sorry." His words sounded civilized enough, but what he really meant was *Who do I kill?* How could anyone treat Addy that way? What was fucking wrong with people?

"It's okay. I've moved on. Look at the well-adjusted woman sitting here with you." Her self-deprecating laughter almost destroyed him. "Talk about too much information, huh?"

"No, it's not too much. I want to know everything." He sighed. "Can I ask you a question?

"Sure."

"Would you be open to having me seek out your enemies, so I can dispatch them in painful and humiliating ways? Because I could. I did a university elective on methods of torture throughout history. I have the knowledge."

Her burst of wicked laughter soothed his need for revenge. For now. "As much as I appreciate your disturbing offer, I'm good. No need to dispatch anyone on my account. Not today, anyway."

"If you say so. The offer remains open."

"I'll keep it in mind." Worry played with the corners of her smile, tilting them downward. "Anyway, I guess this is my way of saying I would not be opposed to trying again. If you're still into it, that is."

She did the most remarkable thing then. She reached for his hand.

To Will, it might have been a life preserver being thrown to a drowning man. "I'm into it." He knew there were people out there who'd recommend he kept things cool, that he kept her on her toes, but that had never been his style and he hated playing games. "I'm just into you, Addy."

Once again, her face lit up. "That's good. Really good."

As soon as the words were out of her mouth, his gaze was drawn to her lips again. There was something about Adelaide that brought forth all his curiosity. It was partly due to the whole medium thing. She was an unknown quantity, another rabbit hole to explore. He wanted to unearth all her secrets.

It wasn't just that, though. She had this amazing combination of strength and vulnerability that spoke to him. And, of course, she was the most gorgeous thing he'd ever seen. She had this amazing girl-next-door quality about her, with her cute haircut and her sneakers, but she also had an undeniable sex appeal. He'd already gotten distracted a few times by imagining himself kissing her, hauling her up against his body to luxuriate in her softness. She had the sexiest mouth, the kind of lips you just wanted to suck on. He wanted to trace her lips with his tongue, learning their shape and texture.

And now she was staring at him like she really wanted to kiss him, and he wasn't sure what to do about it.

This was what he got for not putting himself out there more. Maybe he felt for Addy so much because he sensed a sort of loneliness in her, one he shared. He probably shouldn't have left his relationships on the backburner the past few years. Will wasn't even sure he could call those scattered hookups and failed first dates "relationships."

Although, none of them even seemed to matter right now, not while Addy was gazing at him. For the first time, he noticed there was a tiny scar at the left side of her mouth, right where her lips met. Captivated, he tried to imagine how she might have obtained the scar.

When she cleared her throat, he realized he'd been staring too long. "I, um, I guess I should go." She stood.

"Right. Sure." He jumped up as well. *Take it easy, sport.* She'd only just unburdened herself. Of course, she wasn't going to jump his bones on a cemetery bench. "You'll shoot me a time for the Taylor house visit?"

"Absolutely."

"And let's make some plans soon, for something other than chasing ghosts."

"Yes. Although, for the record, we don't actually chase them. They just seem to follow me around." She arched her left eyebrow. "Still interested in dating me?"

"Yes, ma'am." He drew closer, so that the tips of their shoes touched. "Still interested in dating a history geek with dwindling social skills?"

She looked up from under her lashes again in a display of coyness that just about took a year off his life. "Now, now, Mr. Moran. I'm sure you have some skills."

Saints preserve him. He gulped, at a loss for any sort of response that didn't resemble Neanderthal communication.

Luckily, Adelaide still had control over her motor skills. "I wonder if, I mean..." She rested a hand on his chest, making his skin burn up under the fabric. When she spoke again, her voice was a whisper. "Would it be okay if I kissed you?"

Will almost choked on his tongue. "It would be more than okay."

Being shorter than him, she raised herself on tiptoes. To steady her, Will slid his hand around her waist. Her lilac fragrance went straight to his head. Her mouth, that fascinating, sensuous mouth, looked so plump and soft. Will already knew that once he got a taste of Addy, he'd be coming back for more.

She angled her head and brushed her lips against his. *Fuck.* It was soft. She kissed him twice, each embrace a mere tease. But on the third kiss, Addy let out a quiet moan and opened for him. He touched her tongue with his, seeking something he couldn't even name but that he suddenly needed so badly. It was her moan that did him in. No sound had ever filled him with such urgency and desperation.

He pulled her up against his body, enjoying the crush of her breasts on his chest. Her eyes were squeezed shut and she tangled her tongue with his.

This wasn't just some kiss. It was a damn miracle and it had been worth the time it took to get to this place.

After a few minutes of sheer bliss, they fell apart. Addy was breathing heavily and so was he. She stepped back and ran a finger over her smudged lip gloss.

"You felt that, huh?" he asked.

"Yeppers." Her mouth still hung open.

He made little explosion motions with his hands. "I'm not a geologist or anything, but I think some tectonic plates just shifted."

"See? I knew you had skills." And just like that, Adelaide Darke grinned and waltzed away, a swing in her hips, like the coquettish heroines from the black-and-white movies that his grandmother used to watch. "Bye, Will."

Will waved weakly, then sat back down on the bench, folding his hands in his lap.

He was going to need a minute.

Chapter Nine

That kiss.

Hours later, Adelaide was still thinking about it. Even now, after midnight, she lay in bed, tossing and turning, in awe of what Will's touch had done to her. Kissing Will had been everything she'd hoped it would be. Her body had gravitated toward his, seeming to fit against his so perfectly. The press of his fingertips at her waist and hips made her long for more intimate caresses. She wished she could wrap herself up in his embrace and linger there for days.

She had fought this with all her might, but now that she'd succumbed to temptation, she wanted another taste. Heck, a four-course meal.

For some reason, this felt like the start of something big. She knew better than to get carried away, but she couldn't shake the sensation that there was a curious destiny to all of this. Meeting Will for the first time in the Necropolis, her vision, even the situation with Lottie Taylor. Something was happening and for the first time since meeting him, she didn't want to run away.

She wanted to run toward him.

Although it was on silent mode, her phone lit up on her bedside table. She reached out in the dark and checked the incoming text.

Will: U asleep?

Addy: Are you kidding?

Will: Me neither. I have a big problem.

Addy:??

Will: I can't stop thinking of you.

Addy: Ah. Excitement bubbled up inside her, making her smile. *I can't stop thinking of you either.*

Will: Can I call you? I want to hear your voice.

She gave him the go-ahead and her phone rang. "Hey," he said, when she answered. His voice was full of gravel, as if he'd done his own share of tossing and turning. "So, that kiss."

Her words, exactly. "It was a...decent kiss."

"Decent?"

"Kidding. It was a very good kiss."

"That's better," he teased. "I'd like some feedback, though. On a scale of 'I never want to see Will again because of his weird, wandering tongue' to 'Oh my God, Lord Jesus, take me now,' how did it rate exactly?"

She laughed. "What if I liked the weird, wandering tongue?"

"Nice. If I recall, yours did wander first."

"It did and I regret nothing. In fact, it was an excellent kiss, definitely in 'Lord Jesus, take me now' territory."

He cheered. "Triumph!"

Adelaide wasn't sure what prompted her next comment, but her inner flirt monster roared to life. "Out of curiosity, does that weird tongue of yours ever wander anywhere else?"

"Adelaide Darke! Are you trying to kill me with your salacious comments? Do you want them to find my body tomorrow morning, bereft of life?"

"Just gathering facts and you didn't answer the question."

"I should answer, then. My tongue loves a good jaunt. Do you know of any hotspots it could visit?"

"I can think of a few."

"Well, my tongue happens to be an agreeable sort of fellow. I think it would enjoy those spots very much."

She giggled quietly. "Will?"

"Yes?"

"You're very bad. Keep it up."

"It's up, I guarantee it."

"I'm shocked and scandalized."

"Sure you are." His voice, so low and full of late-night horniness, caressed her through the phone. "Are you curled up in bed right now?"

"Yeah."

"What do you wear in bed?"

"Oh, it could be any number of sophisticated and luxurious items," Adelaide replied with a posh accent.

"Naturally."

"But tonight, I'm wearing an old T-shirt that has a pic from *Nosferatu* on it. Count Orlok, burning up in the sun. You see, I'm not just about the ghosts. I dig vampires too."

"I'd expect nothing less, and I bet you look sexy in it."

"Look at you, getting all hot and bothered over a weird girl."

"I'll have you know I happen to like weird girls. The weirder, the better."

"Lucky me." Her face heated. She rubbed her legs together under the covers, wishing she could feel Will's skin against hers. Her bed seemed so big and empty all of a sudden. It would be a lot cozier with him in it, preferably between her legs.

They were both quiet for a few seconds and a satisfied yawn broke from her.

"Hey," Will murmured, "I should let you get to sleep."

"I guess so. Talk to you soon?"

"You can count on it. Good night, pretty Addy."

She smiled at the description. "Good night." She disconnected the call and turned her phone off, setting it back on the bedside table. Adelaide snuggled in deep, pulling the sheet up to her neck and closed her eyes.

She was still grinning as she drifted off to sleep.

She had to get out of this house. It was slowly killing her, as it had killed so many others.

The house had taken everything from her, leaving her with nothing but an aching hollowness inside her heart. It no longer beat.

That same heart had ominously skipped a beat the first night Aiden hadn't come home, having collapsed outside the tavern. Her heart had stalled when the first of her babies died. And it had stopped beating altogether when she'd buried little Maeve a short time ago.

There was nothing left of her heart now. It was a hard lump of ash, barely connected to its shriveled veins.

God damn you, Aiden.

Despite her anger, she still longed for him, for the man she once knew.

How could he leave her to face this alone? It wasn't fair.

She would find him tonight, she would tear him from his mistress, the Don Vale House, and she would make him understand her pain. She would make him *see* that which he'd refused to acknowledge all these years. How convenient it must be for him to disappear into the drink to forget their shared tragedies. She'd never had that option. Someone had to be strong, and now she was exhausted from carrying two sets of burdens.

Thank the Lord she had Desmond, at least. If it hadn't been for his brotherly companionship, she didn't know what she would have done. She probably would have hurled herself into the Don River ages ago.

Sometimes, she wondered if it would have been kinder to leap from her coffin ship into the ocean long ago. In leaving Ireland and the hunger, she'd escaped one set of troubles, only to be mired in another.

She could still throw herself into the Don. No one would miss her. There was no one left to miss her.

Not true. Desmond would miss her. He would remember her.

Although, in truth, she'd probably come to rely on her brother-in-law too much. In recent months, she'd felt the burn of his gaze at her back. There was an ardor in his voice when he whispered her name and it made her uncomfortable.

It was just another reason her husband had to come home to her. Let Aiden deal with his brother's roving eye. She was too tired to deal with it.

Even though Aiden had warned her from ever venturing near the Don Vale House, she had no choice. She would collect Aiden and bring him home, or else there was nothing left for her. She had to believe a fragment of his soul survived. They'd been in love once, so much in love. Surely that tenderness lingered somewhere in the darkness.

Determined, she tore out of her home and into the night. In a hurry, she avoided Winchester Street and cut through the Necropolis. She wasn't afraid of its gloom. Her heart had known worse.

Fueled by a fire she'd never known, she stepped between the headstones, down the hill and toward the shores of the river. The grimy windows of the Don Vale House beckoned, their lights flickering. The sound of cheering drunkards met her ears.

The tavern was full. She would do her best to empty it of at least one patron tonight...or die trying.

A terrible coughing noise awoke Adelaide from her dream. It was Maria.

"Addy, get up!"

Addy's hands flew to her sides, clutching for bedsheets. She reached for the switch of her lamp on the bedside table and flicked it.

As her room illuminated, a woman appeared at the foot of her bed. Her eyes were murky, void of life.

Tendrils of her brown hair escaped her updo and her old-fashioned clothing was torn and muddied. The aura surrounding her was one of bitter melancholy.

It was the woman from her nightmare, but death had altered her.

Adelaide stared, frozen, unable to recall any of the words she normally used to guard herself from spirits. Maria's painful, phlegmy coughs echoed in her ears.

She suddenly remembered Maria's words the day they saw the spirit woman following Will around the Necropolis.

She is darkness.

No, not again!

The dead woman opened her mouth, as if to speak, but all that emerged was a shivering sort of cry. She reached out to Adelaide, gripping the footrest with her other pale hand.

As the terrible force wafted toward her, another hot rush of energy cocooned Addy, surrounding her in love and strength. It was Maria, acting as her ward, as she always had. She didn't allow the dead woman to come any closer, and Adelaide was grateful. Without Maria's intervention, she wasn't sure what she would have done. The woman's eyes were too hypnotic, too dreadful. They made one want to follow her into the abyss, with no care of what lurked in the shadows.

Because Maria stood firm, the woman faded away, leaving an odor of swampy things behind.

Addy touched the spot on her footrest that the spirit woman had touched, hoping she could glean some sort of detail. Last time at the Necropolis, the woman hadn't revealed much and had cloaked herself in obscurity.

But this time, perhaps without meaning to, she bared a fragment of her soul to Adelaide. She saw a gray headstone, surrounded by leafy trees. A man stood there, his head bowed, his eyes covered by his overgrown sandy hair.

Will.

"'Sheltered and safe from sorrow,'" she whispered. "Maria, that was…"

"Yes, Addy. That was Sarah Byrne."

Adelaide grabbed her pillow and hugged it to her chest. In her considerable experience, she'd learned that the dead appeared for specific reasons.

In this case, the reason was Will.

Chapter Ten

On her way to the Taylor house for the next vigil, Adelaide was fraught with emotion. Will would be meeting her and her sisters there, and she wasn't sure how to break the news that Sarah Byrne had appeared at her bedside. Based on the little she'd seen so far, Will was protective of Sarah's memory. Adelaide understood. Having learned the stories and traumas of so many spirit people, she'd grown protective of those lost souls too.

Something told her she needed to tread carefully.

Nevertheless, considering Sarah had manifested in Adelaide's own home, where she'd placed substantial protections over the years, it was clear Sarah's spirit possessed a measure of power.

What else could she do and what did she want?

Addy wasn't sure she could discuss it with Will until she knew more. He would naturally have questions and she prided herself on being able to provide answers. Right now, all she had was a garbled mess of nastiness in her core.

She hadn't even told Edwina and Susannah about Sarah yet. There had been nothing to tell up until now. Besides, she'd made a pledge to help Charlotte Taylor and she could only handle one paranormal investigation at a time. Even when she did readings for her clients, she had to space them out or all the energies became too draining.

As she arrived at the Taylor house, a sweet noise broke through her worried thoughts.

Chicka-dee-dee.

Black-capped chickadees. Adelaide was suddenly hearing them everywhere she went. It had only been a few days since Will had helped her feed the birds in the Necropolis, but she'd memorized their distinctive call.

One of the little birds flew over her head, singing as if to her. It wasn't out of the realm of possibility that it was one of her little buddies from the cemetery. Will had said it was common for them to follow once they knew people handed out food. Sure enough, the tiny bird landed on the Taylor property fence, a few feet away.

"I'm sorry, friend. I don't have any seeds right now. I'll catch you later."

The chickadee tipped its head, analyzing her, and flew away.

The interaction brought some lightness into her heart, which was something she sorely needed right now. It made her want to go birding with Will, and as soon as possible. In truth, ever since he'd told her about the chickadees, she'd been buoyed by an unfamiliar sort of happiness. He'd shown her something new and exciting, and it had taken her out of herself for a while.

For a few wonderful moments, she'd been able to forget about the unfinished business of the dead and of the phantoms who haunted her world.

She wasn't sure anyone would understand how precious that was to her.

Putting all thoughts of birding out of her head for the time being, Adelaide positioned herself outside the Taylor house on the sidewalk. She was eager to see Will tonight, although she had a feeling their activities would be less joyful than their last moment together. Her sisters had texted and were already inside the house, but she'd told them she would wait outside for Will. Brimming with anticipation, she stared down Sumach Street.

A foul scent hit her nostrils. It only took a couple of inhalations for it to hit the back of her throat, making her want to gag.

"Ugh." It was strong this time. She held a hand to her nose, even though she knew it wouldn't help. There was no way to shield herself from a preternatural stench. She just had to get through it.

Her gaze landed on the gates of the Necropolis across the street. A dead man stood there, clutching the iron bars, staring at her.

Adelaide gasped. He was burned beyond recognition, his face nothing more than a wide-eyed blackened skeleton. His clothing hung from him in tatters. *"Help me."*

She'd never seen this spirit before, not in all her years of wandering around the cemetery.

"What the hell is going on around here?" she murmured. The Necropolis had always been such a peaceful location. It was one of the reasons she liked to go for walks there. But lately, between Lottie, Sarah and this guy? The ghosts were starting to outnumber the living. *Give me a chance to catch up, people!*

Was it possible this new spirit man had a connection to the Taylor house? He was right across the street. If there had been a fire at the property years ago, perhaps he'd been killed.

Moved to tears, Adelaide took a step toward him, but was taken aback by some movement to her left.

It was Will, coming down the street toward her. *Okay, pull yourself together.*

She glanced back toward the dead man, but he was already fading away, taking the stench with him. The last things to disappear were his round eyes, pleading for her help until that last second.

Will greeted her. "Hi, pretty Addy."

"Hey." She blinked several times to remove the telltale moisture in her eyes. "You made it."

"Nothing could keep me away."

"Excited to see the house?"

"Sure." A blush spread across his handsome face. "Among other things."

Oh. He was talking about her. He was excited to see her. Her heart skipped a beat.

He caressed her elbow. "Are you okay? You look a bit shaken."

"I'm fine." Honestly, he wasn't looking so hot himself. There was an ashen tinge to his face today. Dark circles marred the skin beneath his eyes. "Are *you* okay?"

"Yeah. Just tired. Another bad sleep."

Was that normal for him? She knew people who were able to function on only a few hours a night. It didn't ring true in Will's case. She distinctly remembered him saying he hadn't been sleeping well lately, so it had to be a recent problem.

Despite his clear fatigue, he seemed enthusiastic. Would he be okay to do the vigil? Sometimes, spirits liked to play tricks on people who weren't feeling up to snuff and Lottie had proven herself a trickster. She didn't want Will to be susceptible to any of that nonsense.

"You know what would make me feel better?" he asked slyly.

Butterflies clamored high in her chest. "I have a feeling I know."

"I have a feeling you know too." Cupping her cheek, he brought her closer. His eyes searched hers for a tense moment, heightening the anticipation. She wasn't sure what he was looking for but she hoped he saw it in her face. When he finally touched his lips to hers, she sank into his embrace, sighing. He deepened the kiss and her sigh took on a feral quality, a broken moan.

She hadn't realized quite how much she missed being kissed by someone she really liked. Even with two short kisses, she felt a sort of knitting in the space around her heart, as if all her fragments were being stitched back together.

"I've been dying to do that," he whispered, dotting her mouth with quicker pecks.

Adelaide could only stare. This man...he stole her words, and she'd never been short on words.

He brushed his thumb around the edges of her lips. "I messed up your lip gloss."

"You're wearing just as much of it right now."

"Mmm." He smacked his lips. "Don't mind if I do."

She grabbed his hand. "We should go in."

Spurred by a fierce determination to watch over him during the vigil, she led him into the house. Her sisters were standing in the foyer. Adelaide brought him over. "Will, this is Edwina and Susannah."

They all shook hands. "Call me Ed," Edwina said.

"It's good to meet you," Susannah said. "I've read several of your papers. Your piece on Irish immigration to Cabbagetown in the eighteen-forties and fifties was impressive stuff."

"Oh, wow, thanks. It's nice to know someone other than me has read that paper." He laughed at his own joke. "And it's nice to meet you too, both of you. Addy showed me your DPI videos. Fascinating."

Susannah had her wide-eyed history geek face on, and Addy could tell she wanted to pepper Will with all sorts of questions. In the interests of keeping them on track, she took charge of the conversation. "So, a couple of developments. Right before Will arrived, I saw a spirit man outside."

"You did?" Will smoothed his fingers over her wrist. "You didn't say anything."

"He disappeared quickly. It just wasn't nice to see. He was badly burned and he wanted my help."

"Geez, Addy." Will looked horrified.

"I'm used to it," she explained. "There's also this bad smell that's been following me around this place. It's just residual activity, a kind of memory that's stuck on a loop. Unfortunately, in this case, it's gross. It smells like dead animals tossed into a firepit."

"Interesting." Will had a curious expression, but Adelaide wasn't able to read it.

"Well, we're off to an exciting start," Susannah said. "Will, consider that your welcome to the Taylor house. Hold on to your hat."

"Thanks." He chuckled nervously. "I've wanted to see inside this place my whole life."

Edwina cautioned him. "Careful what you wish for. Our last visit was eventful. If this one goes the same way, you might never want to come back."

"As I'm sure Addy has told you," Susannah said, "we believe she made contact with the spirit of Charlotte Taylor, Robert's daughter. Will, I'd imagine your museum might touch on the Taylor family in some way."

"You bet. The Cabbagetown Museum is all about the workers who lived in this area, so we have significant exhibit space dedicated to some of the first industries. The Taylor factory played a huge role in the development of the neighborhood. It was located just up the road, where Wellesley Park now sits, and it provided work for many locals. In fact, lots of those employees ended up working there for years. Many of them rented small company-owned homes right on the factory's doorstep, on streets like Wellesley, Sumach and Amelia."

Amelia Street. Where Sarah Byrne lived. Even the address caused Adelaide's hackles to go up.

"We've all heard about the conditions in Victorian factories," Edwina said, "but was the Taylor factory considered a decent place to work?"

Will grimaced. "I wouldn't go that far. Did it provide employment? Yes. Unfortunately, glue production in Victorian times was a revolting business." He turned to Adelaide. "You mentioned you smelled something like dead animals. That made me think of the factory right away. Taylor created the adhesive in his glue by boiling the connective tissues of animals. The entire neighborhood constantly smelled of animal carcasses and boiling flesh. It was a horrific stench, and if you lived anywhere nearby, there was no way to escape it. It wouldn't have mattered if you were rich or poor, that stench would have been part of your daily life. In fact, there are accounts from people who weren't able to stick around the Necropolis long enough to bury their relatives because the smell was so bad."

"The entire neighborhood," Adelaide said. "Just imagine it."

"On top of that," Will continued, "we also know that Taylor's factory produced a ton of noxious waste. Bits of animal carcasses, lime from the factory's tanning operations and waste products from stove-blacking production all found their way into the nearby creek, and that water spilled into the Don River. Not only did the Taylor factory cause a lot of pollution in the local waterways, it and other industries contributed to sky-high levels of disease in the area."

"That's awful." Susannah shook her head. "Addy, that does sound like the odor you were trying to describe."

Adelaide agreed. "It does. Even as you were describing it, Will, the smell was coming to me. You've hit the nail on the head."

"I'm glad," Will said. "Anyway, it's interesting that you also smelled fire. The Taylor factory was destroyed by fire in 1873. It was a huge tragedy. People died, including Robert Taylor. On top of that, the business was decimated. Still, some might call it a blessing and a curse. It put a lot of people out of work, and it ended the Taylor family's run in the glue business, but people were growing more aware of how their environment contributed to their health. By then, folks were already complaining about having the factory in the neighborhood. I'm sure there were many who were relieved to see it toppled."

"But why have I only just started smelling the fumes?" Adelaide mused. "I mean, I've lived here all my life. I should have picked up on it before. So, why's it happening now? There has to be a reason."

"I had a hunch when you first brought it up, and I could be wrong," Will said. "But we're coming up to the anniversary of the fire. At the end of the month, it will have been exactly one hundred and fifty years since the event. Could that be the cause?"

"It's possible that the anniversary has somehow triggered some of the activity," Adelaide said, "but it doesn't explain the manifestation of Charlotte Taylor. I first saw her years ago, when I was ten."

Susannah began pacing the foyer. "We know Lottie died of typhoid, years before her father died in the fire. Addy, didn't Maria say his spirit was near the river, that he isn't at peace?"

"Yeah."

"Could it be that Lottie was afraid to cross over?" Susannah spitballed. "She's a little girl, asking for her dad. Maybe she's just been hanging around this whole time, waiting for her dad to come get her."

"Based on what I've read," Will said, "they were very close. Robert made it clear in his own letters that Lottie was the apple of his eye. She was the baby of the family and was very attached to her father. In fact, he sometimes brought her to his workplace. She would sit on his office floor and play games while he worked. Despite her young age, he talked to her about how the factory operated. He would stroll her about the site, like she was a visiting princess. He'd hold her hand and introduce her to the people who worked there. So yeah, I can totally buy into Susannah's theory."

"As in life, so it is in death," Edwina said. "Lottie can't move on without the father she adored, but dear old Dad is stuck somewhere else."

"We have to bring them back together," Adelaide said. "Maria said Robert is filled with remorse, that his guilt keeps him here. I have to find out why he feels that way. I think that's the key to what's going on here."

There was a commotion on the top floor of the house. Footsteps pounded the floorboards, as if a child had run from one corner of the room to another.

Will jumped, grabbing Adelaide's arm. "Jesus. Is that…?"

"Yup. That's our cue. I'm going to try to make a connection." Adelaide pulled Will toward the loft room on the top floor, followed by her sisters. The childish footsteps continued as they ascended the stairs, an eerie sign that they were on the right track.

As Adelaide's feet touched the top landing, she called out. "We're here, Lottie, and we're coming to your room. I've brought a friend with me today. His name is Will and he's very nice. He won't hurt you. No tricks this time, please."

The footsteps stopped.

She opened the loft door and walked up the small staircase. The child's energy was all over the room, a cloying, curious heaviness. "Get ready, everyone."

They gathered inside the empty bedroom. Susannah held up a camera, panning around the room. Edwina set down a motion detector on the floor and readied her EMF reader. Will stood close to Adelaide, watching the action.

"I know you're here, Lottie." Adelaide kept her tone light, her demeanor friendly. "I can feel you watching. I'd love it if you could talk to us like you did last time. Or, if it's easier, move in front of the box that my sister put on the floor. It will light up when you come near. Want to see the pretty lights?"

All was silent and still. When the motion detector lit up, Will cursed under his breath.

Edwina checked her device. "Temp's dropped."

"That's good, Lottie, very good. What else can you do? Can you talk to me again?" Adelaide continued to probe with questions. "Were you stuck in this house when you found out your father passed away? We know there was a terrible fire at his factory and he wasn't able to get out. It must have been very hard for you to hear that news when you were alone. Have you been here the whole time, sweetie?"

Will froze. "Someone just grabbed my hand. I feel little fingers."

Adelaide met his gaze, conveying as much calm as possible. "That's okay. She's reaching out to you. You're just saying hello, right, Lottie?"

A small voice resonated in the space next to Will. "Hello."

"Oh my God." Will looked at his hand, speaking in an astonished whisper. "Hey, Lottie. Nice to meet you."

Adelaide addressed the spirit again. "Lottie, I'd like to try to help you find your dad again. Would that be okay with you?"

"Daddy's sad. I keep calling but he can't hear me."

"I'm sorry, honey," Adelaide said. "I think your daddy must miss you so much but he's confused right now. We're going to do our best to bring him home to you. Okay?"

"Yes, please."

Edwina motioned to them to confirm she'd recorded the exchange. She and Susannah did a quiet high-five.

Lottie's voice cut through their reverie. "Are you going to help the lady too?"

Adelaide's body went cold. "The lady?"

"You know. The sad lady in the cemetery. I've seen her from my window."

Adelaide struggled to retain composure but it was hard when her sisters were giving her a 'What the hell' look. "Have you seen the lady a lot?"

"She's always been here, like me. She likes to watch your friend Will." Will's arm moved back and forth, as if a child were swinging it. "I think she's lonely, because she wants him to go live with her."

A visible shudder passed through Will's shoulders.

"Why would you say that, Lottie?" Adelaide asked.

Will brought his hands together and started rubbing them. "She just let go of my hand. Am I the only one who's freezing in here?"

Alarmed at Lottie's words, Adelaide called out to her again, but the girl was silent.

She likes to watch your friend Will.

What the fuck?

She might need to deal with Sarah Byrne sooner than she thought.

The others started talking about Lottie's comments, but Addy tuned out. In her own world, she retreated to the window of the loft room and aimed her gaze toward the dark expanse of the Necropolis.

Something moved between the headstones.

She focused on the hazy figure. There was something about its jerky gait that was familiar. It stood at the far end of the cemetery. It was too distant to make out any other details, but she thought she spied the fullness of a long skirt. Even though Adelaide couldn't see the figure's face, she could swear it was staring at her.

It raised its arm and pointed at her. A mysterious voice sounded inside Adelaide's head. *"Stay away from him."*

It was her, Sarah.

Adelaide's back muscles bunched up into a wad of angry tension. *"What do you want with Will?"*

But the ghost didn't respond. Instead, it dissolved into mist and floated away into the valley beyond the graveyard.

Will approached and she almost jumped out of her skin.

"Sorry to scare you."

"It's okay." She continued peering into the green space, searching for a sign. "Will, about what Lottie said..."

"Oh, that sad lady business? Yeah, that was creepy."

"We need to talk and we need to take this seriously. She mentioned you by name."

Clearly nervous, he babbled as he tried to come up with excuses. "Is it possible we got it wrong? Maybe she said something else?"

She wasn't sure how to explain what went on in her head when a spirit spoke. No matter how fuzzy or muddled those communications might be on a device, they were always clear in Adelaide's mind. At the same time, she didn't want to terrify him. "My sisters and I will review the footage and the audio to be sure, but if Lottie meant you specifically, we'll need to be careful. I don't feel good about this."

"Okay. So, what now?"

"We try again," Adelaide said. "I'd like to do a walkthrough of the other rooms, to see if I can pick up on anything else."

"Awesome."

The group spent the next hour or so going from room to room but where the evening had begun with a bang, it ended with a whimper. Despite a sensation that they weren't alone and that they were being observed, there was no other spirit interaction.

After a time, Addy called it. "I think we should all head out. We won't get anything else out of Lottie tonight."

"I'd like to be there when you reunite her with her dad, if you don't mind," Will said. "What happened here was incredible. *You* were incredible, Addy."

"I haven't scared you away?"

"No. I mean, am I scared? Yeah, shitless, actually. But *you* haven't scared me away." He smiled. "If anything, I feel one hell of a lot safer standing next to you."

Will helped them gather up their equipment and carry it out to Edwina's Jeep. He said good night to her sisters, then Adelaide accompanied him to the sidewalk.

"Thanks for letting me come tonight." Will shook his head, still clearly struggling to process everything that had happened. "I don't even know what to think."

"Thanks for your help. Your info was just what we needed." Full of emotions she didn't recognize, Adelaide reached for his hand. It was a good hand, strong with long fingers. She had an urge to look at it under the light so she could examine each knuckle and vein and luxuriate in the texture of his skin. "By the way, I've been hearing chickadees everywhere I go."

"Oh no." He smiled warmly. "They're wise to you now. My fault."

"No, I love it." This time, she searched his eyes. They were full of mysteries, like the cemetery across the street. "Will, I…"

She had planned to say something more, but once again, her words drifted away. She could only look at him and drink in his unique beauty, marveling at how it resonated for her. At the same time, her sense of danger was growing and now she was getting proof it centered on Will. The need to protect him was becoming a tangible thing. It made her want to grab hold of him and not let go.

He moved a step closer, gnawing on his bottom lip. He was close enough that she got another tempting hit of his pleasant soapy scent.

God, she wanted to close her eyes, breathe him in and forget about the rest of the world. Her eyelids fluttered shut.

When she opened them, he was right in front of her. His lips were parted and his fresh breath washed over her. "I really need to kiss you again, but I know your sisters might see us. Does that bother you?"

"Nope."

"Good." He stroked his fingers over her skin. Sliding his thumb toward her bottom lip, he pressed gently. "You have an amazing mouth. It's so distracting."

She stifled a gasp of delight. No one had ever said that to her before.

Will's longish hairs tickled her face, making her smile. He brushed his lips against hers, softly seeking. He dropped a few light kisses all over her mouth.

Possessed by a sweetness she hadn't quite felt before, Adelaide touched his chest. It was hard and solid and she longed to explore it at her leisure. Needing more, she curled her fingers, grasping his shirt. She parted her lips, sliding her tongue between his, and moaned.

Will was right there with her. On a low note of hunger, he deepened the kiss. Their tongues met again and again, and the hand that had been so gentle on her cheek moved down her throat. His touch less gentle now, Will dragged her closer, and clutched her around the waist.

A deep and vicious desire opened in Adelaide's belly. She wanted to haul him into her home, up to her bedroom and between her legs. She just wanted him, period. Will Moran had been kind and patient and more than tolerant, and she needed more of that in her life.

When they finally fell apart, they were both panting.

"The things you do to me, Addy Darke," he whispered close to her mouth. He licked his lips and smiled.

A chunk of the barrier protecting her heart disintegrated, exposing the tender flesh underneath. And yet, her brain still struggled to protect its sister organ.

"*You're safe with him Addy,*" Maria cooed, "*and he'll be safer with you.*"

Maria was right. It made Adelaide want to be bold.

Edwina and Susannah had been locking up the house and had discreetly held back, lingering on the porch. Edwina cleared her throat. "Sorry to interrupt, kids, but some of us need to get home."

Of course. Susannah lived downtown as well, but Edwina still had a long drive ahead.

"I'll call you tomorrow." Will pulled her into an embrace.

No. He was going to walk away, past the Necropolis, where *she* lingered. If he left, he wouldn't have Addy's protection. She just didn't know how to tell him. On an impulse, she murmured, "Or you could come home with me."

Will hesitated, his eyes bright. He lowered his voice. "Are you sure?"

Not really. She knew what she was asking, and the implications for her heart if it all went to pieces tomorrow, but right now she was powerless to offer an alternative. "Please."

"I'd love to."

Ye gods! He wanted to fornicate too.

Adelaide turned around to face her sisters. "Um, Will and I are going to head out on our own. Have a good night."

Edwina gaped in astonishment, but Susannah put an arm around her shoulders and ushered toward the Jeep. She opened the driver's-side door and put a hand on Edwina's head, like a cop nudging a perp into the police vehicle. "Let's go, big sister. Call us tomorrow, Addy." The tone in her voice made it clear they would hound her if she didn't.

As they drove away in the Jeep, Edwina mouthed, *"You go, girl!"*

Adelaide swallowed hard, more nervous than she'd ever been. How had she careened from a couple of kisses to begging Will to come home with her? This was probably a big mistake.

But when she considered everything that had happened in the past twenty-four hours, and the hungriness of Sarah Byrne's dead gaze, she wasn't about to turn back.

She grabbed Will's hand. "Let's go."

Chapter Eleven

Adelaide's heart palpitated as they approached her home on Carlton Street.

What was she thinking? She wasn't ready for this. Hell, it wasn't all that long ago that she'd been trying to convince Will they were a mistake.

She thought she was stronger than this, that her head couldn't be turned so quickly by a pair of amber eyes and nice forearms. How the mighty had fallen.

And yet, in this moment, she was ready to take that leap. It shouldn't be that big a deal. It wasn't as if she hadn't slept with other guys. Maybe she was overthinking this. It would just be sex. She certainly needed it, and by the famished look on Will's face, he did too.

He mumbled something about her house.

"What was that?"

"Oh." He rubbed his chin. "I was just saying how nice your house is. I've always been partial to Cabbagetown's bay-and-gable homes. It's one of my favorite styles of architecture. I love the glazing over the door and the red brick with the yellow brick ornamentation. It's clever how the narrow window openings draw the eye toward the decorative black gable board. You really feel like you've gone back to the 1870s when you're standing in front of one of these houses…and I ramble on about ridiculous things when I'm nervous."

He just had to say something geeky and adorable to destroy any remaining resistance she might have had, didn't he?

He took a breath.

"I like your rambling." Once they were on the porch and under the light there, she grabbed both of his hands, stood on tiptoes and kissed him lightly on the lips. "And I'm nervous too."

He caressed her knuckles, setting off a chain reaction of shivers up her arm. "We don't have to do anything. I know it's early days. We could just hang out and stream a movie. Or I could go. Say the word, and I'll turn around. No harm done."

"Do you want to stay?"

"Fuck, yeah, but I don't want to pressure you."

"I feel no pressure." As the words tumbled out of her mouth, she understood their truth. "I just want you."

He touched her cheek, slowly dragging the backs of his fingers over her skin. When he leaned in for another kiss, she surrendered to it. *Don't think. Don't question. Just feel.* His mouth opened and he slipped his tongue between her lips, licking as if she were his new favorite flavor of ice cream.

Heavens. It was extraordinary, and no one had even been penetrated yet.

He finished kissing her, sucking her lower lip. "I've had such fantasies about this mouth."

"Really? Maybe you'll share them with me."

He blinked a few times. "Sorry. I think my eyes just rolled back into my head for a second there."

She couldn't help laughing. He treated her like she was some sort of deity and it blew her mind. "I guess I should open the door, huh?" She unlocked it, reached into the foyer and turned the hall light on, and invited him in. "Welcome to my home."

Will entered and kicked off his shoes inside the door. He followed her into her living room and she turned on a couple of lights there.

"Wow," he murmured.

He wasn't the first to have that reaction. She'd worked hard to create the living space of her dreams, and she knew it might not be to everyone's tastes. She called it her "happy jungle," on account of all the plants. They were everywhere. Peace lilies sat on the windowsill, a large anthurium nestled on her hearth, African violets peeked from her bookshelves and large rubber plants sat next to the sleek coffee table.

She'd found most of the furniture in vintage stores and sales, including the avocado-colored sectional sofa and the little green decorative bottles on all the shelves. It was her peaceful wilderness, a place where she could remain calm and remind herself to take a breath.

"This is quite the place."

She smiled as she surveyed the living space. "It works for me."

He fingered one of the plants, one with big elephant ear leaves. "You have a green thumb."

"Not really. I've just learned which plants are harder to kill."

"Why so many? It's beautiful. I'm just curious."

"As much as possible, I want my home to be a sanctuary. Because I deal with the emotions of the living and the dead, it can be a bit much. I need my home to be full of peace and light and greenery. It's important for me to 'touch grass,' so to speak. My plants remind me of being in the outdoors. They help me to breathe and to forget any awful scenes I might have witnessed."

"Like the chickadee effect?"

"Yeah, just like that."

Will's gaze was inscrutable. "This is an amazing place, Addy. It feels good here. It feels...safe."

"That's good to hear." After all the protections she'd placed around the property over time, it should feel safe. "It wasn't always that way, though."

"Are you saying your house used to be haunted?"

"Yup. When I spotted the real estate listing, I fell in love with it. But I knew right away that one of the former occupants was, shall we say, reluctant to leave. I communicated with him during one of my early visits, and I could tell he wasn't a malicious spirit. He just really loved his home. He had a hand in building it, you see, and considered himself a sort of caretaker. Once I was able to make Bob understand that I loved his home too, and that I would also take care of it, I was able to help him move on."

"Wait. Bob?"

"He was a sweet man, a builder by trade."

Will bit back a laugh. "Addy, you're telling me your home was haunted by Bob...the builder?"

She burst out laughing. "I never made that connection! Aw, no wonder he was so nice."

"That was, without a doubt, the best ghost story I've ever heard. I love that you helped Bob earn his wings."

"I try. Spirits were once people like us. At least, most of them were."

"Yikes. Do I want to know what the others are?"

She made a face. "Probably not. Anyway, to help them, I usually just try to find out what was important to them. Sometimes it's reuniting them with a loved one, and sometimes it's just letting them know you'll take care of their home."

"Fascinating." Will peered into the hallway. "And Bob has stayed away?"

"Yes. He's no longer around."

Will smiled and wrapped his arm around her waist. "I'm really glad Bob isn't here right now. Show me your bedroom."

Addy nodded, took his hand and led him upstairs. For a split second, she panicked when she turned on the lights there, half expecting to see the wraith of Sarah Byrne at the edge of her bed. However, after Sarah's last appearance, Adelaide had strengthened the protections around her home, salting around all the doors and windows.

Will walked her to the side of the bed. His gaze locked on her, he removed his shirt. She couldn't help but stare. He was beautiful, lean and strong, with a delectable Adonis belt at his hips. Or, as Edwina called it, "sex muscles."

She gnawed on her lip, unable to tear her gaze away from his abs.

"Hey." He brought her hand to his mouth and kissed her palm. "Say the word and we stop, okay? It doesn't matter when. You're one hundred percent in control here."

But Adelaide didn't want to stop, and he was being so cautious and considerate that she figured it was best to show him she was on board. Being the mistress of seduction that she was, she whipped her top off and tossed it into the corner of the room.

"Okay, then." Will cracked a smile.

"Sorry. I have zero finesse."

"Finesse means nothing to me. I'm glad you're excited." His gaze was full of wonder. "God, Addy, do you have any idea how remarkable you are? I think you're incredibly special."

Addy can't help that she's special.

Even though she knew Will meant it in a positive way, hearing the word stung. It brought back all kinds of bad memories of people who had used her, taunted her and belittled her.

He frowned, touching her chin. "Did I say something wrong?"

"No. I just…" She trailed off, unable to articulate her fears that one day he would treat her the same way. That he'd eventually open his eyes and see her as something to be feared, instead of admired. "My mind spirals sometimes. I'm getting ahead of myself, instead of just enjoying the moment."

"You're worried I'll hurt you."

Yes. I'm worried you'll hurt me. She nodded slowly.

"Because others have."

She dipped her head again.

Will pulled her into an embrace and buried his face in the crook of her neck. "I wish I'd been there to protect you. I'm not a violent person, but when I think of anyone causing you pain, it makes me so angry. I see fucking red."

The tremor in his voice forced all the nerves from her being. She was able to look him in the eye and see her pain held deep in his heart. And somehow, Adelaide knew Will would never try to purposely hurt her. He was too good for that. She wasn't sure how she knew it, but she did.

That knowledge made her brave. She reached behind her back, unlatched her bra and let it fall to the floor.

"Damn." He touched her there, cupping her breasts, stroking the peaks with his thumbs. He had a callous on one of his thumbs and the light abrasion made her nipples pebble. "Amazing."

Will kissed her, slowly and deeply. Each pass of his tongue made her want to weep because her senses could barely handle such an overload of delight. He sat at the edge of the bed and urged her atop him. She straddled his lap, painfully aware of the ridge between his legs, and writhed. Hands clutching her back, he brought his lips to one of her nipples and sucked.

Addy cried out. She couldn't remember feeling so good. She arched her back, wanting him to have more, wanting to give him everything she had. Will's hands were everywhere, squeezing and kneading and gripping, and she didn't think she'd ever experienced such a rush of pleasure.

"I want to make you feel good." His voice, so low and hushed, was a caress on its own.

"You are."

His fingers dipped below the waistband of her shorts. "I think we can do better." He gently moved her off his lap and pulled back the covers on the bed. She lay back and he touched the button at her waist. "Is it all right if I take these off? We can still stop any time you want."

"Don't stop."

His expression was serious, even stern, but still full of adoration. "Tell me what you like, Addy. I want to know."

Aching and timid, never more so in her life, she merely replied, "I like everything."

"No. I'm going to need you to be more specific." He tugged on her loosened shorts, dragging them slowly down her legs, leaving her only in black panties. He knelt at the side of the bed, between her legs, and massaged her thighs. "I want to know what turns you on, and off, for that matter. I've got you, I promise. All you need to do is tell me and I'll give it to you."

I've got you. He'd said that once before. Her heart wanted to believe it.

Adelaide sucked in a breath. She'd never considered herself bashful but, from their first moment, Will somehow transformed her into this fumbling mass of awkwardness.

He ran a finger along the elastic of her panties. "Do you like it if I touch you here?"

"Yeah."

"Good." He tugged on the panties, lowering them about half an inch. "Still okay?"

"Yes."

He kissed her low on her stomach, where all her trembling anxieties and pleasures lived.

"You can take them off, if you want."

"I want that very much." He continued to gently pull, easing them down her hips. His breath came harder and his nostrils flared. With a final tug, he removed them. His gaze was glued to the juncture of her thighs. "So pretty. Do you like being touched here?"

"God, yes. Please, Will."

"I love how you beg, sweetheart, but it's really not necessary." He smoothed his fingers over her skin, and she bucked on the bed. Grinning, he experimented with different types of touches. She knew he was gauging her reactions, which was funny because no matter what he did, she moaned and panted and gasped. Will played with her frazzled nerves until there was a damp spot on the sheet beneath her.

"You're so fucking hot." He dipped two fingers between her lips. "Would you like to be licked here?"

"Uh-huh." Animal noises. It was all she was capable of now.

His smile had a feral curve to it. He withdrew his fingers from her pussy and sucked on them. She couldn't look away. He was magnetic. She wasn't sure how he'd gone from being an adorable history geek to freaking Casanova, but she was eager to get on that train and ride it into the station.

Will spread her legs and lowered his head. The heat! The velvety softness of his tongue. It was perfect. Addy clutched at his bare shoulders, digging her nails into his skin. Still clearly determined to find out what made her tick, Will nibbled and lapped and sucked. When he flicked his tongue against her clit, an anguished cry broke from deep in her being. She didn't even recognize the noise. It was one she'd never made before, and Will seemed to understand it was a milestone of sorts. He stopped teasing her and applied himself to her swollen bud. His kiss was absolutely devilish, and Addy lost any semblance of control that she might have had.

This sinful worship, it was almost too much to bear. Every so often, he'd pull away to look her in the eye, grinning with that naughty mouth. He was enjoying this, possibly as much as she was, and it overwhelmed her with emotion. She was ready to feed him bits of herself, piece by piece, until there was nothing left.

"You taste so good."

The whizzing in her ear had to be the sound of her blood rushing.

He lazily danced his thumb over her clit, manipulating the little button of nerves. "Do you want to come, or do you want me to drag this out? Because I could do this all night long."

When she replied, her voice was hoarse. "Please. Make me come."

"Yes, ma'am." He caressed her, circling his fingers over her clit.

Heat flowed throughout her body, making her feel as if she was carried on a warm river. She closed her eyes, struggling with the swell of feeling that accompanied their raw and unexpected moment of physicality.

Once again, Will used his mouth on her, making those delicious circles with his tongue. When she buried her fingers in his hair, he upped the ante. She fell apart, riding a wave of almost painful bliss. It crested, pummeling her again and again. She groaned as each aftershock left her reeling. Will continued to lap at her until her limbs stopped flailing.

He'd broken her. Her heart was racing and she couldn't move and she'd never felt better.

He finally took pity on her and removed that talented mouth from her skin. "Look at me, Addy."

She raised her head, amazed she could still do so.

"That was incredible. So much better than the falafel salad."

She gave in to an enormous belly laugh.

Will gave her the sweetest smile, as if her laughter gave him life. That smile was her undoing. So full of hope and a willingness to please, his gaze shattered another portion of the wall built up around her heart. It blew it into smithereens.

Adelaide seriously considered getting his name tattooed on her forehead. She suddenly wanted to do all sorts of silly and spontaneous things, like running naked through the sprinkler or chasing an ice cream truck.

And she definitely wanted more moments like this.

"Hmm. So good. I need another taste." To her surprise, he proceeded to lick her again.

"Oh God. You're a dangerous man."

"And you're intoxicating. I can't get enough of you." With a lingering kiss on her public bone, he stood. He tore off his socks, loosened the button on his shorts and dropped them. He retrieved his wallet from the back pocket of his shorts.

Adelaide smiled at the sight of his boxer briefs. They were royal blue and they cupped his straining cock perfectly. She licked her parched lips.

This was going to be fun.

Will fished inside his wallet and produced a condom. Holding it between his teeth, he slid out of his sexy undies. What emerged was perfect, the ideal length and girth for her. With speed and efficiency, he tore the condom package open and sheathed himself. A muscle twitched in his jaw. "Tell me how you want me."

Rolling onto her stomach, she got on all fours.

Will grunted and palmed her ass. "Excellent choice." Without preamble, he nudged her folds and penetrated her. Adelaide cried out, shocked and amazed that her body was still capable of responding. He moved slowly at first, letting her acclimatize to each sensation, then proceeded to thrust deep.

The cry she made was almost embarrassing.

He swore with each thrust. "Yeah. Aw, damn. Fuck. Goddammit."

Addy had never heard anything so sweet as Will falling apart inside her, calling out in blasphemy. He pistoned into her like a machine, clutching her hips.

As his groans became more desperate, he tugged on her shoulders, angling her so that her back was closer to his chest.

He hit a spot, a wondrous spot, deep inside her. Addy gasped. This angle…it was everything. "Oh my."

"Yeah? Amazing." Will continued to pound her until they were both sweaty, their breaths ragged and uneven. He held her tight, one hand at her hip, the other wrapped around her middle. She could almost feel his frantic heartbeat at her chest.

Impossibly, another orgasm rocketed into sight and slammed through her. Addy bit her lip, tasting a hint of blood, and let out a cry. "Yes!"

Will grunted as he came, resting his head on her shoulder. "Jesus, Addy. What the fuck? Unbelievable."

"Yeah?"

"Shit, yeah." He kissed her shoulder, giving her a playful bite, and extricated himself carefully from her body. "So good. I'll be right back."

"There are some clean washcloths next to the sink, if you need one." She rolled onto her back and climbed under the covers. She stared at her ceiling, her head spinning. There were so many stars in her eyes she could have sworn the roof had dissolved.

Yes, it may only have been sex, raw and physical, but there was something about it that had touched her soul as well. As memorable as her orgasms had been, it was the little moments of tenderness that stayed with her. His smile, the careful way he held her and each hungry kiss.

Pure exquisiteness.

When Will joined her in bed, he was all warmth, softness and whispers. Adelaide turned out the bedside light and he dragged her toward him, spooning her. He brushed her damp hairs away from her neck, nuzzling her there. No one had ever made her feel so beautiful, so cherished. So alive.

And, she realized as she closed her eyes, no one had ever left her heart so in peril.

If he broke it, there would be no pretty patch-up jobs, no bandage big enough to cover the tear. It would be broken for good.

Chapter Twelve

"Come, my love."

The songlike voice came to Will as if in a dream, teasing him into a state of semi-consciousness. He lurched into a sitting position, taking stock of his surroundings. It was dark, but a fine light under the blinds, a tease of sunrise, allowed him to see.

Adelaide was asleep at his side. Curled up, she faced away from him toward the window. He leaned over and brushed her hair away from her cheek. She was so peaceful in sleep, so lovely he completely forgot about the voice that had awakened him.

He could make out the curve of Addy's bare shoulder and the dip at her waist. The sheet was bunched up around her arm, covering her only from the ribcage down. Not wanting her to get cold, Will pulled the sheet up over her shoulder. He kissed the shell of her ear and she sighed, burrowing into the mattress.

Struck through the chest with an arrow of happiness, he caressed her arm over the sheet.

What a night. Addy had been a revelation, and on so many levels. Firstly, there was the experience at the Taylor house. He'd never taken part in anything like that and it left him with countless questions.

Then, there was everything that had happened once they got back to her place. Will still couldn't believe he'd held this remarkable woman in his hands, that she'd entrusted him with her body and her heart. He felt this urgent need to take care of Adelaide, to make her not only happy but downright delirious.

His head spun as he contemplated the changes he'd seen in Addy over the past little while. He'd been captivated by the cautious woman that he'd met in the Necropolis, but he loved seeing this new side of her as well. Was it possible that he'd found a way to dismantle the barricade she'd constructed around herself?

Strangely enough, seeing the inside of her house had also helped him feel closer to her. He wasn't sure what he'd expected of her home, but it wasn't the tranquil oasis with all the plants and greenery. Her home inspired unfamiliar emotions in him. He felt a sort of freedom here, a lightness, as if someone had just removed a weight from his shoulders. For the first time in ages, he was unbothered by all the things that normally frustrated him, or at least felt ready to face them.

Maybe he just appreciated getting to see this other side of her, another piece in the puzzle of Adelaide Darke. He wanted to share more of his world with her as well.

Even now, he wished he could gently wake her and peel back the covers from her body. In sleeping with her, he'd become privy to some of her secrets. But Will wanted them all. He wanted to be the keeper of

Adelaide Darke's dreams and hopes and even her fears, so that she never felt alone.

A dull throb started up in his temple, dispersing all his pleasant thoughts. He probably needed some sleep. It had been so hard to get any real rest lately. As his head began to pound, he rolled over, away from Adelaide and curled up in the fetal position. Holding his head, he drifted off into a semi-sleep.

"Come to me."

The voice, so pleasing with its Irish accent, drowned out the pangs in his head. It crawled under his skin, seeping into his blood and marrow. It whispered and cajoled, finding a way into the very heart of him.

"Yes," he mumbled.

Addy's bed, the place that had held such fascination for him, now had the appeal of a doctor's office or a funeral home. He just wanted to get out. Without questioning, without even understanding why, Will slid out of the bed and started putting on his clothes.

"I've been so alone. Come home to me!"

"I'm coming."

As he buttoned up his shirt, Will stared at Adelaide's motionless form, and it was like looking at a stranger. He felt nothing. As he walked out of the bedroom and down the stairs, it never occurred to him to regret leaving. By the time he headed out the door and onto the darkened streets, he couldn't even remember what he'd left.

Only one thought possessed him. *Sarah.* He had to get to Sarah.

Chapter Thirteen

Adelaide awoke Sunday morning in a languorous haze. The sun was streaming through her bedroom window, reflecting off the shiny leaves of the peace lily perched on her windowsill. Her limbs were sore in places, but it was a good soreness, an ache that brought a smile to her face. She rolled over to face the man who'd given her all those tender muscles.

But Will wasn't in her bed and his clothes were no longer on the floor.

For a second, she just listened, certain he was puttering around downstairs or in the bathroom. The floors in her house were old and always creaked, and she'd become familiar with each wooden groan.

The silence told her something was wrong. Her anxious mind supplied the worst possible reasons for his absence. He'd ditched her. He'd gotten what he wanted and now he was gone. He'd wanted to add "weird goth girl" to the notches on his bedpost and she'd never see him again. He'd already deleted her contact info from his phone.

Vesuvius rumbled and spat, quick to protect her as it always had been, eager for a reason to spew.

"Stop it." She bunched up the bedsheet in her fists and forced her mind to slow its frenzied roll. She recalled the advice of her therapist and rested a hand on her heart, giving herself a friendly pat. "Will's not like that, and this isn't how it looks. I'll talk to him and see how he is. Maybe last night was a bit too much for him after all. There's no use in running all the old negative tapes. They're not helping the situation. If there is a problem with Will, I'll deal with it."

There. Her heart rate was returning to normal. "Okay. Make sure he's not just sitting downstairs." She had that nice sunny reading nook in her living room. Maybe he'd curled up there, waiting for her to wake up.

Adelaide threw on yesterday's clothes and went downstairs. He wasn't in her reading nook, nor in the kitchen or her backyard. His shoes no longer sat in the foyer. There was no note anywhere and when she grabbed her cell phone, there were no texts from him either.

He was just gone.

"Nice." She couldn't help her heart from sinking just a little.

Annoyed, both at him and herself, she slipped on her sneakers and went out to her front porch. She wasn't sure what she was looking for but she craved fresh air.

"Addy," Maria warned, *"he's in danger."*

"What?" Her gaze shot toward the Necropolis, on the other side of Riverdale Park.

Sarah.

"Fuck." Adelaide didn't stop to think or lock up her house — she just ran. She tore across the park toward the cemetery, not even sure how she hadn't once considered the spirit woman during her ridiculous pity party.

Has Sarah gotten to him? How?

Perhaps the dead woman had already embedded herself in Will's head. Maybe she'd been there the whole time, just waiting and watching and gathering strength. In the time Adelaide had known Will, she'd seen how fatigue had worn on his looks, making him appear drawn. *Of course.* How hadn't she figured this out? He had mentioned he was tired, that he had trouble sleeping.

Sarah was already inside him. A conductor, baton poised, ready to bring in her orchestra on a shocking chord.

Somewhere in the trees, a chickadee warned. *Chicka-dee-dee-dee-dee-dee-dee-dee-dee.*

Will's words hammered in her memory. *They also use it when predators are near. The more "dees" they add to the call, the higher the threat level.*

She reached the gothic Necropolis gates and ran into the graveyard. A burial was happening over to her right and the people gathered there all turned to gawk at her.

She slowed her sprint to a fast walk. "Sorry. Morning jog."

Like she'd ever jogged anywhere in her life.

"Fuck, fuck, fuck." Once she was past the mourners, she raced past Thornton and Lucie Blackburn, hurried past Ned Hanlan. Adelaide called out to any spirits of light who might be hanging around today. "Please help me."

She spotted Will, standing in front of Sarah's grave, his head lowered. It was exactly like the image she'd seen after Sarah had appeared in her room.

Panting from her run, she paused and approached him slowly. She didn't see Sarah anywhere but that didn't mean the spirit woman wasn't hovering nearby. Besides, a bristly energy gathered at the base of her skull. Something was off here.

"Will?"

He turned and broke into a confused smile. "Addy?"

Just seeing him smile turned her into a puddle of goo. She'd forgotten how it affected her. Any time he turned its full brilliance upon her, her joints became unsteady. But there was something strange about his smile too. There was a vacancy behind his eyes, like he wasn't all there.

"Why are you here?" he asked.

"I couldn't find you back at my place. I was worried."

"There's no need to worry. I'm fine." He motioned to the grave. "I'm here with my Sarah."

No two words had ever hurt so much. *My Sarah.* Adelaide bit back her wounded ego and kept her goal in mind. She had to get him out of there. "About Sarah...we need to talk. I probably should have talked to you about her before." That had been the plan until lust had clouded her brain. "Let's go for a walk."

"I should stay. Sarah needs me."

I need you.

Clouds gathered above them, bringing a curious darkness to that part of the cemetery. Considering it was a bright and sunny day, it didn't seem like a coincidence.

Adelaide would have a fight on her hands. In her own way, Sarah was watching.

"We won't be long, I promise. You must be hungry. You haven't had anything to eat or drink. How about this? I'll make you a strong coffee, then you can come back to Sarah."

His eyelids were hooded and he staggered. "Coffee. Okay."

"Awesome. Let's go." She grabbed his hand and led him toward the Necropolis gates. She silently counted off the graves as they went, knowing each step brought him closer to her home and farther from Sarah's influence.

Chicka-dee-dee-dee-dee-dee-dee.

"I know, friend. I know."

All of a sudden, the bird calls died off mid-tweet.

Adelaide's hackles, which were already up, shot sky-high. The hair on her skin stood on end. "Lady, you'd better not touch my chickadee or we're going to have some words."

Maria pushed forward. *Get him out of the cemetery. Now, Addy!* The warning was accompanied by Maria's unsettling cough. It fractured the quiet of the Necropolis.

She didn't stop to question her spirit guide. She never did. Instead, she hurried Will through the gate and onto Winchester Street.

There, better. The feeling of danger, while still present, lifted somewhat.

Adelaide looked over her shoulder and glimpsed a pale figure. From her spot across the street, she turned to face Sarah head-on.

Sarah skittered between the graves toward them. No one else saw her. The mourners who had noticed

Adelaide running didn't even register the sad and dreadful spectacle before them. Sarah's frantic gaze locked on Will, but she stopped at the cemetery gates.

Addy had won this battle, but the war was far from being over.

As much as she feared Sarah, as much as she wanted to hate her for tormenting Will, she felt sorry for her. There was a reason she kept getting glimpses of Sarah's last moments. Even though she was alarming to behold, the overwhelming emotion that had surrounded her from the very beginning was sorrow.

And she had a suspicion the spirit woman didn't deserve that. She too came from a place of torment and her frightening appearance was merely a reflection of her emotional state.

That meant, as much as Adelaide wanted to remove Will from her sphere of influence and pretend Sarah never existed, she needed to be strong, to face her nemesis and find a way to help her too.

Adelaide tried to reach out to the wraith. *"I want to help you, Sarah, but it can't be at Will's expense. Tell me what you want."*

Even now, the ghost raised an arm toward Will. *"Come home."*

Adelaide wasn't sure whether or not Will could actually hear Sarah's voice as she could, but his face lost all color and his eyes became glazed. "Gotta go home," he mumbled. "To Sarah."

Maria's coughing still rang everywhere. *"This is bad, Addy, very bad. Don't let him out of your sight."*

His eyelids drooped and he extricated his arm from her grip.

"No!" Adelaide seized his arm. "We were going to have a nice coffee, remember? Come back to my place, Will. Just for a few minutes. You don't look good."

"Don't feel good."

"I bet. You can rest your head on my couch for a little while, just until you feel better, okay?"

He was in no shape to argue. Like a zombie, he followed. "'Kay."

Maria's coughs began to fade.

As they walked south on Sumach Street toward Carlton, Adelaide looked back at Sarah Byrne.

The ghost let out a long moan, digging her fingers through her hair. She stared after them for a while, then turned and trudged deeper into the Necropolis. It was only as she became invisible that Adelaide released the breath she was holding.

The effect on Will, however, was longer lasting. Still shuffling at her side, he murmured. "I'm a tired chickadee."

"I know." When they got to her place, she helped him up the front steps. Still holding onto his arm, she ushered him inside and got him settled on the couch. She returned to her door and stood there, staring toward the cemetery.

"You are not welcome here, Sarah Byrne. You will not cross this threshold again, and you will leave Will Moran alone. I will come to you when I am ready and then I'll help you. If you can, please go in peace toward the light." She quietly offered up a prayer for the wandering soul and shut the door, locking it. She hoped they'd seen the last of the specter.

Still, Adelaide knew hope was a flimsy, capricious thing. They would see Sarah Byrne again, and they would need stronger armor for when they did.

Chapter Fourteen

Feeling as if someone had taken a hammer to his skull, Will cracked his eyes open. Light streamed through the windows, harsher than an insult.

Wait. Those weren't his windows.

Where was he?

It was someone's living room.

A sinking feeling took hold of him. It sprouted deep in his gut and spread upward, making him taste bile.

Had he been drugged?

Several soft sets of footsteps padded on the hardwood toward him. The sound shocked him into awareness. It was Addy and her sisters.

Spotty memories flashes before his eyes. *Right.* He and Addy had had sex, amazing, life-changing sex. But he certainly didn't recall Edwina and Susannah joining in. *Oh God.*

Addy crouched in front of him. He didn't like the creases of concern along her forehead or the way she held her hands in front of her, all balled up with anxiety. Her voice was soft and low. "Will? Are you okay?"

"I'm not sure, if I'm honest."

"You haven't been responsive for a while."

"Sorry?"

"Do you remember our last conversation?"

"Um, yeah." He remembered how their bodies had tangled in the sheets, the softness of her skin and the sweetness of each moan. He remembered how everything had felt right just as long as he was in her bed. "But it was kind of private. You don't want me to repeat it here, do you?"

"That was two nights ago, Will."

"But…"

"I found you in the Necropolis yesterday morning. You weren't feeling well, so I brought you back to my place."

"Right. For coffee." Only, he couldn't recall having any coffee. He tried to sit up, groaning when his body fought back. "Wait. What day is it?"

"Monday morning."

"What? I've been on your couch all night long?"

"Like I said, you were out of it. We thought it best to let you sleep it off."

Panic vied for dominance with the sinking feeling. As always, panic won. His breaths grew unsteady. "Holy shit." Once more, he tried to stand, but failed. "I have to get to work."

"Right." Edwina drew out the word. "You might have to call in sick today, friend."

Adelaide shot her a look and turned back to him. "I hope you don't mind that I called my sisters, but I needed to discuss what happened with them."

180

Will struggled to recall their last moments together. "What *did* happen?"

"You don't remember anything?" Susannah asked.

"I…remember hearing a black-capped chickadee?"

"Okay." Susannah narrowed her gaze. "So, aside from bird calls, you didn't see or hear anything unusual in the Necropolis?"

He shook his head.

"Will," Addy said, "the reason you can't remember anything is because you've been under the influence of a dead woman. I believe her attention causes you to zone out. Remember what Charlotte Taylor said? The sad lady in the cemetery?"

"Wait…"

"Will, it was Sarah Byrne."

"*My* Sarah?"

Okay, bad choice of words. Addy averted her gaze but her sisters glared. Edwina raised her left eyebrow in a way that terrified him.

"*Your* Sarah," Edwina repeated. "Should we maybe unpack that?"

"It doesn't mean anything. I just, I work in her old home. I guess I've always thought of her as my Sarah. Oh, man, this is so weird."

Chills skittered down his back. His head still felt heavy and he was starting to think that maybe he had overstayed his welcome at Adelaide's place. A new and uneasy sensation churned in his stomach. Even though his head spun a little, he managed to stand this time. "I should go."

Adelaide put out her hand. "Will, we're dealing with a spirit attachment. Sarah Byrne has latched onto you for some reason and she doesn't seem to want to let go. It has to stop. I want to be clear. You're in danger."

"Spirit attachments are extremely unhealthy for the victim," Susannah explained. "They're also known as entity attachment, a phenomenon in which a spirit attaches itself to a living person's energy field. Kind of like that toxic ex who refuses to stay away. It can harm a victim physically, emotionally and mentally."

Edwina huffed. "That shit'll drain a motherfucker."

"What Ed means is that an attachment can lead to a loss of stamina, mood swings, fatigue, sleeplessness and unexplained physical problems." Susannah rattled off the list of bizarre side effects like one of those voiceovers on the late-night drug commercials. "Attachments can have severe consequences on a victim's life and wellbeing and it's imperative to address the cause immediately."

Will's mind reeled. "Addy, what's going on here?"

Susannah answered instead. "Addy heard Sarah say, 'Come home.' We assume she means the Amelia Street house where she lived, and where you now work. You told Addy that your colleagues thought the museum was haunted. What kind of activity are we talking about? Disembodied voices, cold spots, things moving by themselves, that sort of thing?"

"Um, yeah. All of the above, actually. I've been meaning to talk to Addy about it but, well…" He just hadn't.

And now that he thought about it, he wasn't sure why.

The sisters' gazes met and held. If Will didn't know any better, he would swear they were having a silent conversation.

Heck. Maybe they were. They were the Darke sisters, after all. God only knew what magic powers they had. The possibilities had to be staggering. He shook his head. He was pretty open-minded but he couldn't believe he was seriously having this conversation. His hold on reality was slowly slipping out of his grasp, which was alarming because he really needed to get the fuck to work.

Susannah continued lobbing questions his way. "What about your home? Anything weird there? Maybe feelings of oppression or heaviness. Have you been experiencing mood swings?"

"No." He scoffed. "Or maybe yes. I don't know. I've been under a lot of pressure lately with the museum opening, but that's just work stress. And I have anxiety, so mood swings can happen. I get panic attacks sometimes. Well, they stopped for a while, but they seem to be happening again." Will realized the Darkes investigated the paranormal all the time, but how could they talk about it so calmly, like they were discussing which toppings to put on their pizza?

Once again, the sisters looked at each other.

Okay, those looks were freaking him out just as much as the news about Sarah Byrne. "Addy?"

Adelaide finally put him out of his misery. "I wish I had concrete answers for you as to why this is happening. All I can say for sure is that something has felt 'off' around here for a while. Remember the vision I had on our date? It was of Sarah. I know that now. And it wasn't the only one. I've been getting these little snapshots of her final moments and I don't know why." She shook her head, apparently at a loss.

His cell phone buzzed from the coffee table. Addy must have charged it for him. He grabbed it and saw a text from Miguel pop up. In addition, there were several missed calls. His coworkers were looking for him. "Do you mind if I just call my colleague? Oh, and could I use your bathroom?"

"Of course." Adelaide's smile didn't meet her eyes and only seemed meant to encourage him. "In the meantime, I'll get you that coffee."

He shot off a quick text, telling Miguel he was sick, and put the phone down on the table. He hurried off to the washroom, relieved his aching bladder and cleaned his hands. After splashing cold water on his face and toweling off, he returned to the living room.

A few minutes later, Adelaide appeared with a coffee for him and a small plate of homemade blueberry muffins. Suddenly ravenous, Will blurted, "You smell delicious."

Her face reddened as she set the tray down next to him but at least she was still grinning.

"I mean, *this* smells delicious." He cleared his throat. "Thanks."

Adelaide invited him to tuck in and he did. The coffee was perfect, hot and rich, and the muffins were amazing.

"Mmm, so good."

"Glad you like them. I did some stress baking them last night."

Right. When he'd been passed out on her couch. Once again, the enormity and weirdness of the situation hit him like a punch to the throat.

"I'm glad you have your appetite," Adelaide said. "That's a good sign."

"You've seen...attachments before?"

"Yeah." She gestured at her sisters. "We all have. We can fix this, but we'll need your cooperation."

"You've got it." It occurred to Will that maybe he shouldn't be so quick to agree. What exactly did *cooperation* mean? Would seances be involved? Blood sacrifices? For some reason, he felt like he was signing a contract without having read it first. He just needed to understand better.

At the same time, Adelaide inspired him with confidence. Her dark eyes were so full of empathy, drawing him in. The alluring curve of her lips had him daydreaming about kissing her, even in the midst of this unholy mess.

Geez, he hadn't even been able to enjoy the afterglow. It probably would have been incredible too.

Instead, he'd gone traipsing through the graveyard to liaison with his dead girlfriend.

Okay. He was officially losing it.

"So, tell us about Sarah Byrne." Susannah had perfectly manicured fingernails and when she drummed them on the side table, they made a clicking sound. "Why do you think this is happening, Will?"

There was nothing accusatory in her tone, but he still somehow felt this was all his fault. "I honestly don't know."

"We've been investigating the Taylor house," Edwina offered. "Why has Sarah popped up out of nowhere? Could she be connected somehow?"

"There is a connection between Sarah and the Taylors," Will said. "Sarah's husband Aiden worked for Taylor at the glue factory. His brother Desmond worked for Taylor too. But I don't think she's connected in any way to the Taylors themselves. Sarah died in 1860, well before either Robert Taylor or his daughter did, and she really wouldn't have run in the same circles as them."

"Desmond." Addy frowned. "He was mentioned in my vision. At first, Sarah was grateful for her brother-in-law, for his companionship, but she was also concerned. She felt his feelings for her were inappropriate."

"Des had the hots for his sister-in-law?" Edwina asked. "That would make things awkward."

"Are you sure, Addy?" Will asked. "I mean, Sarah and the Byrne family did come over on the same ship from Ireland. She probably would have had a close relationship with Aiden's brother, but..." *Thwack.* A forgotten tidbit from his research on the family hit him in the face. "Hang on. There's this one detail that came up in my research that's always bothered me for some reason. Desmond was the one who paid for Sarah's headstone. In fact, he made all her funeral arrangements."

"Desmond?" Adelaide asked. "Not Aiden?"

"I always chalked it up to the fact that Aiden wasn't exactly a reliable husband. He was an alcoholic who spent all his wages drinking at the Don Vale House. I always figured he wasn't in any shape to mourn his wife, never mind picking out a headstone. I assumed Desmond did his brother a solid, that he stepped in to take care of Sarah because he felt sorry for her. If what you're saying is true, that puts a different spin on it."

"It does," Adelaide said. "I only saw snippets of Sarah's feelings and I could be wrong. All I really know is that she died that night at the Don Vale House, and some dude was there when it happened."

"So she was murdered!" Edwina exclaimed. "She must want us to find her killer."

"Officially," Will said, "her death record states that she drowned."

"The death record doesn't tell the whole story." Adelaide shook her head with vehemence. "I saw the man put his hands on her. I saw him shove her. Maybe it was the heat of the moment and he didn't mean to kill her, but she still died."

Susannah hummed in contemplation. "I wouldn't have thought the Don River was deep enough to drown in, at least not in that area."

"The landscape's changed since then," Will reminded her. "The Don that we see today is not the Don of Sarah's day. Even now, the river sometimes overflows its banks after a heavy rain. And Sarah died in November, when the water would have been freezing. She probably wouldn't have known how to swim. I would think that if she fell in while wearing heavy woolen clothes, she could have easily been pulled under."

They were all quiet for a time. Will had always felt sympathy for Sarah's plight, but now, knowing that someone might have been the cause of her death, it was even more horrible.

Adelaide reached for his hand and held it in her lap. "As far as I can tell, there are a few questions we need to answer. Was Sarah actually murdered or was it an accident? Why would someone have wanted to kill her? There are connections here, thin threads running through these two hauntings, but I can't tie them together yet. That being said, Sarah definitely has her own agenda, and it's focused on you."

"So, what do we do?" Will asked.

Adelaide gave his hand a quick peck. "*We* aren't going to do anything. My sisters and I will deal with Sarah and *you* are going to rest here and take some time away from work. You've had a shock to your system."

"I...I can't take time off from work." Will stumbled on his words. "I have to get back. I'm fine now, honestly."

"You're not." Adelaide's tone was firm and, frankly, arousing in a way he didn't expect. "And if you insist on going back to work, there are some things we need to do first. One, you need to acknowledge the seriousness of what's happening here. Two, we need to get into the museum so I can cleanse the space. Your house, too. You'll need to practice a lot of self-care in the coming days, and that means taking it easy. And eventually, I'd like you to meet with one of my medium friends, someone who can cleanse your headspace, so to speak."

"Not you?"

"No." She shook her head. "I'm too close to the situation. We need someone objective."

"I really don't want to put you through all that trouble. This isn't necessary."

All three sisters peered at him. They knew he was bullshitting.

Was he bullshitting? He wasn't sure why but for some reason, the idea of letting Addy and her sisters into the museum made him nervous, never mind all that naval gazing and spilling his guts to some stranger.

Something hard and ugly twisted deep in Will's gut, filling him with anger.

A woman's voice echoed in his ear, one with an Irish accent. *Don't let them in. They'll ruin everything.*

"No, stop it," he mumbled.

"Who are you talking to, Will?" demanded Edwina.

He looked up, confused. "I didn't say anything."

They'll take you away from me. Just come home. You're safe with me.

The voice made his head hurt. He rubbed his ear, trying to block it out.

Adelaide sat up straight, her eyes blazing. "It's happening again. She's trying her tricks. I don't know how she keeps slipping past my wards." She turned to her sisters. "Join hands."

Before Will could even ask what was going on, Addy had pulled him to his feet. The sisters encircled him, holding hands.

"I am speaking to the spirit of Sarah Byrne," Adelaide intoned. "I command you to leave this place. You are not welcome here. You will leave Will Moran alone. Do you understand me, Sarah? You do *not* want to get on my bad side." She paused, her gaze landing on several spots around the room. "If you need help, I will help you, but you deal with me. Got it? You need to leave Will out of this. He is not your plaything."

The throbbing in Will's head began to subside. He gawked at Addy. Every time he was with her, he was blown away by the incredible things she could do. "I think she's gone."

"Good."

Will hung his head, overwhelmed. Sarah Byrne was squatting *in* his head. How fucked was that? And he'd pretty much opened the door to her.

"Hey." Adelaide urged him to sit back down. She crouched in front of him and grabbed his hand. "We're going to fix this. I know it's a lot to accept. I'm sure you must be thinking all sorts of things right now. Can you trust me? I just want you to be safe."

Sarah had said the same thing. *You're safe with me.* This was Addy, though. "I trust you." There was honesty in Adelaide's eyes, and somehow, he was able to forget the pull of Sarah's strange voice. "You think she'll come back?"

"Yeah, but next time we'll be ready for her."

"Fantastic." A dead woman was talking to him, and Addy and her formidable sisters were preparing to banish her. *All perfectly normal. Nothing to see here, folks.*

Edwina and Susannah went into the kitchen to make themselves coffees. Adelaide put her hand on his cheek and made him look at her. "I promise you, I'll find a way to help Sarah. But I will not let her, or any other dead things, fuck with you."

Wow. Will had never been the sort of person to enjoy displays of possessiveness, and had rarely shown them himself.

Coming from Addy, however? He liked it a lot.

Chapter Fifteen

Tonight, they would go to the museum, or as Adelaide had started thinking of it, Sarah's house.

First, they'd made a pitstop at Will's place, where he'd picked up some fresh clothes, toiletries and his laptop. They decided it was best that he hang out at Addy's for the day. She had had client readings scheduled but she'd postponed them as soon as she'd realized what they were dealing with. Edwina and Susannah had called their respective partners to let them know they'd be at Addy's for a time as well.

At lunch, they ordered in a couple of pizzas. Will seemed nervous so Addy was grateful when Susannah and Edwina got him talking about his family. He told them that he had an older brother, Frank, and he regaled them with stories from their childhood. He let it slip a couple of times that Frank was their father's "favorite son" because of his love of sports and shouting at the TV. It gave Adelaide some insight into Will's family dynamics and the comments he'd tossed out about his dad before. There was definitely some tension between Will and his father, but he seemed close to his mom. All in all, it was a nice lunch and she'd appreciated not having to talk about Sarah Byrne and other assorted ghosts.

But as evening drew near, Adelaide prepared for what was ahead. She wasn't sure what they would encounter at the museum, but if she could nip this thing in the bud in one visit, she would do her darndest. Before she left her house, she went out into her backyard and sat alone for a few minutes, meditating under the sunset. She called on all her angels in preparation for the museum visit. It wasn't so much that she believed in Biblical angels but she'd always known there were spirits of light around her. Not just Maria, either. Every soul had them, whether they be relatives who'd passed or wise souls who remained on this plane to help the living. As far as she was concerned, she would take all the help she could get.

Will held her hand as they headed toward the museum. As they arrived, she was hit by a wave of tremendous sadness. Like the merciless ocean, it pounded her again and again. It just about brought her to her knees, tearing down any newfound joy that she'd felt in getting closer to Will. Adelaide sucked down a few cleansing breaths, composing herself.

She touched her heart necklace, drawing on her grandmother's strength. *Focus on what needs to be done.*

This little house had seen catastrophe and lots of it, so she was determined to come to it with a sense of humility, respect and empathy. The form in which Sarah appeared nowadays was unnerving to say the least, but there was a time when she'd been a regular

person, just like any of them. She would be strong for
Sarah.

Will pulled his keys out of his pocket, unlocked the
door and disarmed the building's security system.
"Welcome to the Cabbagetown Museum. It's not the
introduction I would have liked. Come on in and I'll
show you around." He held the door open so that
Edwina and Susannah could pass.

As Adelaide crossed the threshold, he stopped her,
tipped up her chin and kissed her. Despite the creepy
circumstances, his kiss was somehow full of passion.
He wrapped his hand around the back of her neck, in a
possessive move that made all the swoon fairies flit
around her head. She was reminded of their night
together, and realized how much she wanted more
nights like that. She sighed into his embrace, reaching
up and tangling her fingers in his hair. He slid his
tongue against hers, seeking. For a sweet, sweet
moment, Addy was lost to sensation. She wanted him
inside her, so badly it hurt.

Unfortunately, that would have to wait.

They disentangled themselves and Will smiled.

"Not that I'm complaining, but what was that for?"
she asked.

"It was for good luck, and to remind you that my
only interest in Sarah was scholarly. I need you to
understand that, Addy. My interest in you, on the other
hand, runs much deeper than that."

Aflutter with new emotions, she appreciated the
reminder more than he knew.

She gathered her wits and walked into the museum
entryway. Once again, she was met with a surge of
sadness. She offered up a quick prayer, as she did
whenever she entered a location that set her on guard.

Addy reached out to any spirits who might be present. *We come here in peace. I mean you no harm.*

Something gathered outside her peripheral vision, a reluctant darkness. It hovered, not wanting to reveal too much of itself, but its message was clear. *Tread carefully.*

Maria rushed forward, ready to protect Adelaide, but stopped short of manifesting. She too lingered on the sidelines, watching for any danger.

I'm okay, Adelaide assured her spirit guide.

Be on guard, Maria said. *You are not welcome in this place.*

Adelaide braced herself. No wonder Will's colleagues felt uneasy in the museum. Between the aura of sorrow and the underlying hostility, no one would be truly at ease there.

Will brought them into the museum office, which sat off the main entrance. "This is where guests will start their tour. As you can see, we've set up this area with display cases featuring information about Indigenous peoples. Even though the focus here is the life of a typical nineteenth-century Cabbagetown worker, we wanted to start the experience with Indigenous histories."

"Of course." Adelaide inspected the display cases, taking a moment to read and absorb the land acknowledgment. It also made reference to groups that had visited that area thousands of years ago, such as the Laurentian people, the Point Peninsula people and the Iroquois.

"When things quiet down, Will, I'd love to do an article about this place," Susannah said. "I write for *Ontario's History* magazine. The story behind the museum would be perfect for our readers."

"I'd love that, thanks."

Edwina already had her EMF reader out. She tinkered with the settings and walked around the space. "I feel something, Addy. Actually, I think it's more than one presence."

"I agree." The shadows in Adelaide's mind's eye lengthened. "Sarah isn't the only one here."

"Aside from the Byrnes," Will said, "there were several other families that lived in the house through the years. Could it be one of those people?"

Addy shook her head. "No, this person has been here a long time, almost as long as Sarah. I see the form of a man, hovering far in the background, watching us. He won't come forward."

"Could it be Aiden Byrne?" Susannah asked. "Or Desmond?"

"I'm not sure." Adelaide shrugged and addressed the spirit directly. "I would like to talk to the man in the shadows. What is it that keeps you here?"

The man's presence was so vague it was almost insubstantial. The faintest of breaths. A sheer layer of gauze. Adelaide perceived him, nonetheless.

"Okay, have it your way. We'll talk when you're ready." Adelaide turned to Will. "While we're here, could we see the exhibits on Robert Taylor and the factory?"

He brought them into another room, one that had blown up photos of Cabbagetown during industrialization. In the display cases here, there were many interesting artifacts from the age, everything from old work shoes to food product tins to bits of machinery. What drew Adelaide's eye right away was a set of two large photos hung next to each other. One showed the Taylor factory in its heyday, the other, after its destruction. All that was left of the factory in the second image was ruins. A description next to the photos featured a map, showing where in Cabbagetown the factory would have been located.

Susannah surveyed the map image. "It looks like it was a massive factory. The floorplan spans blocks."

"It was the largest industrial complex in the area," Will said. "Although there were originally five buildings connected to the factory, by the time it was destroyed, it was a sprawling set of twelve. It took up the entire space where Wellesley Park now sits and it would have just about reached the river, ending where Rosedale Valley Road runs."

"Do we know how the fire started?" Edwina asked.

"Unfortunately not," Will answered. "Even though the buildings were made mostly of brick, there was a significant amount of wood used throughout the complex. The fire would have taken hold quickly."

As Will was talking, Adelaide meandered toward one of the displays. Sitting on a pedestal was a chunk of machinery that appeared to be some sort of gear. The label next to it stated that it had come from the Taylor factory, and it welcomed guests to touch it, undoubtedly to keep younger visitors engaged. Because Adelaide was often able to get strong impressions by handling an object, she put her hand on the gear and closed her eyes.

Pandemonium erupted in front of her as she was thrust back in time to the day of the factory fire. The sky was a wound, more red than blue, as the flames roared. People were shouting, running back and forth with buckets of water. Screams echoed in the distance, as men succumbed to their injuries. And the smell...the horrible, toxic smell, was everywhere. It leeched from the buildings, from the tools, from the very air itself into the ground, scarring the site for generations.

In that awful moment, Adelaide not only witnessed the death of Robert Taylor as he furiously tried to save documents in his office, she also saw six other men perish. Even more upsetting, she envisioned their spirits wandering now, lost and confused in the place where they died.

Adelaide let go of the gear, pulling her hand back as if it had scalded her.

Will put his hand on her lower back, gently rubbing. "Hey. Did you..."

"Yeah. I saw the fire. I saw everything."

Susannah pulled out a bottle of water from her knapsack and handed it to her. Grateful, Adelaide took a sip.

"I'm sorry." Will brought her into his embrace.

Comforted in a way she'd never experienced, Adelaide soaked it up. She closed her eyes and buried her face in his shirt. His fresh smell, body wash and clean laundry, helped the Taylor factory stench evaporate.

Will might never fully comprehend the scenes that appeared in her head, but he'd shown more compassion and patience than any man she'd ever hoped to trust. And he just felt so good. His embrace was the coziest, safest place she'd ever known. She could get used to this.

"Do you want to step outside?" Edwina asked.

"No, I'm okay. It's passing." Adelaide looked up from her comfy place on Will's chest. "Thanks."

The heat of the sun was in his smile and she was tempted to bask in it.

Will slung his arm around her shoulders. "We know of six individuals, aside from Taylor, who died as a result of the fire, either onsite or in hospital later. It really was a terrible event."

"They're still there, the men who died in the fire." Adelaide thought back to the burned man from the Necropolis. "They're wandering this neighborhood, trying to find a way to cross over. They've probably always been here, trying to communicate. I think the anniversary of the fire has somehow enabled them to show up on some other frequency."

"We'll help them," Susannah declared. "For now, why don't we split up? Ed and I can take the second floor." She and Edwina headed toward the stairs.

When they were alone, Will pushed a stray hair out of her face. "Are you sure you're okay?"

"Yeah. It's always overwhelming when it happens, especially with a scene like that, but it always passes."

"I wish I could take it from you."

"I'm not sure I would give it away, even if I could. It's too much a part of me. It's my purpose."

He held her hands and studied her. "Not too many people I know speak in terms of having a purpose. Addy, I... My head is all over the place right now."

"I'm sure it is."

"But there's one thing I know for sure. You're amazing."

Once again, her heart's rhythm hitched. This rush, it was something she'd never dared to feel before and it was happening all so quickly. "I think you're amazing too. Being with you helps me forget the bad moments."

"I'm very glad to hear that, but I still wish I could stop those bad moments from happening."

Holding hands, they made their way toward the next set of rooms on the main floor. She murmured in awe when she saw the setup. It was as if they'd walked into a home from the mid-nineteenth century.

Sarah's home.

The exhibit consisted of a small living room with a kitchen adjoining it. There were a couple of plain chairs in the living room. Handmade doilies sat atop the accent tables. A cabinet in the corner displayed a few cups, saucers and more precious keepsakes such as candlesticks. The kitchen doubled as a bathroom. In fact, it had been set up as if it were bath night for the family, and a washtub had been placed in the middle of the floor, a few inches of fake dirty water floating inside. A threadbare towel sat next to it over a chair. The description next to the washtub said many worker families would have bathed once a week, sharing the same water. Baths would have been done on Saturday nights, so that the children looked clean for Sunday church services. It was all cramped and dark, and it made her uncomfortable.

One of the first things that struck Adelaide was the cold. It was just like walking into a cold spot created by a spirit person, but instinctively, she knew that wasn't the case. She shivered.

"We pump cold air in here on purpose," Will explained. "Heating was a real issue for worker families at this time period. Many of these homes were heated by wood fire or coal, but those items were not always affordable. I've read accounts about how some children were sent to the St. Lawrence Market to collect discarded wooden crates. They'd bring them home and cut them up for firewood."

"There was a lot of hardship here."

"Absolutely, but you'll notice we've kept things neat and tidy, and that was done to a purpose too. When you read the stories shared by these workers, it becomes clear they took a real pride in their homes."

Adelaide nodded, overcome by emotion. She walked over to a small display case, one that had a write-up on the Byrne family. In the case was a photo of Sarah's headstone, as well as some personal items like a lady's glove, a comb and a slipper. There was also an old newspaper account of the "coffin ships" that brought Irish immigrants over to Canada during the days of the Famine. They'd been called that because so many passengers died enroute.

"These items, were they Sarah's?"

Will nodded. "Yeah. Desmond survived until his eighties and he still had some of her things. He'd passed them on to other members of the family and they ended up donating them to the museum."

"He kept Sarah's things?" Adelaide reeled. This felt like an important piece of information. "Interesting. Is it okay if I touch one of the items? I can wear gloves, if you'd prefer."

"Sure." Will popped back into the office and returned with two pairs of latex gloves. He put one pair on himself and handed the other to Adelaide. He unlocked the case. "How about the comb? The glove and the slipper are more fragile." Using two hands, he scooped up the comb and instructed Adelaide to hold it with both hands.

As she ran her finger on the edge of the comb, her field of vision changed. She saw a woman in Victorian garb kneeling at a child's empty bed, bent over the threadbare blanket. Her body shook as each sob broke from her. She cried out a name. *Maeve.*

Adelaide's heart broke for Sarah.

Oh, Maeve, my darling girl. Not you too. Sarah gathered sections of the blanket in her hands and pounded the bed in desolation.

A man walked into the bedroom. It was Aiden. He was swaying and Addy could smell the booze coming off him in waves. *I'm going to the Don Vale.* As he turned, she got a good look at him. He was tall, lean, had pronounced cheekbones and a wave in his light brown hair.

He was a dead ringer for Will.

Sarah watched her husband go, then looked right at Adelaide, like an actor breaking the fourth wall. Although she was a lovely woman with pale green eyes and pink lips, as she stared at Addy, she transformed into the wraith from the graveyard. Her skin became a deathly white and her eyes clouded over. She grimaced, showing yellowed teeth, and the scene faded away.

Adelaide sucked in a breath. As she exhaled, she rid herself of the vision. Still taking care with the old comb, she handed it back to Will.

"What did you see?" Will closed and locked the case and disposed of their latex gloves.

"I saw Sarah and I saw Aiden." She quickly surveyed the displays in the room. "Do you have any photos of them? I want there to be proof for what I'm about to say."

"Sorry. If there ever were any photos of them, they didn't survive."

"I think I know why she's been targeting you. You look exactly like Aiden."

His eyebrows shot up. "Really?"

"Will, are you sure you're not related to the Byrne family? Because I can see why Sarah might feel an attachment for a family member."

"Definitely not. My grandmother created detailed family trees years ago. If there had been a connection, even a minor one, I would know it."

"Maybe she has you confused with Aiden. He broke her heart. I've seen hauntings that originate from far less than that."

"That makes sense."

"She mentioned another name. Maeve."

"Maeve was one of their children. She died young, like all the others."

"How many were there?" Adelaide asked.

He indicated a piece of paper that sat in the display case. It was a record that showed the deaths of Sarah and Aiden's children. "Five."

Adelaide perused the information. "They were all so little. I can't even imagine how someone would cope with that sort of loss. It's unfathomable."

"I know. It's an incredibly sad story but an important one, I think, because it clearly illustrates how difficult life was for these people. If they weren't contending with sickness and poverty, they were dealing with all sorts of other hardships."

"It's possible Sarah glommed on to you because she sensed your empathy for her situation. She might see you as a kindred soul. On top of that, you've had a lot on your plate and some mental health challenges, so your guard was probably down. Sometimes, spirit people see the dents in our armor. It's like a window into our psyches, and it allows them to creep in."

"I...talk to her sometimes."

"Oh?"

"When I come to work in the morning, sometimes I'll say hello to her. I don't know why I started doing that. Knowing she had such a hard life, I guess I wanted her to know her legacy was in good hands." He brought his hand to his mouth. "I brought this on myself, didn't I?"

"Not at all. You're a victim here. For all we know, Sarah may have been a wonderful person in life, but she can't be allowed to continue on this destructive path. On some level, her spirit has been searching for something. Attachments happen when spirits are attracted to something in us, whether it be our light, our humanity, or even just a way of satisfying urges that never died." A thought occurred to Adelaide. "And sometimes, all they need is an acknowledgment, to be seen."

"Meaning?"

"Meaning I'd like to try something." Adelaide went out into the hallway and called for her sisters. Once they were downstairs, she had them all stand in a semicircle around the display case, holding hands. She closed her eyes. "I'd like to talk to Sarah Byrne. Sarah, I'm so sorry that you experienced so much sorrow in this life. It truly isn't fair. I saw you mourning little Maeve and my heart went out to you. I know you felt alone for many years because Aiden didn't know how to support you. I think you've been reaching out to Will because he reminds you of Aiden. I can understand why you would do that, but it's not right. Will is not your husband and you need to leave him alone. Aiden is dead. You are dead and you need to move on. We now extend all the love in our hearts to you so you may be reunited with your children and your husband.

They're waiting for you there. Go now in love to the place of peace."

They were all quiet for several minutes. Edwina spoke first. "I don't want to jump the gun but I feel like the energy has shifted in here. I don't have the sense that I'm being watched anymore."

Addy nodded but was unwilling to make a call yet. "How do you feel, Will?"

"It's weird, but I feel lighter. There's a knot I've been carrying at the top of my spine for weeks." He rolled his shoulders. "It's gone."

"I think you did it, Addy." Susannah patted her on the back. "You helped Sarah cross over."

Adelaide tried again to connect with the energies that she'd sensed upon walking into the house but came up against a wall. If any spirit people remained, they were hidden so deep they might as well have been in a crawlspace under the building. They were imperceptible. She checked in with Maria. *Do you feel her?*

Maria was cautious as well. *"She's gone, but I don't know if it's for good."*

"Let's keep an eye on things, I guess."

Adelaide smiled at Will. "I think you should be okay to work here now. I just don't want to make any promises. I'd like to monitor the situation."

"You're a star, Addy." He hugged her tight. "Thank you, and not just from me. You helped Sarah be at peace."

"I think she just needed someone to acknowledge her pain. Anyway, I hope she really is at peace because we still have Lottie and Robert to deal with."

"The anniversary of the fire is coming up," Will reminded them.

"That means we'll have a date at the site of the factory that night."

"We have very interesting dates," Will teased.

Was it finally sinking in for him, the fact that he was dating a weird girl? Was he having regrets?

Her worries must have been written on her face because Will leaned over and whispered, "If it means I get to spend time with you, I'm there."

She forced a smile, wondering if he'd tire of her otherworldly shenanigans.

They said goodbye to her sisters. Adelaide waited for Will as he turned off the lights in the museum and grabbed his keys. He locked up the building, setting the alarm. As they headed down the walkway together, Adelaide grabbed his hand, marveling at how easy it was to be with him, and at how content she suddenly felt.

He was right. There was a certain lightness in the air now. It no longer seemed oppressive or claustrophobic. She allowed herself one small moment of triumph.

They headed down the sidewalk and Addy glanced back toward the Amelia Street house.

For a fleeting moment, she thought she saw the silhouette of a woman in profile move across one of the upper windows. She waited for the soul-crushing sensation of sadness that she'd felt on the way into the house, but it never manifested.

Throughout their time with Darke Paranormal Investigations, Edwina had cautioned them over jumping to conclusions and attributing anomalies to the supernatural when they didn't have proof. Adelaide had argued with Edwina many times, but this time, she was inclined to take her point of view.

Perhaps the shadow she'd seen in the window was merely a trick of the light.

Or, if it was Sarah, maybe that was her way of saying goodbye.

Chapter Sixteen

Will was just setting the box of donuts on the office table, the last bit of preparation for their staff meeting, when he heard the knock on the open door. "Terri, thanks so much for coming in."

Terri entered the office, her gaze flitting around. "Hey, Will."

He gestured to the chairs and they both took a seat. "I wanted to speak with you before the others get here. First of all, thank you for coming back. I can't even tell you how much I appreciate it."

"I love this job. I hope you know that."

"I do. Even in the short time we worked together, your passion for the work was evident and I value your contributions." He paused. "I want to apologize as well. I didn't take your concerns about the atmosphere of the place seriously because I was too caught up in making sure the museum opening would be a success. My mind has been...a little cloudy. At any rate, I should have listened better and acted sooner. I'm sorry."

"Thanks. I hear you brought in Darke Paranormal Investigations. I subscribe to their YouTube channel. They're awesome."

His cheeks heated. "Yeah, they are. Anyway, Addy feels it should be safe for us to work here, but she'll be popping in to keep an eye on the situation."

"If Adelaide Darke gave it the all-clear, then I suppose I can give it another shot."

"Great. I know I speak for Miguel and Alison and the volunteers when I say we're all happy to have you back on the team."

"You know," she said, laughing quietly, "I've always been convinced that I have some sensitivity to the paranormal. When I was young, I used to see shadows in my house and I'd have these really intense dreams about relatives who'd died, kind of like they were visiting me. I went to see a medium once. He told me I have abilities but I've never explored them. I was always too scared to open that door, in case I couldn't close it again."

"I hear you. I doubt I'd want to explore those sorts of abilities either. I'd never get any sleep. I don't know how Addy does it."

Will and Terri chatted for a few minutes about the volunteer program, then Miguel and Alison arrived for the meeting. They greeted Terri enthusiastically and they all took their seats.

Will sat at the far end of the table and began the meeting. "Thanks, everyone. I'm really glad to have this entire team back together and I'd like to offer a huge welcome and thanks to Terri." He rubbed his hands together. "Thank you all for your hard work and for the tremendous effort you've put into this place. As we near the opening date, there are a few things I want us to concentrate on. I'm going to be doing another media blitz. Press releases have already gone out. Miguel, I believe you've been confirming programming details with the local schools?"

"Yeah. Our first visiting classes will be from Orde Street Junior Public School and Our Lady of Lourdes."

As Miguel continued to speak about what he had planned for the two schools, Will's eye was drawn to the open office doorway.

A shadowy outline blurred the edges of the door, almost as if someone were peeking around the corner. Slim fingers gripped the edge near the hinges and slid away.

Will blinked. In the time it took him to do so, the shadow disappeared.

He braced himself for the voice, *her* voice, but didn't hear it.

"Will?" Miguel stopped giving his report. "You okay?"

"S-sorry," Will stammered. "Just thinking ahead. How many classes was that from Orde Street again?" He smiled at Miguel as his mind raced.

You're just seeing things. You've had some wild experiences since meeting Addy and it's perfectly normal they would have an influence on you. It's like watching a scary movie and being afraid to look under your bed. It's called imagination.

His throat tightened and he forced himself to look toward the door again. *There. It was nothing.* He was the leader of this team and he needed to keep his shit together. He'd only just convinced Terri to join them again. He certainly couldn't afford to lose her or anyone else.

As Miguel relayed a few more details, Terri glanced at the doorway, then at Will. Her gaze darkened, as if in awareness.

Fuck. Had she seen it too?

However, she smiled and went back to jotting notes down on her pad of paper.

Okay. He really was getting carried away. Terri was fine. He was fine.

The museum was fine.

Determined to believe it, Will reached for the donut box. He grabbed a huge cruller, took a bite, and sat back as the hit of sugar calmed his nerves.

* * * *

When Adelaide heard the doorbell early Saturday morning, she jumped and hurried to open the door.

Will stood outside, wearing jeans and a T-shirt, hiking boots and a baseball cap. "Ready to go birding?"

"Yes!" She launched herself at him and kissed him, knocking his cap off.

He kissed her back, laughing as he did. As their tongues touched, his laugh turned into a low moan and he ran his hands down to her backside, pulling her against his body. She dug her fingers into his mop of hair, enjoying the sensory overload. He smelled so good, of citrusy shampoo and coconut-scented sunscreen. She wanted to eat him up.

Maybe she would in the car. They had a short drive ahead of them. She might be able to convince him to pull over for a few minutes on a quiet road so she could use that mouth he was always talking about.

He stroked her cheek and bent down to retrieve his cap. "You have a mischievous look on your face."

"Do I? I'm just excited to go birding with you. Let me grab my backpack." She popped inside, got her things and locked up. They walked hand in hand to his car, which was parked down the street.

They were going on a real date, one that had nothing to do with dead people. *Amazing.*

Even though she'd been to Will's house a few times now and had seen the cute red Mazda parked in the driveway, this was the first time she'd seen it in action and it took her aback. Because they lived so close to each other, they'd been walking around Cabbagetown on all their adventures. Sitting in his car was such a pleasant hit of normalcy. The plan was to drive out of town to the Royal Botanical Gardens Arboretum in Hamilton, to the west of Toronto, to spend a fun day together. The sort of thing regular people did.

Adelaide couldn't quell her happy nerves. She and Will had been hanging out a lot, usually late in the evening after he finished work, but this was a date. An actual date, not some lusty fumbling on her couch. People had dates all the time. It wasn't a big deal.

It just felt vaguely momentous.

Even now, as they set out on their road trip, she had the excitement of someone going on safari or on a world tour. Of course, she knew better than to put too much stock into one morning of birding, but at the same time, she just wanted to enjoy being swept away. It was a curious sensation and it bubbled inside her, as if a hundred balloons had carried her off her feet. It was exhilarating and frightening and awe-inspiring, all at once.

Elated, she called to her spirit guide. *"What is this, Maria?"*

"Oh, Addy. It's joy, and you deserve it."

Joy. She had trouble wrapping her head around the concept. She'd encouraged her sisters to embrace love and happiness when they'd begun to fall for Simon and Noah, but it was strange applying her advice to her own life. She'd been let down too many times.

As she looked over at Will, admiring the way his knuckles settled around the steering wheel and listening to his happy chatter, she marveled at how easy it was to go with the flow. It was one of the things she liked most about him. From the beginning, even in their tense and awkward moments, he'd made everything easy. She felt like she could be herself with him. It was something she hadn't experienced with many people in the past, so much so that she now regarded it as a gift.

They chatted on the hour-long drive out of Toronto about fun things like recent movies and books that they'd enjoyed, where to find the best hot dog in town—the street vendor outside the Royal Ontario Museum—and their thoughts on different scenes from the *Star Wars* franchise. They sipped their coffees and nibbled on the homemade granola squares that Addy had baked for their date. By the time they got to the Arboretum, she could have sworn minutes had flown by instead of an hour.

Will had a couple of pieces of equipment with him, a fancy camera, two pairs of binoculars and something called a spotting scope which allowed him to see at greater distances. She helped him grab the items, as well as a couple of water bottles, and they set out on one of the paths. Adelaide was instantly calmed as the tree canopy enveloped them. There was something so wonderful about being outside in the fresh air, surrounded by mature maples and oaks and cherry trees.

It wasn't long before she heard the familiar *chicka-dee-dee*. They'd come prepared with a bag of seed. As soon as they dropped a few kernels into their palms and held them up, a small group of the birds alighted.

Strangely emotional, Adelaide cast her eye toward Will. "I will never get tired of this."

"I'm so glad you enjoy it."

They fed the birds for a few minutes, then left little piles of seed on a nearby tree trunk. After sanitizing their hands, they carried on, farther into the wooded area. It was very early and although they'd encountered a couple of dogwalkers when they'd approached the path, there was no one else near. All she heard was birdsong, the rustle of undergrowth as squirrels and chipmunks ran by and a croaking bullfrog at the edge of the Cootes Paradise Marsh.

Will set up his scope at the edge of the marsh and adjusted it for her. "I've seen all kinds of birds out here, everything from tiny warblers to bald eagles."

"No way."

"Would I lead you astray?" Something trilled in the woods behind them and he held up a finger. "I hear a red-eyed vireo but there are other birds too. The vireos are really hard to spot because they tend to stick to the trees. Why don't we try the binoculars?"

"Okay."

He handed her a set, then put on his own. "Now, if you spot some movement in the branches, look with your eyes and bring the binoculars up to that position. It makes it easier to spot the bird."

Adelaide looked up into the tall trees, keeping her eyes peeled for shaking leaves. "I think I've got something, up near the top." She kept her gaze trained on the spot and brought up the binoculars. "I see a bright yellow bird!"

Will followed her lead. "That's awesome. It's a yellow warbler, one of my favorites."

"It's beautiful."

"You're going to develop something many birders get. It's called 'warbler neck.' Warblers tend to keep to the higher branches so they will stretch your neck muscles. You know, you can start a list of the birds you've spotted. There are some apps that will help you track them. I can show you later."

"I would love that."

They spent the morning at the Arboretum, talking about birds and plants and their shared love of nature. Will knew of many parks where one could spot different varieties of birds, and they made plans to visit all of them. By the time noon rolled around, and they decided they were hungry for lunch, Adelaide was floating on a cloud. After having seen so many cute birds, and feeding so many chickadees, she felt like fricking Snow White.

They had lunch in a small pub not far away. In their corner booth, they held hands and whispered like giddy teenagers. Will had gotten a bit of sun on his nose and he looked healthy and recharged, so different from the pale man of a short time ago.

It once again gave Addy hope that Sarah Byrne's influence had worn off and that the spirit woman had found peace.

By the time they started heading back to his car, Adelaide was full of good food, good experiences and overwhelming emotions. It had been a perfect day so far, and she wanted more of them with Will.

Will had parked his car at the far end of a quiet lot. Before she even opened the passenger door, a fantasy unfurled in her mind, one of her going down on him right there.

How better to show her appreciation?

Rather than open the passenger side door, she opened the back door.

He gave her a quizzical look over the top of the car. "You getting in the back?"

"Yeah." She licked her lips. "And I'm really hoping you'll join me there."

His eyes narrowed in lust and he checked the lot to make sure no one else was near. One eyebrow quirked, Will got in the back.

They came together in a crush of lips and tongues and teeth. He cupped her breasts, urgently seeking, but she pushed him so he sat back.

"Uh..."

"I'm going to give you a blowjob, Will. Is that okay?"

His mouth fell open. "It is so okay, but I got a little sweaty on our walk."

She winked. "I don't share your concern."

"Aw, fuck."

Delighted and beaming, Addy undid the button on his jeans and slowly pulled the zipper down.

Another curse spilled from his lips as she eased his jeans and boxer briefs over his hips. His cock, already hard and throbbing, sprang free. The light was good and she had a chance to admire it for a moment, wrapping her hand around his girth and teasing her fingers along its veins. It was gorgeous and it made her mouth water.

"Geez, Addy." Will tangled his fingers in her hair but didn't push her downward. He drew in a deep breath and let her set the pace. "You'll destroy me one day. You know that, right?"

"I think you'll survive." Feeling naughty, she leaned over and gave him a slow series of licks.

"Goddamn." His hips jerked and he let out a moan.

She cupped his balls, trying her best to draw this out, even though he was already straining. "Keep an eye on the lot so we don't get arrested."

"I make no promises. I can't take my eyes off you."

Adelaide took him into her mouth, giddy at his reaction and her power over him in that moment. He tasted so good—a little salty—and it was intoxicating. She licked and teased him until the curses erupting from him verged on the blasphemous. His movements became tense and his grip on her head and neck firmer. She indulged in daydreams of doing this to him in other places, of getting kinky and wild, exploring each other's desires and limits. Will was panting, writhing below her, and her need to drive him to the brink was all-consuming.

He'd shown her a new world today. He'd brought her a measure of peace. Now, she wanted to leave him spent and delirious, totally safe in her arms.

"Addy." His voice was low and dangerous. "I'm going to come."

"I know. I want you to." She pulled out all the stops, taking him as deeply as she could.

He let out a cry and thrust his hips toward her face. When he unraveled, she swallowed, happy to give him this moment of ecstasy.

"Good Lord." He caressed her scalp, his hand a little shaky. "Did you take a class or something? Because that was outstanding."

She laughed softly and wiped the corner of her mouth with a finger. When she sat up, Will was staring at her like she was a sunrise after a long, stormy night.

"You are so fucking beautiful. Thank you."

Adelaide's heart rejoiced. Being with him was such a rush, better than riding her favorite rollercoaster. It was like that heady moment at the top of a big hill, catching air before shrieking with abandonment on the descent.

His gaze of adoration transformed into one of pure lust. He leaned over and kissed her neck, just under her left ear. "I want to return the favor."

"Oh, you will, but let's go home first."

"Are you sure? I can be very discreet."

"I bet you can, but I'm not sure I can be. Something tells me I'll want to make a lot of noise and we probably shouldn't do that here." She nodded toward a car about forty feet away, one that a family was approaching.

"Damn. I'm not sure I can wait." He kissed her, flicking his tongue across her bottom lip.

"I believe in you. Let's go."

On the drive home to Toronto, they were both quiet and contemplative. As he drove, Will touched her frequently, either by giving her hand a quick squeeze or tracing his fingers along the length of her thigh. With every kilometer they logged, Addy's anticipation grew until it was a living, pulsing thing. She wanted him so badly it was all she could do not to demand he pull over and service her at the side of the highway.

Once they got back to her place, Will grabbed a parking spot right in front of her house. It was as if the sex gods had decreed they should be naked as soon as possible. They jumped out of the car and raced into her house, tearing at their clothes as they rushed upstairs.

Wearing nothing but a smug smile, he crawled onto her bed and lay back. "Climb on up, my pretty girl."

Her hands tingling and her pussy wet from sheer anticipation, Adelaide scrambled atop him. He grabbed her ass, dragging her toward his open mouth. Then, Will returned the favor. Several times.

Chapter Seventeen

On the anniversary of the R. S. Taylor Glue and Blacking Manufactory fire, Adelaide met Will and they walked together up Sumach Street toward Wellesley Park, where they would meet Edwina and Susannah. It was another typical pocket of Cabbagetown. There were historic homes from various time periods, bordered by small but pretty gardens. Idyllic, aside from what awaited them.

As they turned right on Wellesley Street, it hit her. Her senses inflamed, warning her of spirit activity. All at once, she smelled it. Burning and the vomit-inducing stench of dead animal flesh.

She stopped in her tracks and Will touched her shoulder in support.

That was when she saw the man. At first, she thought he was just some guy hurrying down the street, but she realized there was something wrong with his gait. He was clutching his head and moaning.

As he drew nearer, she got a better look. The man was white, perhaps forty years old. Like the spirit in the Necropolis, he was also badly burned. His clothing, an old-fashioned suit, looked well-made but was torn in places and charred in others. His hair had been burned off one side of his head and his skin showed raw underneath. Moving through Will's body, he seized Adelaide's arms. *"Help them. The fire, it's everywhere!"*

Her lungs began to constrict, just as they had on their first visit to the Taylor house. Although her body was only reacting to the memory of smoke, it behaved as if the fire blazed in front of her. She automatically coughed, as her heart raced in panic, but she reminded herself it was just spiritual activity. She didn't believe the spirit man was in actual pain either. He was simply trapped in the memory, making her feel what he had once felt.

He tugged on her arm. *"Help!"*

Details of his life popped into her head. His name was Harold Painter and he'd worked in the offices of the factory, as a clerk to Robert Taylor. He'd had a wife and two children, with another one on the way at the time of his death. She saw him as he used to be, ruddy of skin, with a full head of bushy brown hair.

She called on Maria for backup, then faced the poor soul. "Listen to me, Harold Painter, you are not bound to this place anymore. The factory fire happened a long time ago and you no longer need to relive your pain. You are free to go in peace and love. Your wife Fran is waiting for you on the other side. Look to the light."

His gaze traveled over her shoulder. *"I see a woman with black hair. She's standing on a long path."*

"That's my spirit guide Maria. She'll show you the way to your family. Go with her."

"I'm afraid."

It was fear that had kept the factory men here all this time. Adelaide had seen that many times. She'd encountered numerous souls who'd been frightened to make the transition. "There's no need to be afraid, Harold. I promise you."

"She'll take me to my Fran?" Tears flooded his eyes. *"I'll be able to see her and the children again?"*

"Yes. I feel them, waiting for you on the other side. They just need you to take that first step. Go to them and be at peace."

He released her arm and grabbed Maria's hand. As soon as he did, the burn marks disappeared from his head and his brown hair filled in. Restored and full of wonder, Harold turned to Adelaide. *"There are others here."*

"I know, and I'm going to help them."

He smiled. *"I couldn't see the way before. Thank you."* With those final words, the man disappeared, accompanied by Maria. The terrible odor faded almost immediately.

"Jesus, Addy," Will said. "Harold Painter. That was the name of one of the factory fire victims."

"I know. He was stuck but he's crossed over now." She braced herself. "Will, he confirmed that there are others. I think I'm going to have my work cut out for me at Wellesley Park."

"Tell me what to do. How can I help?"

"Just be with me."

He held her hand. "Absolutely."

* * * *

Will was still clutching Adelaide's hand as they arrived at the park. He wished he could do something significant to help her. After her encounter with Harold Painter, her energy had flagged. The spark had gone out of her eyes and her shoulders drooped. It was all he could do to resist swooping her up into his arms and taking her away from all of this. However, at the edge of the park, she took a breath, straightened her spine and was somehow ready to confront what lay ahead.

Edwina and Susannah stood near the park entrance, by the splashpad. Because it was now dusk, the park was officially closed, but there were no gates to keep people out so they had free run of the place.

"Addy, are you okay?" Susannah asked. "You don't look good."

"I'll be okay in a minute." Adelaide sat on a nearby bench.

"She helped a factory victim cross over," Will explained. "Addy said that he came right up to her, that his face was burned from the fire. She said he warned her there'd be others."

"I feel it too." Edwina glanced over her shoulder at the dark expanse of green space. "The moment Suz and I stepped onto this parkland, there were eyes on us. The men are watching from behind the trees."

Will stared into the darkness but saw nothing. That didn't stop chills from going down his spine.

Her sisters had brought them all headlamps. They took a moment to put them on, adjusting the lights. With Addy leading the way, they walked farther into the park.

Adelaide headed slowly toward an enclave of trees, then stopped. "I see them."

Edwina gasped. "They're coming toward us. Oh my God, they're all burned."

"I see Robert, standing apart from the others," Adelaide said. "Maria was right. He's tormented by guilt. He wears it like a cloak."

"Why does he feel so guilty?" Susannah asked. "The fire was deemed an accident."

"Let's find out." Adelaide took a few more steps and stopped. "I see you, Robert Taylor. My name is Adelaide Darke and I'm here to help you and the men who worked with you."

Will gazed in wonder, trying to see what Addy saw, aiming his headlamp in the direction she was facing. All at once, the shadows shifted. Several pale figures became visible. He couldn't make out any faces or distinguishing characteristics. All he saw were their faint outlines. They moved in a jerky fashion toward Adelaide, like children's chalk drawings come to life. "Fuck. Me."

Edwina turned to him. "You see this shit too?"

"Normally, no, but I see it right now." Maybe Grandma Nell had a point about Irish blood having a direct line to the spirit world. Had she been able to see dead people?

On second thought, he wasn't sure he wanted to know.

The chalk drawing men crept toward them.

Will moved closer to Addy, ready to defend her, although he was pretty darn sure she was more capable of defending him in this situation. "What are we supposed to do?"

"It's okay." She gave his shoulder a squeeze. "I've got this. We're not in any danger from these men." She turned back toward the ghost. "Mr. Taylor, why does your guilt bind you to this place? You can tell me."

At first, all Will heard was wind whistling through the trees, but it wasn't long before he could distinguish some words. It was as if they were being carried to them on the breeze.

Adelaide was having a conversation with Taylor, and Taylor was answering.

"So much death."

"He keeps telling me about all the deaths," Addy said, "but he's not just talking about the fire. Toward the end, he began to understand the effect his business was having on the neighborhood. He knows his factory poisoned the air and the water." She paused. "He's saying something about typhus and cholera."

"There were typhus and cholera epidemics in early Toronto," Susannah explained. "There were several outbreaks between the 1830s and the 1850s."

"He's saying his factory killed people just like those epidemics." Adelaide frowned.

"I killed my Lottie."

"I mean, if you want to get specific, Robert," Adelaide said, "typhoid killed Lottie. I understand that you feel a level of responsibility for not taking care of the land around you, but maybe you didn't know any better. There are people today who are destroying the environment, and they definitely know what they're doing and they don't care."

"My fault. Must make amends."

"He's tearing at his hair," she continued. "The guilt is almost unbearable. He feels the need to punish himself and that's why he stays here, on the land he poisoned."

Will watched in wonder, his chest weighed down by an invisible heaviness. Taylor's guilt was so oppressive it seemed to be affecting everyone there. Susannah was rubbing her stomach and even the normally indomitable Edwina was misty-eyed. As for Addy, even though she remained focused on the spirits, her lips were drawn tight in frustration.

Would others feel this way when they visited the park?

Edwina piped up. "Addy, if we help the other men cross over, do you think that'll persuade him to go too?"

"It's worth a shot. Let's join hands." The sisters formed a line, holding hands, and Will linked up on Addy's right. She closed her eyes. "Spirits of the Taylor factory, you are no longer bound to this place. Your time on earth has ended and you may now go in peace to your everlasting home. May the Creator watch over this land and the people connected to it, cleansing it with holy light. May all lost souls be permanently healed and reunited and taken into the light. Go now to the place of peace." She opened her eyes. "The other men have gone, thank goodness, but Taylor's still here. He's determined to stay."

Will put his hand on her lower back, gently rubbing. She looked so damned tired. "What can I do?"

"Nothing." She stood on tiptoes and kissed him on the cheek. "But thank you. He wants me to go with him, so he can unburden himself."

"But it's dark out there. At least let me walk behind you."

"I'll be okay, I swear." With that, Adelaide turned and walked deeper into the park. Aside from the light of her headlamp, the darkness swallowed her.

Will watched until he could no longer see the bobbing light. His stomach turned over in utter helplessness.

"Don't worry," Susannah said. "She has done this before. I don't sense any malice coming from Taylor, just a heavy heart."

"Right." He gnawed on the inside of his cheek. "How long do you think she'll be?"

"As long as it takes." Edwina steered him back toward the park bench and patted the seat next to her. "Long enough for us to grill you about your intentions, I'd say."

"Intentions, huh? Okay, let's do this." All of a sudden, a part of Will wished he could go hang with Addy and the dead guy, but judging from the amused expressions on her sisters' faces, he didn't need to be too intimidated.

In truth, Susannah and Edwina took it much easier on him than he expected. They were cool and even shared stories of how their significant others had been impacted by previous paranormal investigations.

"Maybe we'll introduce you to Simon and Noah," Edwina teased. "They'll prove to you that a man can emerge unscathed after being in a relationship with a freaky Darke sister!"

"I think Noah emerged unscathed." Susannah laughed. "Then again…"

Edwina scoffed. "Nonsense. He worships the ground you walk on."

Susannah smiled in a secretive way, one that made it very clear her partner did indeed indulge in a bit of worshiping from time to time.

"Well, I've never been worried about being scarred by our relationship. And for the record, I do plan to stick around," Will said. "If that's cool with Addy. I think she went into this with more reservations than I did."

Her sisters dipped their heads in identical nods. They weren't surprised.

"She told me she was bullied in school."

Susannah's mouth opened. "She told you that? She's never told anyone about the bullying, aside from family, and even then she barely mentions it."

"Hopefully that means she's comfortable with me. I gather it was bad?"

"Oh, yeah. It was bad," Edwina said. "A lot of school kids got involved. Hell, even our cousin bullied her."

"Geoffrey," Susannah muttered and made a gagging noise. "Sorry. When I hear his name, I become a petulant tween again."

Will fumed. "Is it wrong that I want to find all those people and smack them upside the head?" Actually, he wanted to do a lot worse. "Addy cares so much. Why would anyone do that to her?"

"Because people suck sometimes," Susannah said. "Personally, I think they were all secretly afraid of her."

Edwina nodded. "Oh, they were totally afraid of her. Remember Cheryl Ladmore's face that time Addy told her off at choir practice? That was brilliant." She elbowed Will. "Our little sister might be sweet, but she's also a badass. She has no trouble standing up for herself."

"So I've noticed."

Across the park, a light bounced over the grass. It was Adelaide, heading back.

Will jumped up to meet her. "Hey. How'd it go?"

Surprising him, she walked right up to him and wrapped her arms around him.

"Oh. Come here." He enfolded her in his arms and moved her headlamp off her forehead, then kissed her brow. For a minute, he just held her, giving her what she needed. "Is everything okay?"

"Yes and no. Robert appreciated being able to talk to someone but he has concerns." She glanced over her shoulder. "But he wants to see Lottie so he's willing to come back with me to the house."

Sure enough, a shadowy figure hovered a few feet behind Adelaide.

Will exhaled on a long breath. "This is turning into quite the outing."

He reached for Addy's hand. Forming a somber parade, they headed down Sumach Street toward the Taylor home.

As they reached the sidewalk in front of the Taylor house, Adelaide saw Lottie appear at the window. When she saw her father standing next to Addy, she jumped and waved, mouthing, "*Daddy.*"

"*My little girl.*" Taylor's eyes filled with tears as he faced Adelaide. "*I'll never forgive myself.*"

Adelaide was torn. On one hand, she understood and respected Robert's need to repent for his sins. As a lover of the outdoors, she hated seeing the environment destroyed. On the other hand, she didn't believe in eternal punishment. "*Let's not keep your daughter waiting.*"

On Adelaide's nod, Susannah unlocked the front door. They had arranged with Cindy to have the keys for what would hopefully be one last visit. Once they were inside, Robert disappeared, but she wasn't worried. She could feel his energy in the house and he was already running to the loft room.

Edwina hit the lights and they followed. When Adelaide reached the upper landing, she saw that the loft room door was ajar. Leading the others, she walked up the short staircase and entered the room.

The bare space had miraculously transformed. What had once been a dusty vacant loft was now full of color and texture and light. It appeared as it had in Lottie's day. The dainty furniture was restored. On the white bedframe was a mattress and a lovely handmade quilt. The dresser was laden with ribbons and doilies and a pretty set of silver brushes and combs. There were clothes in the closet and the window seat was full of dolls and books.

The bedroom had come back to life.

As poignant as the sight was, Adelaide couldn't help but think of Sarah Byrne's poor children. They'd never had the chance to experience such splendor. There had been no ribbons and bows in the Amelia Street house, no pretty dolls. As much as Addy sympathized with Lottie's situation, the disparity shook her.

Will came up behind Adelaide and put his hands on her shoulders. "Oh my God."

She turned to him, only to find him wide-eyed, looking about the room. "You can see it?"

"See it, hear it." He grabbed her hand. "And I feel it."

As did Edwina and Susannah. Her sisters stood nearby, still and astonished.

In the middle of the room, Robert kneeled in front of his young daughter. Around them, a soft light shone, making each strand of hair glisten and each teardrop sparkle.

Robert took Lottie's hand. "My princess. I'm so sorry."

Lottie, her sweet face beaming, touched his cheek. "It's all right, Daddy. You're home now. We can go see Mommy now."

Crying, Robert clasped her to his chest and they embraced. After a long moment, he wiped his eyes. "No, my love. This is one journey you'll have to take without me. I promise I'll join you one day, though."

"But..."

"Lottie, I still have to repent."

The girl quirked her head. "What does 'repent' mean?"

"It means I hurt many people with my business, with my greed. I made people sick. I may even have made you sick, and I have to take time to consider what I've done. I should have known better, Lottie. I should have done better."

"But I'm afraid to go by myself." Lottie whimpered. "I want you to come too."

"You'll be fine," her father promised. "And Mommy will be so happy to hold you in her arms. You will see me again, I swear it. Now, I need you to be brave for me. Can you do that?"

Lottie nodded reluctantly.

Robert turned to Adelaide. "She'll be safe?"

"Yes, and she won't be alone. My spirit guide Maria will help her." Although she didn't feel right about leaving Robert behind, she'd given him her word when they'd had their conversation at Wellesley Park. If he wanted to remain and contemplate his life and his actions, that was his prerogative. She didn't believe in crossing anyone over who wasn't ready. She didn't even believe it was possible.

"Imagine," Will whispered. "An industrialist who feels the need to atone for his environmental sins. I never thought I'd see the day."

"It's his choice," Adelaide said. "If Robert wants to atone, this is really the only way he can." Taylor had been a man of wealth and privilege, a man whose actions had impacted an entire community. Although some of his actions could be chalked up to ignorance, others had been driven by greed, as he'd stated himself. It wasn't as if she could send him back in time in order to change his ways and preserve the cleanliness of the local waterways and air, but she could give him this.

"Thank you, Adelaide." Robert hugged his daughter one more time. "I'll come find you soon, Lottie. You have my word."

"Okay, Daddy. I'll be brave."

Adelaide called on Maria to help Lottie make her transition. "Lottie, my friend Maria is going to take you to your mom now. Can you see her?"

"Yes," said Lottie. "She's already holding my hand. She's very nice."

"Perfect." Addy quietly recited a prayer to help the little girl cross over and another for her father to find peace in his own way. "Lottie, it's time for you to go home. You'll never be lonely again."

"I see flowers and trees, Daddy, and so many colors! It's beautiful." On a laugh of pure happiness, she was gone. A brilliant light filled the room, then faded.

Robert gazed at the empty spot his daughter had vacated and smiled. "I won't forget your kindness, Adelaide."

"Are you sure you don't want me to help you too?"

"If you want to help me," Robert said, his voice taking on a hollow quality, "help the one I wronged so grievously. Help Sarah."

"Sarah?" A terrible shiver insinuated itself along the length of Adelaide's spine. "You don't mean…?"

But Robert had faded away, taking all the light and color in the room with him. The loft was dark and empty again.

Will ran his hand through his hair. "Jesus, that was intense."

Choked up, Adelaide shook her head. She wasn't sure what to say. Did he mean Sarah Byrne? Why would Taylor make reference to the dead wife of one of his employees?

She'd really hoped that Sarah had found peace as well, but a kernel of uneasiness had implanted itself in her brain that day at the museum. Now, it threatened to pop.

And yet, Will looked so healthy. He'd been happy and energetic.

Maybe Robert meant a different Sarah. The name was a common one. It could be someone else.

However, even as she considered the idea, she knew she was wrong.

Her true reckoning with Sarah Byrne was yet to come. That meant Will was still in danger. Sarah had merely been biding her time.

If only she could get some kind of confirmation...

Susannah interrupted her scattered thought process. "We should finish up here, Addy."

"No, I need to summon Robert again. I have to talk to him. Maybe I should go back to the park."

Susannah grabbed her hands. "You've done enough for one night. I know you have questions. We all do, but the main thing is you helped Lottie find peace. That was always the goal here. We'll figure out the rest later."

"You're right." Adelaide clung to that thought. They'd helped the lonely little girl in the window. It was something she'd wanted to do since she was ten years old.

"You did an incredible thing tonight," said Will.

Addy shook off the praise. "We all did."

Edwina patted her shoulder. "Nah. You're our fearless leader."

"Don't be silly," said Adelaide. "You've always been the leader of DPI."

"No." Showing her softer side, Edwina kissed Adelaide on the forehead. "*You* have always been our leader."

Adelaide chewed on her lip so she wouldn't cry.

Will wrapped her in a warm hug, whispering, "You're a fucking badass."

Exhausted, she lingered in his arms for a while. As much as she tried not to cry, tears finally coated her eyelashes. Her tears may have been inspired by Lottie's situation, but part of her emotion was because it meant so much to have Will at her side tonight. Even still, the little kid inside her bristled, always expecting a rejection or an insult.

She was so tired of anticipating rejection.

She'd freed Lottie Taylor. Maybe it was time to free little Adelaide Darke as well.

Susannah walked around the room. "You know, I think Cindy can go ahead and stage this room."

Edwina agreed. "It actually feels kind of cozy in here. I bet Cindy will get that sale any day now."

Adelaide didn't have anything else to add to the conversation about the real estate agent. She needed to be in her pajamas at home right now, surrounded by her plants, preferably with a big bowl of mint chip ice cream in her hands. Then, she needed a nap, a long one.

Will nuzzled her head. "You look shattered."

"I feel shattered."

He reached for her hand. "Let me take you home."

Chapter Eighteen

By the time the weekend rolled around, Will was still on a high. After witnessing everything that had gone down at Wellesley Park and the old Taylor place, his mind was still wildly processing what Addy had done.

She was a veritable miracle. She had saved not one, but a group of people from an eternity of unrest. Will was now questioning everything he'd ever known, but in a good way. He'd always been of the mind that when someone died, they just ceased to be. Death was a big sleep and nothing more. Despite growing up in a Catholic family, he'd never really bought into the whole heaven and hell scenario. As far as he'd been concerned, life on earth was probably as hellish as it ever got and St. Michael and his pals were fictional.

He didn't get the impression that Adelaide subscribed to the Catholic playbook, but she clearly knew something he didn't. She saw stupendous things and the scholar in him was thirsty for more knowledge.

Since knowing Adelaide, right from that first meeting in the Necropolis, Will couldn't help wondering if there was something more out there.

There certainly had been for Lottie Taylor and the men from the factory, and Will had seen that with his own eyes.

His week at work had been a busy one but a good one. Terri remained with them and she had resumed working with their team of volunteers. Will had been doing the rounds of local press for his media blitz, even garnering a couple of spots on morning TV shows. He'd made sure to get a haircut before filming.

Thanks to those TV appearances, an elderly brother and sister had come forward to donate some family heirlooms to the museum. Their parents had lived in Cabbagetown, in a similar worker's cottage, and they'd held on to a lot of knickknacks. Alison was currently in the process of cataloging the artifacts and adding them to the collection.

Susannah had been true to her word and had visited the museum one afternoon to interview Will for *Ontario's History* magazine. People were getting excited for the opening, and Will couldn't have been happier.

He hadn't had a panic attack in a couple of weeks. There had been one time when he'd been sleeping at Addy's place and had woken up in a sweat because he thought he'd heard voices in his head. But the moment had passed, thanks to Addy's calmness and her patience, and he'd pretty much forgotten about it.

There was something about her that brought peace into his life and he wanted more of it. When she wasn't near, he craved her. She'd forgotten a T-shirt at his place one night, and the day after, he'd caught himself picking it up and sniffing, just so he could smell her lilac perfume.

He was falling in love and it scared the hell out of him, mostly because he expected it would scare the hell out of her. At the same time, it was exhilarating and it felt right. *She* was right for him. Because of her, the things that usually pissed him off didn't seem to faze him anymore, and she made him feel strong enough to confront the rest. He now had these long, drawn-out fantasies of building a life with her and he couldn't wait to see what that entailed.

They hadn't seen each other for a couple of days because they'd both had a week full of commitments but they'd been texting and calling each other practically non-stop. On Saturday morning, he texted her.

Will: Hey. I have something for you.

Adelaide: Is this a gift…or are you being filthy?

Will: (shocked emoji) Madam. Our conversations have never been filthy.

Adelaide: Your memory is selective.

Will: You're probably right. Are you around this afternoon? I would like to bring you your gift. I miss you.

Adelaide: I miss you too. Give me until lunch. I have to do a couple of readings, then I'll be free. I can't wait to see your "gift."

Will had never seen such sexy quotation marks in his life. He hardened, just considering the grammatical implications.

He responded by sending a gif of Darth Vader, saying 'Prepare for my arrival.'

Will took the morning to do a bit of work from home. After showering, he got dressed in his best pair of jeans, a short-sleeved shirt that matched the brown of his eyes and added his favorite vintage-look sneakers. He dragged a comb through his fancy new haircut and raced downstairs. After grabbing his wallet, keys and the sizable gift bag, he headed out of the door.

As he locked up, a woman's voice whispered in his ear. *"Stay with me."*

The barest of tingles danced across his shoulders. For a good few seconds, Will couldn't move.

On the sidewalk in front of his house, a couple of women jogged by, chatting with each other. He stared after them, his stomach turning over in apprehension.

He'd probably just heard part of their conversation. Nothing insidious about that.

Feeling foolish but also unnerved, he headed to Addy's house. Even as he walked away, he couldn't shake the sensation that he was being watched.

In truth, he'd been nervous ever since Robert Taylor's ghost had asked Addy to help Sarah.

So Sarah Byrne hadn't gone into the blasted light after all.

"Your Sarah." Again with the voice.

He grunted. "No, not mine." He did his best to ignore it, even though it seemed to come from inside him.

He had to get a grip. He was just imagining things. Life at the museum had been quiet. There had been no misplaced footsteps, no voices, no feelings of heaviness.

He was fine, and if Sarah really was back, Adelaide would have a plan.

As soon as he got to her house, he would tell her about the voice.

Resolved, he cut across Winchester to Sumach, passing the Necropolis. As he walked alongside the wrought iron cemetery fencing, the creepy sensation heightened. Given his recent history with Adelaide, he now understood that ghosts walked among the living. Even though it scared him shitless to do so, he angled his head toward the Necropolis.

Nothing but headstones today. Maybe his experiences had left him more unsettled than he'd realized.

Shaking it off, rolling his shoulders, he left the cemetery behind and headed to Carlton Street.

He rang the doorbell. When Adelaide appeared, all his nerves melted away. She was a mouth-watering picture. She wore a pleated skirt in pale pink that came to just below her knees. Her gray T-shirt bore the Harley-Davidson logo. The shirt itself was slightly cropped, showing just a tantalizing glimpse of waist. Still, the most intriguing part of her ensemble was her bare feet. Her toenails were painted with a glittery black polish and he wanted to get down on his knees to check out all the little sparkles in greater detail.

"Hey," she said quietly.

"Hey." He swallowed and put his bag down on the porch. "How is it that you get prettier every time I see you?"

"You need your eyes checked. I look the same as I did yesterday and the day before."

"Nonsense, and I'll have you know I have twenty-twenty vision. Now, come here."

Smiling, she clung to him and kissed him.

She felt so good, so soft and warm. She smelled like lilacs and her toes were adorable. He wanted to eat her up. Just a taste even. A nibble, and he could go to his grave a happy man.

"Can I get you anything?" she asked as she closed the front door behind him.

"Just more of you." He smacked her on the ass.

She jumped and laughed. "Excuse me, but didn't you say something about a gift?"

"You want to see it that badly, huh?"

"Yes. I love gifts."

"All right. Have a seat."

While Will grabbed the bag from the hallway, she sat on the sectional. She leaned back and ran her toes along the seams of the area rug in excitement.

Will wanted to grab those pretty feet of hers and bring them to his lap so he could stroke them. He wished he could lower his mouth to the arch of her foot, kissing his way up to her ankle and beyond. His daydream grew more pornographic as he imagined himself pushing her skirt up over her knees and thighs, then hauling her toward him. He dreamed of hooking his fingers in the elastic of her panties and dragging them slowly down her legs, tossing them onto the floor. He would get on his knees, would spread her legs and worship her, and it would be incredible. She would taste incredible and he would never want to stop feasting.

She cleared her throat.

"Sorry. I was having a little daydream."

"Of what?" she asked, the picture of innocence.

"You know exactly what. That's a very nice skirt, by the way." He handed her the giftbag. "Here. I hope you like it."

She pulled the old volume out of the bag. "*People of Cabbagetown*."

"It's an antique, very hard to find. It's out of print now, but back in my university days, we had a weathered copy in the library and I referred to it a lot. It's full of info and pics that aren't necessarily available online. I found this copy at a sale years ago. Anyway, I want you to have it. I thought that it might be a nice memento, considering what you did for some of the people of Cabbagetown."

She stared at the book's cover, flipped slowly through the first couple of pages then closed it. She didn't look up. When she spoke, her voice was quiet. "I don't know what to say."

Did she not like it? "You don't have to keep it, if it's not your thing. I know not everyone likes old books."

When she met his gaze, her eyes were shining with unshed tears. "No, I love it. It's a thoughtful gift. Thank you."

"You're welcome."

She set the book down on the coffee table and scooted closer. The gratitude in her expression took on a new heat. "Will?"

"Yeah?"

"I really do love the book but I'm going to look at it later, okay?"

"Okay." The earth shifted beneath him as he realized what was happening. They'd had sex many times now, but every time she so much as batted her eyelashes at him or licked her lips, it rocked his world. "Is there something else you want to do?"

"I think you know what I want you to do. It's all I've been thinking of since you mentioned your *gift*." She waggled her eyebrows.

"It was the Darth Vader gif, wasn't it?"

"Oh, totally. Who doesn't love a bad boy?"

"I can be bad. Very bad. In fact, when I was eight years old, I stole a chocolate bar from the corner store to impress a rascally friend. I mean, I immediately returned it and confessed because the guilt was too much to bear, but for that moment, I was really bad."

She pushed up her skirt and straddled him, smiling against his lips. "I love that story but we're going to stop talking now."

"Sounds good." Will leaned back against the sectional, thankful it was an oversized couch. They had plenty of space and no pesky armrest at the far end. He curled one hand possessively around her waist. Her shirt rode up and his fingers got a tantalizing touch of bare skin at her waist.

So soft.

Of course, she was soft everywhere. Even though the fact had been cemented in every one of his senses, he couldn't wait to discover her all over again.

It occurred to him that he was supposed to tell her something, but suddenly, he had trouble remembering what it was. Funny. He couldn't even remember the walk to her house.

Must not have been important.

Their lips touched, their tongues connected and Will set about making his daydream reality.

Adelaide's mind reeled.

Why was it that Will felt so good? She pulled at his shirt, trying to get at his skin, desperate to figure out why her fingers sizzled when she touched him. When she made contact with his flesh, little trumpets sounded inside her, the clarion call of her libido blazing to life.

Maybe her nerves just needed a break, a moment of recalibration. Since seeing Will last, she'd been figuring out ways to tackle the situation with Sarah. She'd even reached out to a couple of medium friends, asking for their perspectives on dealing with severe attachments. They'd been in agreement.

Sarah had to be dealt with, and soon, preferably in a place where she didn't have the upper hand.

But first, Adelaide needed more information on Sarah. For that reason, she had also quietly asked Susannah to do some research for her. Her sister had met her recent deadlines and had jumped at the chance to help.

"I take it you haven't asked Will," Susannah had commented. *"You're worried he's still under her influence?"*

"He seems fine," Addy had replied, *"but you never know."*

What if Will had withheld information? What if he resisted in some way? They'd already had proof that Sarah knew how to get into his head.

So, Addy had gathered her facts and done her best not to stress Will out. As for Sarah, she had an idea or two on how to deal with the troublesome spirit, but she hesitated in putting them into action just yet. She needed to understand Sarah first, and as intimately as possible.

In the meantime, she would take as much pleasure with Will as she could.

He ran a hand up her leg, dipping under her skirt. "Did I mention how much I like this skirt?"

"You may have mentioned it."

He kissed her again, licking at her lips, playing with her tongue. He slid his hand up her bent leg, meeting with the tender skin at her hip. With his thumb, he traced the elastic of her panties. He toyed with it as if he'd been dreaming of nothing else.

She shivered in delight. Her body responded instantly to every touch. Her nipples pebbled and the fabric of her panties was already wet and uncomfortable.

Every moment she'd shared with him had been memorable and intense, but she already knew this time would be powerful. The air around them crackled.

He brushed his lips against her throat. "I want you so much. You're all I think about."

"I want you too," she whispered. "So much."

He stopped kissing her long enough to give her a smoldering look. He was so sexy with his new haircut, although she sometimes missed the way his longish hair used to tumble over his eyes. It was still fun to play with, though. She danced her fingers over the short bits around his ears and he shivered.

"God, Addy." When he purred her name like that, she felt secure and treasured and free of all worries.

He stroked his tongue into her mouth, clearly as hungry as she was. He danced his fingers toward the hem of her shirt, slipping under it.

Adelaide groaned, desperate for deeper touches, for penetration.

He cupped her breast over her bra with his free hand. The delicate layer of lace and silk did nothing to protect her from the power of his roving thumb. Over and over, he flicked at her nipple, rendering it painfully hard. She ached to feel his tongue there, wanted it all over her body.

"Are you happy here, or do you want to take this to the bedroom?"

Adelaide didn't want to waste a single second. She stood and reached for the throw blanket that she kept folded over the back of the couch. She unfolded it and tossed it onto the sectional, covering the fabric. "Here's good."

"Awesome." Will stood. He unbuttoned his shirt and removed it.

Adelaide touched his chest. She could look at him all day long and never get bored. She loved the shape of him and loved dragging her fingers along each lean muscle.

He caressed her nipple where it stood out through her shirt. "Your turn." Will lifted her T-shirt up over her head and tossed it onto the floor. He unfastened her bra and slid it from her shoulders.

For a moment, he just looked at her, a delicious tension at his jaw. "You're so beautiful. I can't stop looking at you."

Adelaide smiled, her heart full.

Will sat on the sofa and urged her to straddle him again. At first, he smoothed his fingers over her breasts, plucking at her nipples.

"Will, please."

He gave her a devious grin. "Oh, yeah? You want more?"

She nodded, on the verge of pouting.

He gave her what she wanted. He brought his mouth to her breasts, moving from one swollen nipple to the other. His tongue felt so good fluttering against her skin, but when he sucked, gently biting down, Adelaide saw stars.

He continued to tease her like this for the longest time. "Addy," he said on a breath, "I want to taste you so badly."

"I want that too." She writhed atop him, groaning at the hard ridge inside his jeans.

He fumbled with the catch and zipper at the back of her skirt. Once it was loosened, Will laid her back on the blanket. He pulled her to the edge of the sectional and kneeled at its edge. Little by little, he dragged her skirt down over her hips. He moved slowly, deliberately, as if he were unwrapping the most delicate of presents.

She wore her flimsiest pair of silky pink panties. She could feel the wet patch, so it had to be evident to him as well. Will grinned, stroking one finger over it. "I can't tell you how happy this makes me, seeing you so wet."

She clutched at his shoulder. "Please."

He hooked his fingers in her panties and she thought he was going to pull them off. However, he tightened them against her skin and licked her over the fabric.

Adelaide wiggled and groaned. He hadn't even taken off her underwear and the sensation was cataclysmic. What would it be when he touched her bare skin? She'd probably dissolve from the euphoria.

She dug her fingers into his soft hair, urging him closer. She raised her hips, offering him everything, hoping he'd take it. Her clit was so swollen under the fabric and she was dying to get rid of her panties. "Please."

"You want me to taste your skin?"

"Yeah."

"You want to feel my tongue inside you, pretty Addy?"

"Do it."

Showing mercy, Will tugged at her panties, whipping them off her legs and into the air over his shoulder. He spread her legs and brought his face close to her core.

Just not close enough.

Oh God, he was teasing her. She wouldn't survive this.

With one finger, he slowly explored her folds. "So fucking pretty." He slid his digit inside her. "Beautiful."

Adelaide thrust against his hand, ready to take anything he gave her. She wriggled and writhed, unable to get release.

Finally, he removed his hand, his very talented hand, and lowered his head. It only took a few well-placed licks to devastate her. He had already come to know her body so well. When she came, she came hard, and Will groaned as much as she did.

Adelaide had had lovers in the past who would get her off speedily, then take care of themselves. It was what she'd come to expect from sexual partners. Will was different. He acted as if her pleasure gave him life. Even after her orgasms, he would linger there, softly toying with her, taking his time.

He dropped a few kisses on the inside of her thigh. "I love doing that to you."

"New hobby?" she drawled.

"Yes. Birding, cemetery tours and making you come. I'm very well-rounded."

She laughed, but when he grazed his lips against her there again, she held her breath. "How do you do that?"

"Do what?"

"You make me want more. I don't even want a break. I just want more of you." She reached for his shoulders, urging him upward. Will settled in between her legs, his cock thick and hot between them. *There.* That was where she wanted him.

Always.

The thought came from nowhere, astounding her with its clarity and gravity. She needed Will in her life, in her bed and in her heart.

He brushed his lips along the length of her neck and all the hairs on her body stood at attention. He had magical lips. She didn't want to day to pass in which she didn't get to taste them or feel their softness on her skin.

I love you, her heart cried, although Adelaide didn't dare say the words. It would be a huge leap of faith for her to admit something like that, and she wasn't prepared for it yet.

But she felt it. Keenly. It underscored the way she touched him and she hoped Will would somehow understand.

"Condom," she whispered.

He kissed her lips. "Yes."

Will slid away from her and her body immediately registered the loss of his heat. Shivering, she watched as he retrieved a condom from his wallet. As he bent over, his leg muscles flexed. She followed their sleek lines up to his round ass. She became wet just looking at him. "Hurry, Will."

He nodded, his face stern and handsome. He rolled the condom on and joined her on the sectional, sliding deep on the first thrust. He came at her slowly, setting up a punishing rhythm that made her doubt her senses. Each time he entered her, he went so deep it was almost painful. And yet, there was no way anything this blissful could count as pain. It was too beautiful.

Adelaide clutched his ass, bringing him closer to her body. Will buried his face in the crook of her neck, nibbling her tender flesh. "Yes," she cried. He hadn't used his teeth on her before and she suddenly wanted to feel the sting all over her body. She hoped he'd leave marks so that she could admire them later. "Yes."

"Addy." He was starting to quiver. His pace was no longer slow, leisurely. There was urgency in each thrust. "I'm close."

"Me too. Do it."

Will fucked her like he was being judged on his performance. Addy screamed as she unraveled once more.

He fell apart a moment later, collapsing on top of her, groaning out his orgasm. "Fuck."

Spent, she let her hands fall from his back to the sectional. She was a ragdoll, completely limp but happy to have been used so well.

He propped himself up on one arm, wiped his sweaty brow and grinned. "I'm really glad I came over today."

She knew he was being cheeky but she was still swimming in the solemnity of her emotions. *I love you.* "I'm really glad you did too."

They kissed and Will touched her hip, gently squeezing. If she weren't already delirious and exhausted, she would have pushed him back onto the bed and mounted him again.

She still might, if he didn't stop touching her that way.

He brushed her hair away from her face. "Let me clean myself up." He arose and went to dispose of the condom in the powder room. When he returned, he lay next to her on the sectional and wrapped them up in the blanket they'd been using.

She burrowed into his side and closed her eyes, full of contentment and wonder.

Will combed his fingers through her hair, then traced the lines of her face with a finger. When he reached her mouth, he moved his thumb over her lips. He touched the little scar at the corner of her mouth. "How did you get this?"

She hadn't thought of it in a while, but the unpleasant memory came rushing back. "That was courtesy of my cousin, Geoffrey."

"Hmm. Your sisters mentioned him, not in a flattering way."

"He was never nice to me. This one time, when his parents dropped him off at our house to hang out with us, he got annoyed at something or other and shoved me. We were in the driveway at the time and I fell over and cut my lip on the asphalt."

"For fuck's sake. You could have gotten a head injury from that."

"I know. My parents didn't allow Geoffrey over again after that."

Will grunted. "If I ever meet this cousin..."

"I doubt you will. He never comes to family stuff anymore. The last I heard of him, he was trying to lock down his fourth wife." She tried to leave the mischief out of her smile, but it was hard. "Besides, during the asphalt incident, I gave as good as I got."

"Adelaide Darke." He pretended to be shocked. "Did you bust Geoffrey's lip? Or was it a black eye? I'm trying to picture it in all its glory."

"It was a decent side kick and he had it coming. By then, it was long overdue. I'd been taking tae kwon do classes, because of the bullying. Even though my instructor always used to say that the best defense is just walking away to defuse a situation, I sort of snapped and gave Geoffrey one of the kicks I'd been learning. Like I said before, I have a temper."

"It sounds like Geoffrey got what he deserved." Will sighed and kissed her scar. "I know you don't need protection from a mere mortal like me, but I would love to be there the next time someone crosses you."

"Oh, yeah? You want to be my hero?"

"Actually, I just want to be there to watch you decimate the poor bugger." He grew serious. "But yes, I want to be your hero. I want to be worthy of you."

"Will, you're more than worthy." Awash in sentiment, Adelaide played with the hairs on his chest. "Tell me what you were like as a kid."

"Me? Oh, I was serious and studious and I usually had at least one Jack Whyte fantasy novel tucked under my arm at all times. I listened to morose music and dreamed of working in the Sir John Soane's Museum in London. It's this eclectic old house that belonged to a famed English architect. It's filled with antiquities and sculptures and paintings that are scattered all over the house. I used to picture myself holed up in one of its rooms, elbow-deep in treasures."

"Maybe you'll get there one day."

"Nah, I'm happy where I am. Especially right now."

They snuggled for a while, whispering their dreams and most private of thoughts. But eventually, Will glanced at the clock on the wall and sighed. "I actually need to get going. My mom asked if I would swing by tonight to help her with a few things at the house. I should probably go home and tidy myself up."

"Of course." It was fine. He had to go but she already knew she would miss him fiercely.

"I would really like to introduce you to my family, though. Would you...be into that?" There was such hope in his eyes as he asked the question.

"Yes. I would love to meet your family. Maybe I could introduce you to my parents too."

"Great. We'll set it up."

With a satisfied grin on his face and his hair a mess from their activities, he stood and dressed. Addy watched him, fascinated by how he zipped up his jeans and the way his long fingers worked his shirt buttons through their holes. They were normal actions and shouldn't have been fascinating in the least, but she couldn't look away.

As for Will, he kept his gaze trained on her as if she was the most ravishing creature in the world. When he was ready, he leaned over and kissed her. "Stay here and rest. I can let myself out."

"No, it's okay. I should probably wash this blanket." She stood and wrapped herself in it. "Or maybe I'll frame it."

His laughter echoed through the room. "A great work of art, if I've ever seen one."

She walked with him to the front door. Once they were standing there, it was hard to let him go. They held each other's hands and she played with the fingers that had so recently been inside her.

"I'll call you later." There was such tenderness in his eyes, a depth of feeling she wasn't sure she'd seen before.

It rattled her and thrilled her. "I'd like that."

After another long kiss, Will walked down her front steps, glancing over his shoulder at her. Adelaide closed and locked the door. Fairly bursting, she walked into the middle of her living room and let out an enormous squeal of happiness.

She was in love with Will Moran, and she was pretty sure he loved her too.

* * * *

As Will walked home, his fingers strayed to his lips. His sexy afternoon with Adelaide had been incredible, and he was on such a high. Her kisses had electrified him. He was surprised his hair wasn't standing on end. And the way she touched him...amazing.

He wanted that feeling in his life from here on in. No more messing around. Everything had changed. She'd brought joy and adventure into his life and there was no way he would ever let that feeling go.

He knew it was still relatively a new relationship, but this felt different than any other. This was it. He wanted Addy, plain and simple.

Dude, you are so getting ahead of yourself. Maybe take a minute before you go down on bended knee.

His head swimming, Will picked up his pace. He was due at his parents' place and he was already late. He quickly shot off a text to his mom, letting her know he was running behind and that he'd be there as soon as possible.

An evening with the parents would probably give him the clarity he needed. He was so caught up in Addy right now, and as much as it was mind-blowingly good, it was also scary.

He walked up Sumach Street, when a thought popped into his head.

He was supposed to have mentioned something to Addy, something important. *Wait.* He remembered standing on his porch, seeing the two women joggers.

He'd heard a voice. *Her* voice.

All of a sudden, his head began to pound and the memory floated out of his reach. With every few steps, he could feel the headache gathering strength. It went from distracting to painful in a matter of seconds.

He'd had a few headaches lately. This one, like the others, had cropped up out of nowhere. He'd felt just fine a few minutes ago. Maybe he'd skip visiting his parents tonight and just go home and pop a couple of headache pills.

He was probably just a little dehydrated after his sex fest with Addy.

The throbbing sharpened, making him wince. When his sight darkened for a few seconds, he began to worry. Was this what a migraine felt like?

Lost in thought, he stumbled toward the next intersection and glanced at the sign.

Amelia Street? What the hell?

He must have walked right past the cut off for Salisbury. How had he come that far without noticing?

Another deep throb in his brain made him squeeze his eyes shut.

"Come home, my darlin'."

The woman's voice drifted over his right shoulder, sweeping all thoughts of Adelaide from his mind. He heard it as if in a dream. Miraculously, upon hearing it, his headache disappeared.

Dazed, he turned around, looking for the source of the voice. He was the only one standing at the corner of

Sumach and Amelia. A short distance away, the residents of the Necropolis slumbered, but they certainly weren't making any noise.

"*Come home.*"

The voice was strange and familiar all at once, but for some reason, he couldn't place it. He barely had the wherewithal to question it. It just *was*. A fog settled all around Will. It cushioned him, taking away his ability to protest. It stole his breath, leaving him dizzy.

In that fog, one thought came to him with perfect lucidity. He should go to the museum.

Of course. It was where he belonged.

Once more, the siren-like plea landed on his ear. "*Come home.*"

Will understood exactly what "home" was. Home was Amelia Street. Home was the Cabbagetown Museum.

Home was with Sarah.

Chapter Nineteen

Still glowing later that night, Adelaide grabbed herself a snack of cheese and crackers and padded into her living room. When she realized her throw blanket was still lying across the sectional, she smiled, remembering all the things Will had done to her on it. She put her plate down on the coffee table, gathered up the blanket and tossed it in the washing machine.

She grabbed the book that Will had brought her and curled up on her couch. She popped a slice of cheese into her mouth and began to flip through the book. *People of Cabbagetown* appeared to be mostly a collection of old photos from various time periods. The book itself looked fairly old. She carefully flipped to the copyright page and was immediately hit with old book smell. It had originally been published in 1960 but it appeared to be a reprint from the seventies.

Robert Taylor and his glue factory had a prominent place in the book, of course. In fact, there was a chapter dedicated to the 'Captains of Industry.' She recognized some of the names. Gooderham and Worts, owners of a grist mill and distillery, whose factories had been cleaned up and transformed into Toronto's trendy Distillery District not long ago. There was also Enoch Turner, a brewer, who had established Toronto's first free schoolhouse to serve the working class. That building still stood a few blocks south of where Adelaide lived and functioned as an event space.

She continued to page through the book, not seeking any particular info. She was intrigued by the nineteenth-century images of places that she knew so well. There was even a chapter on the Necropolis. Most of the photos in that chapter were what one would expect, somber images of families paying their respects. However, there was one that struck her as sort of funny. It was of a family having a picnic in front of one of the graves, having a grand old time. Of course, she remembered Will saying that cemeteries were used back then as parks were used today.

Nibbling her cheese and crackers, taking care not to drop crumbs in the pages of the book, she continued skimming through the pics of the Necropolis. Eventually, a name caught her eye.

Desmond Byrne. Sarah's brother-in-law.

She recalled Will's comment. *Desmond was the one who paid for Sarah's headstone. In fact, he made all her funeral arrangements.*

In the photo, Desmond stood before Sarah's grave. Adelaide read the caption.

Cabbagetown resident Desmond Byrne pays his respects to a family member, 1885.

"Hmm. They couldn't bother to put Sarah's name in there." As she studied the photo, an oddity struck her. It was the date. 1885. A full twenty-five years after Sarah had died in the churning Don River.

Desmond's mouth was turned down at the corners. His eyes were wet as he held back tears. He clenched his hands in front of his body. Grief radiated from him.

"You look like someone just ran over your puppy, Desmond, old boy."

It didn't sit right with her, this level of anguish from a brother-in-law. Adelaide loved Simon and Noah, her brothers-in-law, but she had a hard time believing that if she passed away today, they'd still be visiting her grave on their own almost thirty years later. Hell, she wouldn't even want them to.

Sarah had believed that Desmond's feelings were inappropriate, that his eye had been "roving" in her direction.

For Adelaide, one thing remained unclear. Sarah had clearly been uncomfortable with Desmond's attentions, but was it because she remained loyal to Aiden? Or was it possible she'd been fighting feelings of her own for Desmond?

She peered at the picture. "What's your story?"

It was then that another detail hit her. He looked familiar.

Of course, she'd seen his brother Aiden in a vision, and there was clearly a family resemblance. Desmond might be much older in the photo, but he had the same wave to his hair, the same light color. He was tall and slim, with those striking cheekbones.

Just like Aiden.

Just like Will.

She brought the book closer to her face. *Yes.* Desmond looked like an older version of Will. The only difference was Desmond sported a mustache. In fact, if she didn't know any better, she would have thought Will had visited one of those old-timey photo booths where the sitter could get dressed in period costume and be given a sepia-toned print at the end.

Was it possible that Sarah was fixated on Will because he looked like Desmond, and not Aiden?

"Oh my stars." The realization filled her with angst.

She remembered Robert Taylor's words. *If you want to help me, help the one I wronged so grievously. Help Sarah.*

How on earth could Robert have wronged Sarah? Their only connection was the fact that Aiden had worked at the glue factory.

Hold on. Desmond had too. Will had said as much.

She texted Will.

Adelaide: Hey. Would you happen to know what Desmond Byrne did at the glue factory? I assume he and Aiden were both laborers of some sort?

If they had been laborers, she didn't imagine they would have socialized with the man who owned the factory. So, why on earth would Taylor still feel remorse over something done to Sarah?

She kept coming back to her initial vision of Sarah. There had been a man there, at the river's edge and that man had pushed her into the water. Unfortunately, she hadn't been able to make out the man's features.

Had Robert Taylor done it? Maybe he'd been attracted to Sarah and had made a pass, one that she'd rejected?

Or had it been Aiden on the riverbank that night? It made more sense. After all, Sarah had been determined to get to him and bring him home from the Don Vale House. If he was an alcoholic, he probably wouldn't have been inclined to leave.

Or was it Desmond, the brother-in-law who'd offered her companionship on those long, lonely nights…and more?

Adelaide glanced at Desmond's photo again, taking stock of his evident woe.

What if there had been more to Desmond and Sarah's relationship than simple brotherly love? What if simple caring had turned into flirtation, into stolen kisses and passionate love?

After a few minutes, Addy realized Will hadn't responded to her text. A frisson of dread skittered across her shoulders.

Help Sarah. Taylor's plea ran through her mind over and over again.

It didn't take long for Will's words to echo in a strange counterpoint. *My Sarah.*

Adelaide set the book aside and began to pace. Something felt wrong. Something was off and Will wasn't responding to her message. He always responded right away.

She urged herself to calm down. There were plenty of reasons why Will might not message her immediately. He might still be at his parents' place. They could be in the middle of something. He could be using the bathroom. He might be charging his phone. Heck, after their exertions, he might have even taken a nap.

Even though there were a thousand possibilities for Will's silence, the longer it went on, the more Adelaide worried.

"Okay, settle down." She sat back down and stared at the old photo from the Necropolis and at Desmond's pained face. Unsure if she'd find any info online, she pulled out her laptop and began a search on employees of the Taylor glue and blacking manufactory. There were plenty of articles and blogs about Taylor and his impact on Cabbagetown, but nothing on the people who worked for him. "There has to be something on this guy."

She kept scrolling, amazed at how many people were interested enough in the neighborhood's history to build websites around it. After about fifteen minutes of searching, she landed on a site connected to the University of Toronto archives. She plugged in Taylor's name as a keyword and a few photos appeared on her screen, ones she hadn't seen in *People of Cabbagetown*, or at the museum.

The name Desmond Byrne lit up like a fireworks display. In that photo, Taylor was standing in his factory, talking to another man. The caption read *R. S. Taylor and factory foreman Desmond Byrne*.

A foreman, not a manual laborer. Desmond would have had some authority at the factory. He may even have reported directly to Taylor. Certainly, they would have had conversations.

Adelaide picked up the Cabbagetown book again. She touched the photo of Sarah's brother-in-law, wondering if she might get some passing insight into his character, but any images that flitted past were too fuzzy, too vague.

"Give me something," she murmured. "Anything." She moved her fingers over to the picture of Sarah's headstone and closed her eyes, willing the information to come to her.

What she got instead was another image.

It was Will, collapsed across a desk. Above him, a black cloud swirled, draping him in despair and confusion.

Maria came forward. The sound of terrible childish coughing filled Adelaide's living room. It shook the fucking timbers. *"She's back, Addy. She has him."*

Her heart pounding, Adelaide pushed the Cabbagetown book off her lap onto the couch and stood. "My phone. Where's my phone?" She spotted it, where she'd left it on her occasional table and seized it, dialing Will's number

It went to voicemail. She tried calling again, several times, but Will didn't pick up.

"Oh my God, Maria. Can you see where he is?"

"Her house. She's strongest there."

It was nighttime. Why would he have gone to the museum?

Maybe Sarah had drawn him there and Will had been powerless to refuse. Perhaps she was more powerful, more present, than Adelaide had first guessed.

She didn't stop to change out of her light pajama pants and top. She simply stuffed her feet into a pair of shoes, threw her phone and keys into her small cross-body bag, slung it over her shoulder and ran out through the front door.

She hurried up Sumach Street, even though she wasn't exactly sure what she'd do once she got to the museum. She could try banging on the door, but if Will was under Sarah's influence, he probably wouldn't respond. Besides, she'd wake the neighbors and probably get arrested before she could even shake Will out of his stupor.

She had to think outside the box and lure Sarah away from him.

Resolved, Adelaide ran into the Necropolis. It was dark in the cemetery, too dark, but she didn't let it dissuade her. Addy knew its layout as well as the floorplan of her own home. Still, she pulled out her cell phone and aimed the flashlight in front of her. *Nothing like tripping over a grave marker or tree root.* Picking her way among headstones old and new, she made her way over to Sarah's grave.

She set her cell phone down on the headstone for some light. Taking a breath for courage, she put her hands on the monument. Addy closed her eyes and called out in a firm voice. "I am calling to you, Sarah Byrne. I am here, at your resting place. It's time we talked. I demand you to join me here. Now!"

The graveyard was still. Not a leaf shivered in the trees.

But Adelaide sensed a shiver of another sort. She had Sarah's attention.

Adelaide's breaths came quickly. Communicating with the hostile dead could be dangerous, even for someone like her. She normally had her sisters nearby whenever she attempted anything reckless, but if it meant she could draw Sarah away from Will, Adelaide was willing to take the risk.

"Stay with me, Maria."

"I'll always be with you."

"Sarah Byrne," Adelaide called, "I saw a photograph of your brother-in-law Desmond earlier. He was standing at your grave and he seemed sad, very sad. Lost, even. I think he really missed you after you died."

Prickles of energy gathered at the edge of the Necropolis, creeping toward her. Yes! She was on the right track.

"Tell me about Desmond, Sarah. I know you appreciated his companionship. You showed me that. But did your feelings run deeper than that? It was clear he had the hots for you. Did you fall in love with him? I know about Aiden's alcoholism. Did you go to Desmond for comfort?"

Like electricity, Sarah's attention crackled in the night. The little sparks of energy combined, lengthening into tentacle-like feelers. They slithered along the cemetery floor, moving toward Adelaide. They came from several directions, peeking around the headstones.

Sarah was trying to scare her. Little did she know that Adelaide didn't scare easily.

As they drew closer, the feelers gathered behind Sarah's stone. They entwined, rising upward, taking the form of a woman.

It was her, just as Adelaide had seen her that first time. Her brown hair was coming loose from its updo and there were a few twigs and leaves caught up in her tresses. Her outfit was muddied, but Addy could make out patches of gray and blue, its original colors. She was taller than Adelaide by a couple of inches, and willowy. Hollows of malnutrition marked a face that was once lovely. Her teeth were yellowed. But, worst of all, were her eyes. Despite the fact that they were cloudy and pale, they blazed at Adelaide, veritable pools of misery.

As dreadful as she appeared, Addy knew it wasn't her true form. Sarah's ghostly appearance was merely a manifestation of the dread she carried. She drew closer to Adelaide, white hands clutching at her own headstone, and smiled through those horrible teeth.

"I'm not afraid of you," Adelaide said.

"You should be."

"You can't hurt me, Sarah. If anything, I'm more afraid of what you're doing to Will."

Maria whispered in Adelaide's ear. *"She's going to touch you."*

Sure enough, Sarah rounded the gravesite, disappearing for an unsettling moment, then crept up behind Adelaide. Even though she no longer needed oxygen, her breath landed on her neck. She ran her fingers through Addy's hair, doing her best to invade her space. "So pretty. That's what he calls you, isn't it? Pretty Addy." She sighed, her breath reeking of the river. "I was lovely once."

Mustering every ounce of bravado in her body, Adelaide turned and faced the wraith, looking her right in her dead eyes. "Why have you attached yourself to Will?"

Sarah didn't answer. She turned and meandered amongst the graves, touching every headstone that she passed. "They took my babies and put them in a hole in the ground, every last one. They should have taken me. Why was I left behind?"

"My heart breaks for you, it really does." As much as she sympathized with the dead woman, she knew Sarah was trying to distract her. "Tell me about Desmond Byrne. Why was he still visiting your grave thirty years after you died?"

Sarah spun around and flew toward Adelaide. "Don't you dare speak his name to me!"

"You loved him, didn't you? Is that what keeps you here? Your husband caused you nothing but pain so you turned to your brother-in-law for comfort. Did Aiden find out? Is he the one who pushed you into the river? If you loved Desmond, you can tell me. I would never judge you for seeking out love. You were in a terrible situation. Just help me understand. Help me to help you."

Sarah let out a shriek that shook the cemetery trees. "No one can help me!" With that, the troubled soul picked up her dirty skirts and ran to the far end of the Necropolis. Her voice echoed long after she'd disappeared. "Why did he leave me alone in this place?"

"Sarah, wait!"

But Sarah was gone.

Adelaide was ready to tear her hair out. She felt badly for this woman that life had so mistreated. So much loss. How had she endured it?

At least Sarah was no longer hovering around Will. Adelaide could feel her presence leaving the area. She pulled out her cell phone and tried reaching him again, but he didn't answer. She tore out of the cemetery and up Sumach, toward the house on Amelia Street. Adelaide knocked on the door, conscious of the fact that there were houses on either side of the museum. "Is he okay, Maria?"

"He's sleeping soundly," Maria replied. *"The scent of decay no longer surrounds him."*

"But he's safe?"

"Yes, he's safe for now."

He would stay safe, if Addy had anything to do with it. That thought in mind, she sat down on the museum steps and waited. If he woke up, she would be there for him. If Sarah returned, Adelaide would be able to intercept her. She didn't want to fight with the spirit woman, but if that was what it took to keep Will free from harm, Sarah would have a battle on her hands. At least it was a warm night and she wouldn't get too cold.

Her gaze pinned on the darkness of the Necropolis, Adelaide brought her knees to her chest and hugged them, hoping no raccoons would try to nibble her toes in the middle of the night.

Chapter Twenty

Will's head snapped up, but immediately lolled again.

Tired. So tired. Just a few more minutes.

If he could just get a bit more sleep, he'd be refreshed and ready for work. He reached his arm out to angle his clock radio so he could see the time, but his hand met with air.

Disoriented, he opened his eyes and realized he wasn't in his bedroom. "What the…?"

He was in the museum office but had no recollection of getting there. He swallowed, tasting bitter saliva and fuzzy teeth. Did he forget to brush his teeth that morning? He honestly couldn't remember.

And where was everybody? Why was he all alone?

He took note of his outfit. Brown shirt and the same jeans he'd worn when he had brought the Cabbagetown book to Addy.

Acid churned in his belly, crawling up his throat. Something was wrong here.

He reached for the cell phone in his shorts pocket. It was at five percent charge, just enough to see that Addy had left him numerous texts and voicemails, as had his mom and dad.

Right. He was supposed to have gone to his parents' place. Had he?

Will's heart leapt into a terrible beat.

His laptop was open in front of him. He jiggled the mouse, refreshing the screen. It was open to a document that he and Miguel had been working on for the museum programming. Had he seriously come to work instead of helping his mom, as promised? As he stared at the doc, his eye was drawn to a shadow on the office wall.

Several words had been scratched into the paint, into the drywall behind it.

COME
DEAR ONE
TO THE RIVER

"Jesus Christ."

He pushed away from his desk, muscles groaning when he stood because he'd been sitting in the same position too long. His bladder ached from not having any relief in a while but he pushed through the discomfort and walked over to touch the wall. The words had been gouged into it with some sort of knife or sharp implement.

"Who would do this?"

He was the only one here, and he was starting to think he'd been there a lot longer than he'd first suspected.

Did *he* do this?

The museum would be opening soon. Finding a contractor to fix this mess at this late date would not be easy.

He was so screwed.

Panic rose through Will's chest, thick and vile, coating his throat with the taste of bile. "No, no, no, no."

Okay, calm down. This is not a disaster. It can be fixed.

His voice of reason came to him a moment too late. Irrational alarm had set in, taking hold. His heart pumped for all its might. Suddenly short of breath, he opened his mouth to force air into his lungs.

Can't breathe.

Out of instinct, he looked around for someone to help him, but of course, no one else was in the goddamned museum. He was the foolish one who'd somehow decided to camp out there all night long.

What the hell had he been thinking? He might be a bit of a workhorse, but he'd never done anything like this.

Dread took hold of Will's soul.

Need to get out.

All at once, icy fingers danced across the back of his neck. Frigid and silky, they tempted him to stay. The pressure from those fingers caressed his skin, sliding toward his throat. They tightened.

Will broke into a run, toward the museum entrance. Desperate for air, he yanked open the door and almost tripped over a figure on the ground just outside it. "Addy?"

She had been asleep but upon hearing his voice, she jolted awake. Her eyes were bloodshot and she was shivering.

Seeing her like that made his panic attack subside. His own fears faded in the face of her troubles. He crouched next to her, drawing her near for warmth. "Hey. What are you doing here?" Something told him he already knew the answer.

She wrapped her arms around his torso and hugged him hard. "Are you okay?"

Christ. She was so cold, even through her pajamas. He rubbed her back. "I think Sarah's back."

"I know. Last night, when I was looking at the book you gave me, I had a vision of her hovering around you like a cloud."

"Wait. You've been here all night long?"

"Maria sensed that there was something wrong, that you were under her spell. I figured my best shot was drawing Sarah away from you. I lured her to the cemetery, where we had a little confrontation, then I came here to wait for you."

"A little confrontation?"

"Maybe not so little."

"I'm so sorry." He kissed her temple. She smelled of faded perfume and the outdoors. What had she done on his behalf? It terrified him to consider it. "There's something you should see."

Will led Addy back into the museum. The moment he crossed the threshold, it became difficult to breathe, but he pushed through it. He led her into the office and gestured at the defaced wall, but nothing was there. The message was gone. He touched the wall again, feeling for the deep scratches, but the surface was smooth under his fingertips. "I don't understand. I found a message scratched into the wall. Deep scratches."

"What did it say?"

"Come, dear one, to the river."

"The river. Of course." She grunted and punched her thigh a few times. "Why didn't I think of that?"

"Hey, hey, hey. Don't hurt yourself." He gently grabbed her hand, releasing her fingers from their iron grip.

Adelaide took a deep breath. "Listen, let's stop at your place and get some clean clothes for you. You can come back to my house and rest. I could use some rest too. Then, we'll make a gameplan."

"Okay." Frankly, he welcomed an opportunity to stay with Addy in her sanctuary-like home.

As they left, Will was never so relieved to leave the old Byrne house. And yet, with every step he took, something tugged at him. Like a tiny hook, embedded in the skin near his spine, it pulled and scored his flesh.

"Come back."

When the hypnotic voice whispered in his ear, he swatted at it. "No. Let go of me."

Adelaide tightened her hold on his hand. Just like that, the hook unlatched. The ache ceased but he knew Sarah was only playing with him. The allure of her voice was undeniable. It was a part of him now.

It would only be a matter of time before she dragged him into the depths with her.

Chapter Twenty-One

"Sorry, Addy. Did you say 'Tiny Joe?'"

Her client's question brought her back. *Focus!* "I'm sorry, Marjorie. Yes, 'Tiny Joe' is the name I'm getting. Ask your grandmother if your grandfather ever had that nickname amongst his friends. When I see him standing around you, that's what he says. 'Tell her Tiny Joe is here.'"

"Fascinating. I've never heard that nickname in the family. Joseph was his middle name. He never even used it."

"He would have been called that when they were quite young, teenagers even." Adelaide glanced at the clock on the kitchen wall. "Anyway, he wants you to know that he doesn't feel any pain anymore. He knows that you worried a lot at the end about whether or not he was in pain, but he wasn't."

Marjorie sniffled. "I'm happy to hear that."

Adelaide smiled as the spirit man behind Marjorie hopped around, showing off his ease of movement. "He just did a couple of squats. He says that even his bum knee isn't a problem anymore. He feels like a teenager."

"Wow. That knee bothered him the whole time I knew him. He was always talking about how stiff it was."

"It's no longer an issue. Anyway, I'm afraid that's it for today, but let me know if you want to book another reading. I'm blocking off the next few days for some personal time, but I have some openings later in the month." She ended the session by reciting a prayer so that Marjorie could go in peace, then walked her client to the front door.

She stood on her porch for a moment, looking toward the park, and beyond it to the Necropolis. Her encounter with the spirit of Sarah Byrne had rattled her and she'd been alarmed to see exactly how much sway she'd had over Will. Even now, a few days later, fear insinuated itself under her skin, causing it to erupt in itchy hives.

Will was currently upstairs in her spare bedroom, working, and she knew he was frustrated at not being able to go into the museum. But after his last encounter with Sarah, he didn't even try to force the issue. In fact, he'd done something that had made her proud. He'd closed the museum site for a few days, asking all his teammates to work from home as much as possible, so everyone was safe.

Adelaide had managed to pull Will out of that environment and she still didn't know how Sarah would react, but she hoped this would give her a cooling off period of sorts.

At the same time, she knew another confrontation was in order. It would be difficult. She would need to channel every ounce of strength she had to bring Will peace, and Sarah as well.

Adelaide padded to the kitchen and brewed some chamomile tea for the two of them. As it steeped, she considered what was to come and all that had happened. She was determined to help Will break free from the destructive influences in his life.

She kept reliving their moments together. His touch, his smile, everything that had brought joy to her heart. Adelaide had shared more of herself with Will than she had with any other guy.

Will had slipped through the cracks in her walls. After being so determined to keep him at bay, she'd done an about-face and had allowed him in and it hadn't destroyed her. *Imagine that.*

Of course, she was still conscious of the fact that things could sour. Will was wonderful, but she'd been burned by men who were far less wonderful. She'd made some bad choices and a lot of mistakes. There was still the possibility that Will could hurt her, but given her own unique set of faults and foibles, she had the power to hurt him too. It wouldn't be intentional, of course. But what if her temper got the better of her? What if she said the wrong thing?

After all, it was what people did. They hurt each other, all the time. She'd had ample evidence of it in her conversations with the dead. Those interactions were full of betrayals, deceptions and broken hearts. Like Edwina often said, sometimes people sucked.

A memory from her school days sliced through her thoughts. Grade ten. The gym changeroom. Cheryl Ladmore, the ringleader of her group of bullies, had cornered her after gym class. A few of the other girls had hung back to taunt Adelaide as well.

By then, Adelaide had had more than enough.

A couple of them had shoved her, uttering threats, and Adelaide had snapped. She'd told those girls exactly what she'd seen in some of their futures, every heartache, every loss and every failure. She had let loose a litany of profanity-laced horror and they'd been stunned into silence. As her sisters had often said, those girls were probably secretly afraid of Addy and they'd shown it in that moment, cowering in a locker room.

Of course, she'd regretted it later, but what good did regret do? It didn't change anything. Besides, they'd hurt her many times over, and in more damaging ways.

She shook her head now, unsure of why those people were even crossing her mind. The last time she'd heard from her old nemesis Cheryl was about three years ago. Darke Paranormal Investigations had started getting some acclaim and a couple of articles had been written about the Darke sisters. Addy had been bewildered when a friend request from Cheryl had come through on social media. To this day, she still wasn't sure why she would have reached out like that. Maybe, after all these years, Cheryl wanted to apologize. It didn't matter. Adelaide hadn't been interested. She'd promptly deleted the request and had blocked her.

She had enough questionable energy in her life as it was. No need to invite more in.

Once the tea had steeped, she poured out a couple of mugs and brought them upstairs. She poked her head around the corner of the spare room. Will was sitting at the desk there, his head in his hands. He was breathing heavily. "Will?"

He looked up and smiled but was too slow to mask the lines of pain on his forehead. "Hey, pretty Addy."

She set the mugs down on the desk and stood between his legs. He wrapped his arms around her middle and rested his head on her stomach. Adelaide tangled her fingers in his hair, gently massaging his scalp. "Another headache?"

"Yeah. I took a couple of pills but they're not helping. I can barely do my work."

Pills wouldn't help this kind of ache. It was Sarah, trying to get in. "I'm sorry you're suffering. I'm going to fix this for you, I promise."

"I don't like the idea that you'll be putting yourself in harm's way for me. Are you sure I can't communicate with Sarah in some way?"

"Hell, no. The last thing we need is you calling out to her." She moved the mug of tea toward him. "Here, drink some chamomile tea. It should help."

Will let her go and took a couple of sips of tea. "I feel badly for being in your space."

"I like you in my space." She pushed his hair away from his face. "I love...having you here." *Say the words. You love him. Just say it.*

But she couldn't. Adelaide had faced all manner of phantoms and demons, but saying 'I love you' scared her more than anything.

He set the mug back down and stood, enfolding her in his arms again. "I love being here with you. Very much."

When he kissed her, it was soft and gentle. A whisper of a kiss that somehow carried tremendous weight.

The emotions sitting on her chest were almost too much to bear. She didn't understand how something could burden her and fill her with lightness at the same time. She was thrilled to be reaching this new stage of intimacy with Will but it was terrifying too. Adelaide knew she would have to make some sort of declaration soon, if only to relieve the pressure. She felt a need to open her heart and show him what was there. It might be messy and confusing, but it was all her, and she wanted to share it with him.

But first, she needed to send Sarah into the light.

"You should lie down," she said. "Get some rest."

"You're right. I can't concentrate anyway." God bless him, he tried to flirt, offering her a sad wink. "Want to 'get some rest' with me?"

"Not when your head's hurting. I'll join you in a little bit, okay?"

He nodded and kissed her again. Taking his tea with him, he padded off to her bedroom and shut the door. Adelaide waited a few seconds, grabbed her mug of tea and went downstairs.

After taking a few fortifying sips, she grabbed her cell phone and headed outside to the porch where she could have some privacy. She started a video chat with her sisters.

"Yo." Edwina was eating a croissant, probably one Simon had baked. As the co-owner of a bed and breakfast, Simon had picked up some culinary skills and he often baked as well. As Edwina had admitted herself on more than one occasion, she was trash for his pastries.

Susannah adjusted her headphones. Her blonde waves were up in a high ponytail and her eyes were bright with excitement. "Hey. I have info."

"I'm ready," Adelaide said.

"I was able to connect with another Cabbagetown historian. I'm sure Will must know her. Her name is Julie Hubbard and she runs the local history society. She was able to provide some details on our friend, Desmond Byrne."

Addy's legs bounced up and down. "Uh-huh?"

"It seems that Desmond wasn't always the foreman at the glue factory. He worked as a laborer at first, just like Aiden did. At least, he did until the day that Robert Taylor found himself choking on a piece of food while in his office. The story is that Taylor became frantic, that he ran out of his office and onto the factory floor. It seems our boy Desmond was standing nearby and he took it upon himself to give the old man some wallops on the back. Luckily for all involved, the chunk of food was dislodged. Apparently, Robert was feeling rather grateful, and all of a sudden, Desmond Byrne was moving up in the world."

"Interesting," Edwina said. "So Robert actually rewarded this guy."

"Not only that," Susannah continued, "he seems to have taken an interest in him. Taylor nurtured Desmond, right up until the day of the fire. He saw intellect and drive in the younger man. I remember reading somewhere that Taylor was kind of disappointed in his own sons. He thought they were layabouts, only interested in mooching off Daddy. But here was this young Irish dude who had no money and very few prospects, but he worked hard and showed Taylor he wanted to learn. Taylor helped him do just that."

"Thanks, Suz," Adelaide said. "It's clear the two men were close, despite their differences in wealth and status. But what did that mean for Sarah?"

"Robert said he wronged her," said Edwina. "I can think of a few ways a rich dude could wrong some poor woman."

"But how does Desmond fit into that? In the dream I had of Sarah, she was grateful for Desmond, but concerned his feelings had deepened. When I confronted her in the cemetery, she flew into a rage at the mention of his name. At first, I thought maybe they were having an affair, but it just doesn't ring true.

Could he have been the one who pushed her into the river?"

"Based on the fact that she's been haunting Will, a lookalike for the Byrne boys, my guess is on either Desmond or Aiden," Edwina said. "But what led to that push?"

"I need to find out." Adelaide squared her shoulders. "Suz, did you find an answer for my other question?"

"You mean, where the Don Vale House was situated exactly? Yep. It sat where the Lower Don River Trail now runs, at the trailhead, right at the east end of the Necropolis."

"Is it even accessible?" Addy asked.

"You bet," Susannah replied. "There's nothing there, just a bike path."

Adelaide nodded, more than satisfied with her sister's research. "Then it's time to visit the scene of the crime. You guys free tomorrow night?"

* * * *

Come, dear one, to the river.

Will had almost forgotten about seeing those words scratched into the wall of the museum. However, now that he and the Darke sisters were headed to the location of the Don Vale House, the words flashed in front of his eyes again. It didn't even matter that the words had been some sort of hallucination. They'd felt too personal. *An invitation from Sarah.*

And now, they were giving her exactly what she wanted. He and Adelaide and her sisters were picking their way along the Lower Don River Trail at dusk, and his nerves were having a riot.

It was bad enough his head was killing him. The headaches hadn't ceased, no matter how many pills he popped or how much of Addy's chamomile tea he swallowed. From the moment he woke up every morning, *she* was there, pounding on his brain, demanding to be let in.

As hard as Addy was fighting to keep him safe, Sarah was fighting to take him away with her. Sometimes, late at night when the headaches threatened to break his skull in two, it was tempting to give in. During those moments, he just wanted to head back to the museum, lock himself in and let her do her worst, if only to end this strange saga.

But then he'd look at Adelaide, would feel the heat in her gaze and the tenderness in her touch, and he knew he had to be strong for her. For them.

He wanted a future with Addy. He loved her.

He didn't ever want to spend a day without her. The feelings might have come fast and unexpectedly, but they were fierce. As much as he was tempted to surrender to Sarah, he wanted that future with Addy more.

She'd been so strong for him. He had to be strong for her and he had to fight.

"Here we are." Susannah indicated the area of overgrown bushes next to the river. "I've consulted numerous sources. This is pretty much where the Don Vale House would have stood. Do you agree, Will?"

He nodded. "It's about as close as we can get." Although busy Bayview Avenue now bordered the east side of the Necropolis, in Victorian times, there would have been no such barrier. One could have walked directly from the cemetery to the tavern and the river's edge, as Sarah had on her final night on this earth.

Come, dear one, to the river.

From somewhere over his shoulder, Will heard a woman's tinkly laugh. When he looked around, there was only shrubbery.

He pinched the bridge of his nose, determined to shut her out. At the same time, he wanted a showdown with Sarah. Why was she doing this to him? He'd only ever shown interest in her story, in teaching others about her life and the lives of those around her.

Somehow comprehending his inner struggle, Addy grabbed him by his upper arms. "Listen to *my* voice, not hers. Okay? Mine. I'm going to get some answers tonight. It's going to be all right."

Even as he tried to focus on her lovely eyes, they changed. A film covered them, turning them opaque and pale, like Sarah's eyes. Startled, Will pulled away.

"Hey." Addy didn't give up. She reached for his hands, bringing them to her mouth so she could kiss them. "It's just me. Just me."

He blinked a few times and the mirage faded.

"There's no time to waste. Sarah's just playing with him now." Addy turned to Edwina. "Keep an eye on him?"

Tight-lipped, Edwina nodded and stood closer to Will.

Adelaide had come prepared. She wore jeans, a light jacket and tall rubber boots. Inspecting the area near the shrubbery, she pushed aside some of the longer branches.

Susannah made a face. "We'll need to check you for ticks when you're done."

"I'll be fine." Moving as close as she could to the river's edge, Addy got down on her knees in the grass. She touched the soil, facing them. "I'm here, Sarah Byrne. We're here, at the place where you died. I want to know more. I want to help you."

As Will watched, the pain in his head began to quickly subside. It was almost as if Sarah had left him and was concentrating all her attention on Addy now.

"That's it," said Adelaide, her breath coming fast. "I can feel you approaching. Tell me everything. Take me there. Do it, Sarah!" She shook and her eyes rolled back into her head.

In horror, Will gritted his teeth. He couldn't do a thing to help Addy.

Sarah had her.

Chapter Twenty-Two

Toronto, November 1860

Sarah Byrne stood at the front room window, staring unseeing toward the Necropolis, the cemetery where she had just buried the last of her babes. Rather, the ones who'd survived their births, to be precise. Her first, wee Thomas, hadn't seen his first birthday. His sister Sarah had made it to her second before typhoid found her. The twins, Aiden and Bridget, had expired a few short days after their entry into the cold world. And Maeve. *Ah!* Maeve had been Sarah's golden child, her great hope. Sarah had gone to sleep every night, her knees sore from all her bedside praying. She had begged the Heavenly Father to spare Maeve, to let her thrive in this harsh place where so few of their acquaintance seemed to. Surely the Lord wouldn't be so cruel as to take Sarah's remaining child. Maeve had only just reached the age of three.

But Death had struck again, and swiftly.

The Lord, it seemed, had turned his back on the Byrne family.

Sarah had never felt more alone. For all her twenty-eight years, her faith had sustained her. Even as a youngster in County Galway, when the Great Hunger had devastated the majority of her kin, she had maintained her belief that God would save her nearest and dearest. Even as she'd watched her mother, father and sister wither away on their coffin ship, Sarah had remained steadfast.

Her parents had promised that a new life awaited them in Toronto, a place where they'd never go hungry. When her family members had breathed their last on that ship, just a few days from shore, Sarah had faltered in her beliefs. She'd only been thirteen years old then. Too young to be left alone.

When Mary Byrne, one of the mothers aboard the ship, had spotted Sarah crying one evening, she'd called to her. Mrs. Byrne had been gentle and kind, and Sarah had fallen into her arms, exhausted and terrified and stupefied that she'd somehow escaped Death's clutches.

"There, there, child." Mrs. Byrne had squeezed her hand. "You aren't alone. You're part of my family now."

To young Sarah, Mary Byrne might have been an angel. Despite her dirty, sweat-stained clothes and her unkempt hair, she radiated goodness better than the archangels Michael or Gabriel or any of their lot. She'd been true to her word too. The Byrnes had taken Sarah in and had raised her as one of their own, alongside their own children Aiden and Desmond. As close to twins as any two brothers could be, they shared the same honey-colored eyes, the same unruly hair and similar temperaments.

Aiden, though, had always had a certain charm about him. Quick with a smile, he was a natural storyteller, the sort who'd wink at you so you knew he was telling tall tales.

When, several years later, the time had come for Aiden to take a wife, Sarah had happily filled the vacancy. Besides, she and Aiden had always been sweet on each other. They'd married, and for a short time, she'd been optimistic.

Sarah wished she had taken greater notice of those blissful times, those years when it seemed the Angel of Death had forgotten all about her.

Standing at the window now, she barely noticed the sun going down. It was only as the shadows lengthened in the cottage that she realized how late it was.

Aiden should have been home by now. He worked at the R. S. Taylor factory, the glue and blacking manufactory, just a few short minutes' walk from their Amelia Street home.

But he never came straight home anymore. He spent all his evenings at the Don Vale House, mired in sin.

Sarah probably should have been angry at being abandoned every night, but in a way it was also a blessing. It allowed her to plumb the true depths of her grief without having to worry about upsetting Aiden.

At the same time, she wanted to rage at her absent husband. One would think that he could be persuaded to spend an evening with her after the death of their fifth, and probably last, child, but no. The boxing contests and cockfights at the Don Vale House were the only things that held his interest now. That, and the drink. When Aiden did come home, he would reek of whiskey and a sadness he'd never dared confront.

Once again, Sarah was on her own. There was no motherly Mrs. Byrne to help her now. She and her husband were also dead and rotting in the Necropolis. Oh, there was Desmond, for certain. Her brother-in-law was a good soul who'd stood by her as she'd mourned each child, but she feared Desmond wanted something she could not give him.

Love.

She had none of that left to give. If any remained, it was for Aiden. It would always be for Aiden. Even now, when he did manage to stumble home on occasion, she'd get a glimpse of the cheeky young man who'd stolen her heart. Not long ago, she'd caught him watching her from the doorway of their home, drowning in his own grief and unable to extend a hand for help.

"I'm sorry, my Sarah," he'd whispered. "This isn't the life I would have chosen for us."

He suffered too. He just didn't have the stomach to withstand it.

Not for the first time, Sarah wondered if she might have been better off dying on the coffin ship. At least, she wouldn't have had to endure the destruction of her family.

Grief, fierce and merciless, took hold once again. She glanced across the street, toward the headstones in the Necropolis. Wind whipped up autumn's dried leaves, making them look like the souls of the departed, flitting upward. There was a sort of beauty to those cold monuments, a deep sense of peace.

Were her children at peace?

Come, Mama. Come to us.

She'd been hearing their voices lately, even though most had perished before learning how to string two words together. It didn't matter. She recognized them.

They whispered to her the moment she awoke. They slipped their little hands into hers as she fought to sleep. They clutched at her skirts, greedy for her affection, and oh how she wished she could give it to them!

Come, Mama.

But she did not have the nerve to follow them into the darkness. She had been spared from the illnesses that had claimed others time and again. There had to be a reason for it. Did God really have a different plan for her?

One thing was certain. She would never discover it sitting in this dark cottage every night, hoping for a passing glance of her husband. Aiden might be content to drink himself to death, but Sarah wanted more, just a few more precious moments of happiness. Was it too much to ask? She was still young and full of vigor.

Desmond told her she was beautiful, that he would be proud to have such a wife. Whenever he spouted such malarkey, she shushed him and reminded him of his place, and she knew it grieved him.

But what of her place? What if she just…walked away from all of this?

A wild scheme hatched in her brain, one in which she left Aiden and changed her name. It wasn't as if she could end their marriage, but perhaps she could just disappear.

It would be hard, but did she really have a choice? Aiden showed no signs of changing.

She could find a job, something to distract her and give her a new purpose. Sarah had heard talk of several schools for ladies in Toronto. One of them had even been run by a Dubliner woman up until recently. She had no hopes of attending any of them as a student, but perhaps she could find some work in one of the establishments as a cleaner.

There had to be more to life than tending to the cabbages and potatoes in her front garden. There had to be more than staring out of the window, hoping Aiden would see sense and come home.

Memories of Mrs. Byrne flitted in front of her eyes. She'd been so happy when Sarah had agreed to marry her son.

She would give Aiden one last chance, for his dear mother's sake. Sarah would march down to the Don Vale House right now, collect her husband and bring him home. And if he refused, well, he'd never see her again.

No one was coming to save her this time. She would have to be her own savior.

That thought in mind, she stepped away from the window and left her home. Her legs shook as they took their first steps toward her new existence. She'd forgotten to throw on her shawl, but hope lit a fire in her heart, warming her through. She walked across the dark road toward the Necropolis.

"God damn you, Aiden. God damn you," she cried, her passion tinged with fury.

The smells from the glue and blacking manufactory immediately assaulted her. She wasn't sure she'd ever be immune to the stench of dead animals and rotting flesh. Aiden, when he did come home, would bring that foul odor into their cottage.

Still, the farther she walked through the Necropolis, the more Sarah was able to forget it. She trudged around the plots, taking care not to step directly on anyone's grave, touching headstones as she went.

It really was beautiful here. The moon cast a soft light over the graves, as if welcoming her into the cemetery's ethereal splendor.

Come to us, Mama.

"Not yet, my darlings." Sarah took a deep breath for courage. "One day, but not yet."

She headed toward the grand entryway of the cemetery and continued along Winchester Street. It was quiet and dark on the plank road now, but it would have been busier a couple of hours ago as the workers from the nearby businesses flooded toward the Don Vale House on the promise of cheap liquor and cheaper entertainment.

As she followed the desolate road around the final bend, lights flickered ahead. Tallow candles illuminated the windows of the simple wooden tavern. Once a dwelling, but a public house for the last ten years or so, it stood alone, aside from a barn for horses and a small shed. Across from it, a small bridge traversed the Don River. The river was swollen due to recent heavy rains. The water levels had risen, spilling over in places.

Raucous cheers and curses emanated from inside the Don Vale. Sarah made her way toward one of the back windows, careful to avoid a small huddle of men who'd gathered out front. They'd probably needed to take the air for a few minutes. She couldn't imagine the air inside was pleasant.

Still, she didn't need to attract their attention.

She peeked inside the window. A boxing contest was underway. Dozens of shouting men surrounded the competitors. One of them, a hulking Irishmen that she recognized, pummeled the other. He landed three vicious punches in a row and the other man hit the floor, blood spurting from his face.

Aiden was right in there with the lot of them up front, his hands clenched, his eyes trained on the men's violent movements. From the way Aiden swayed, she knew he was well on his way to being pissed. It wouldn't be long before he was drooling on the floor too.

Seized by a terrible loneliness, she shook her head. This was a terrible idea.

What had ever made her think she could walk into this building, this den of vice, and convince her husband to come home with her? There wouldn't be any coming home for Aiden, not really. She'd known it when he'd first started to withdraw after the death of wee Thomas. She'd spied the gloom in his eyes then. It overwhelmed her now.

"I'm sorry, Mother Byrne," she whispered. "I don't know how to help him."

Confused and feeling foolish about her short-lived bravado, Sarah turned around and readied herself for the walk back up the hill. From where she stood, she could make out a few of the Necropolis headstones. They stood like sentries, pale and patient in the moonlight.

"Sarah."

Sarah turned toward the voice, her arm hairs rising. However, upon seeing her brother-in-law, Desmond, her heart stopped racing. Thank God it wasn't one of the delinquents from the tavern.

He stormed over to her and grabbed her by the arm. "What are you doing here, Sarah?"

The four men who had been standing near the tavern door stumbled past. One of them looked her up and down and whistled.

Desmond moved in front of her, anger flashing in his eyes. "Move along, or I'll move you." He pulled himself up to his full height and clenched his fists. Desmond was an imposing figure and a sober one, whereas the men were clearly in no shape to fight.

He pulled her away from the tavern, toward the river's edge. He ran his hands along her arms, as if to convince himself she was really there. "Why are you here?"

Sarah wriggled out of his grip. "Same reason as you, I suspect."

He spat on the ground in disgust and paced the riverbank. The soil there was like a sponge. Water seeped into his shoes, but he didn't seem to notice. "I'm done with him, Sarah. You should be too. Aiden doesn't deserve you. He doesn't deserve either of us."

The weight of it all came crashing down. *So much loss. When will it ever end?* "I know." Exhausted from trying to be strong, she gave in and wept into her hands.

"Oh, my darlin'." Desmond rushed over and pulled her into an embrace. He ran his hands up and down her back. "My love."

"No." Placing her hands on his chest, she pushed him gently away. "Desmond, I've told you before. I appreciate all the kindness you've shown me, but I just don't see you that way. You're like a brother to me."

"I don't want you as a sister. I want you to be my wife."

She turned from him. Why did he persist in this foolishness? She'd been very clear. Perhaps she'd been too kind, too careful in sparing his feelings.

Desmond reached for her hand again.

"Stop it. Don't touch me."

"I would take care of you, Sarah. I could make life better for you. I've been talking to Mr. Taylor at the factory. He likes my work. He made me foreman, you know. There are great things in store for me, you wait and see."

Mr. Taylor. Her lip curled. How wonderful to know he'd taken an interest in Desmond. He certainly hadn't taken an interest in her when she'd gone to him, begging him to turn over Aiden's wages to her instead of to her husband. She'd explained he would only piss it away, but he'd insisted on putting the money right into Aiden's hands. "I wouldn't trust your *Mr. Taylor*, if I were you."

"He's been good to me, I swear."

"And what of Aiden?"

"You saw him in there. He'll be dead inside the month, if not sooner. He could barely hold up his head. If the liquor doesn't kill him, he'll find trouble somewhere else. You know he will. Frankly, it would be a blessing. Do you know how many times I've had to make excuses for him at the factory?"

He was right, she knew it, but old bonds were the toughest to break. "How can you say that about your own brother, your own blood?"

He moved toward her. "You're the only one I care about, Sarah. Just give me a chance." He touched her cheek. "Let me shelter you. Let me take you away from all this sorrow and keep you safe. I could give you more children. You'd like that, wouldn't you?"

She gawked at him. She didn't want more children. She wanted her other babies back! Why didn't he understand?

"Please, my darlin'." Desmond held out his hand. "Let me take you home. Let me take care of you."

"I said no!" Sarah retreated, stumbling as she neared the river's edge. The sound of the rushing Don filled her ears, competing with the cheers from inside the tavern.

"Step away from there," Desmond cautioned. "You'll get hurt." Once again, he reached for her.

"Stop touching me."

"Sarah, please. I'm just trying to help."

Help. He would help her straight into his bed was what he would do. She inched farther away.

Come, Mama. Come to us.

Another raucous shout went up inside the Don Vale House. Of all the voices, Aiden's was the loudest.

His eyes wide with worry, Desmond grabbed her by both arms. "What's wrong with you? Stop pulling away from me!"

She couldn't even think when he was touching her like that. She jerked her arm away, but he was holding her so tightly that he tore her sleeve. "I just want Aiden to come home. I just need to see him." She screamed his name, hoping she'd be heard over the din. "Aiden! Come home, my love!"

"Can't you see I'm offering you freedom?" Desmond shouted. "You'd rather pine for the miscreant inside that tavern than spend your days with a man who adores you?" He clutched her shoulders in an attempt to move her out of danger's way.

Tangled up in each other, they drew perilously close to the edge of the river.

"I don't love you and I never will. I'd be trading one prison for another."

"Prison, eh? Well, isn't that grand?" His mouth twisted. "You're no better than my brother." Without warning, Desmond shoved her.

Sarah struggled to find her footing, but the ground was too wet, icy in patches. She fell into the river, dropping like a stone. The water immediately drenched the layers of her clothing, adding weight to her slight frame. She flailed but the fast-moving river knocked her off her feet. She went under once, then again. Each time, she swallowed mouthfuls of the putrid liquid, the runoff from the Taylor factory. It choked her, but every time she opened her mouth to gag, more filth poured in. She went under a third time, chilled by the Don's wintry embrace, and this time she couldn't get back up again.

It was cold, so very cold.

From somewhere outside her body, she heard a cry. It was Desmond, realizing too late what he had done. As he called out in horror, she silently pleaded with the God who had forsaken her so many times before.

Her clothes were so heavy and she couldn't move her limbs.

Before long, little hands seemed to bear her up. They reached into her hair, tugging playfully. They cupped her cheek, filling her with a strange sense of calm amongst the chaos.

Come, Mama.

Sarah stopped struggling and let the rushing waters take her. *I'm here, little ones.*

Desmond Byrne, unable to move, stared at Sarah's limp figure as she went under that final time. Dread filled his soul.

"What have I done?"

He knew he should venture into the water to try to save her, but she'd gone under so quickly. She had to be dead. There was no way she could still be alive.

"Sarah, no!" he screamed into the night. But no one heard him, not with the noise inside the tavern.

He crept toward the water's edge, in case she popped up again, but couldn't see her. The river had swallowed her whole.

He hadn't meant to push her, he really hadn't. He'd just been so angry, so frustrated that she couldn't see the love in his heart. "Why, Sarah, why?"

All at once, he was gripped by fear. What if someone had seen him shove her? He'd surely hang.

Desmond spun around, his eyes raking the darkness, but there was no one there.

"What should I do now?"

Panicked, he did the only thing he could think of. He ran. He tore up the hill toward the cemetery, running as if Sarah's ghost was already nipping at his heels. Racing between the graves, he headed toward the cemetery entrance and arrived at the corner of Sumach and Winchester Streets.

Mr. Taylor's house loomed ahead. *Yes.* Mr. Taylor would help. He'd know what to do. Certainly, he would understand.

He slowed his pace, gulping down huge mouthfuls of air, and climbed the front steps. As he stood in front of the door, he smoothed his hair down and knocked.

After a short time, a tired manservant appeared, wearing night clothes. He looked Desmond up and down and scowled. "What is it?"

"I'm sorry. I know it's late, but I need to see Mr. Taylor. It's an emergency. Tell him it's Desmond Byrne. From the factory."

The man ushered him into a room and told him to wait, sneering as if he expected him to steal something. Desmond perched at the edge of a dainty chair, wringing his hands. Once he was alone, he uttered a prayer.

What if coming here was a mistake? What if Taylor delivered him to authorities? *I should leave. Now.*

But there were footsteps on the stairs and they were coming toward him.

Also in night clothes, Mr. Taylor came into the room. His brow was lined in apprehension. "Byrne, what on earth are you doing here at this hour?"

Desmond opened his mouth to speak, but all that came out was a cry. "I didn't mean to hurt her. I swear."

"Who did you hurt?"

"Sarah Byrne. My brother's wife."

Mr. Taylor stared at him for what felt like forever, his mouth tight. After heaving a great sigh, he poured him a beverage and made him drink it. It was strong and sweet and it helped him calm down. He made Desmond tell him the whole story.

At the end of it, Taylor shook his head. "Listen here. There's nothing we can do to help Mrs. Byrne, and I don't see why you should lose your life over some poor judgment on her part. You tried to help. You offered her a better life. It's not your fault she refused."

"But…"

"It's possible she'll never even be discovered. Her husband is certainly in no shape to notice her absence."

Desmond clutched the fancy crystal glass. His stomach turned.

"*If* her body is discovered in the coming days, it will look like a tragic accident. She wouldn't be the first person to drown in the Don. If I were you, I'd make it clear to anyone who asks that the last time you saw her, she'd gone out looking for her husband. It's the truth, after all. It's easy enough to imagine she might have slipped into the water. Or, quite frankly, that she encountered someone unsavory near the tavern."

She had encountered someone unsavory. *Him.* "There were some men out there."

"See? If anyone should ask me, I'll vouch for you, Byrne. You're the best foreman I have. It would be a great inconvenience to train another. Now, drink up, go home and get some sleep. We'll sort this unfortunate business in the morning."

Desmond did just that. Stunned, he walked home.

But he did not sleep.

All night long, he stared at his ceiling, unblinking. He couldn't stop picturing the look on Sarah's face as she fell, her wide eyes trained on him in accusation.

Chapter Twenty-Three

Later that night, Adelaide stood at her bedroom window, staring into the darkness, contemplating all she had seen. When her vision had ended, at the site of the Don Vale House, she'd almost been nauseous and she'd had to take several deep breaths to keep the contents of her stomach intact.

Sarah had died because Desmond had lost his temper. He hadn't set out to kill her that night. Quite the opposite, in fact. Nonetheless, he hadn't been able to take no for an answer and she had suffered for it. Then he and Robert Taylor had hushed it up. They'd chosen to sweep the death of a poor woman under the rug.

She now understood why Taylor wanted to atone. *Good. Let him.*

But Desmond had never accepted responsibility for what he had done. He might have gone through life regretting what he did, but he'd hidden from justice, and now he was dead too.

Something told her Sarah would appreciate an opportunity to address her brother-in-law. It might even be enough to help her finally achieve peace.

Will approached her from behind, massaging her shoulders. "How are you feeling?"

"Better, thanks."

"I ran the bath water. Nice and hot, just how you like it." He tucked her hair behind her right ear and kissed her lobe. "Want some company or would you rather be alone?"

She turned around in his arms. "I want you with me."

Smiling, he offered her his hand and led her into the bathroom. Will quietly helped her get undressed, even crouching to pull off her socks and to ease her panties down her legs. He disrobed, tossing his clothes on her pile of discarded garments. Gloriously nude, he extended his hand. "Come here."

He helped her into the tub and got in as well. As soon as the hot water hit her calves, she sighed. "This is perfect."

He sat down at one end, and slid her toward him, between his legs. His knees stuck out of the water and she poured water over them so his legs wouldn't get cold. Running her hands over his kneecaps, she memorized their shape. She leaned against his chest, eager to soak up a moment of peacefulness before the storm.

"I need to go back there tomorrow," she murmured. "I'm scared, Will. Scared I won't know how to help her when the time comes."

"It's okay to be scared. You're the bravest person I know, and you're still allowed to get frightened. But if anyone can help Sarah, it's you."

"What if I screw up? What if I say the wrong thing? I want you to be free. I want you to be happy."

"Addy." He whispered her name. "You've already made me happier than I ever thought I would be. Anything else is gravy." He tipped her chin, feathering his lips against hers in the lightest of kisses.

She moaned softly, resting against him once more. With the water gently lapping and their hands exploring under it, she began to feel a measure of calm.

Will kissed the back of her neck. "Hey. Didn't you say you had a bath bomb?"

"Yeah. On the shelf behind you."

He reached around, laughing when he saw the sparkly skull. "A skull."

"Not just any skull. It's rose-scented and it bleeds from its eyes."

"Of course, it does. Are we going to be red when we get out of the tub?"

"It rinses off. Put it in."

He dropped it in the tub in front of her, chuckling at the display of red ooze and froth. "I feel like I'm in a cauldron."

"I know," Addy said, snuggling against him. "Isn't it awesome?"

They sat quietly, watching as the bath bomb slowly disintegrated. Will held her, his hands wrapped around her waist. It wasn't long before he explored the length of her thigh. His semi-erect cock was wedged between their bodies, reminding her of its presence. He brought his lips to her skin over and over, dropping kisses on her spine and shoulders.

Adelaide was glad they'd found a few moments to cherish each other because she wasn't sure what tomorrow would bring. Will's headache had disappeared after their visit to the trail by the Don

River, but Sarah's influence still hung around him. Adelaide slid away so she could turn in the tub and face him. He brought his legs together and she straddled him. He was pale, so pale, and the dark circles she'd previously glimpsed under his eyes were now somewhat sunken. His sharp cheekbones seemed even more prominent this evening. He looked like he needed a good meal, or four, as well as a week-long sleep.

She would get him what he needed when this was all over.

Adelaide caressed his cheek, smiling at the trail of pink water that it left behind.

Will gazed at her, suddenly serious. "Addy," he began, his voice cracking, "I love you."

Her chest quivered with the beginnings of a happy laugh. *He loves me!*

Even with so much going on inside his head, he'd found a way to be brave and open his heart. She needed to be brave too. "I love you too."

"Yeah?"

"Yeah." She crawled closer, needing to touch him with more than just her fingers.

Will curled his fingers around the back of her neck, bringing her in for a kiss. He slid his tongue slowly into her mouth and she tangled it with hers. This right here, this was what she wanted for the rest of her life. This easy intimacy. A passion that blossomed from a look, from a touch, from the knowledge that she was safe. That he was her person and that she was his.

Will grabbed her ass, kneading. She rubbed herself against him, wanton and hungry.

He looked into her eyes and smiled. "I've got you, beautiful."

On a groan, he slipped one hand between her legs. It only took a few seconds. He caressed her there, drawing those leisurely circles that drove her mad, and she fell apart. She rested her head on his strong shoulder, dazzled by each sweet spasm.

"I've got you," he repeated, between kisses. His cheek was hot and damp. He throbbed with need.

She wanted to give him everything he'd given her.

"Bedroom," she whispered.

Will helped her stand, then grabbed the handheld showerhead, removing it from its spot on the wall. He turned the water on and rinsed them both off so that no one would think a crime had been committed there.

They toweled off quickly but were still damp when they hit the sheets. Goose pimples arose on her skin from the blast of air conditioning, but Will covered her body with his own. "I'll warm you up."

They came together, a tangle of legs, arms and mouths. He caressed and teased, until she was ready for him again. He reached for a condom from the bedside drawer that he now used and put it on.

"How do you want me, love?" He palmed his cock.

Addy welcomed him between her legs. "Like this."

Will made love to her unhurriedly that night, deliberately. Often. And even though Adelaide was begging him to stop at the end because her body could handle no more, she knew she would always be hungry for this.

She would do anything to preserve their little sanctuary, their home.

As Will fell asleep later in her arms, she stroked his hair and whispered it as a promise.

Chapter Twenty-Four

They approached the Lower Don River Trail in silence the next evening. Will held Adelaide's hand, while Edwina and Susannah followed them. The sun had already started setting, casting a coral glow over the bushes. As Addy and her sisters set up, readying their handheld recorders and a couple of flashlights, Will said a silent prayer. He'd never really been the praying sort, but this time, his prayer was for Addy, and he wasn't above begging for help. *Please just keep her safe.*

Addy stood off to the side, preparing herself mentally. He had no idea what to expect this evening. He knew Addy would be attempting to make contact with Sarah, but beyond that, she'd been close-lipped about her plans. Her sisters had been quiet too, both of them clearly worried about what the night would bring.

"*She's dealt with difficult entities before,*" Edwina had admitted earlier at Addy's place, "*but this just feels different. I don't know what it is.*"

Will knew. His relationship with Addy made things different. There was a personal nature to this haunting, which meant the consequences could be devastating for both of them if something went wrong.

Once she was ready, they formed a circle. Addy said a prayer of protection and made her address. "I am calling out to the spirit of Desmond Byrne."

Will turned to her, confused. He'd thought the plan was to connect with Sarah. He didn't like the idea of her reaching out to a murderer.

"We're here, Desmond," Adelaide continued, "at the place where you killed Sarah and I want to talk to you. You've been hiding in the shadows for far too long, watching, just like you watched Sarah all those years. I felt your presence when I first entered the house on Amelia Street, even though I didn't realize it was you. Nevertheless, you were there, lurking. Hiding from me, even hiding from Sarah."

Even though the forecast had called for a clear night, a dark cloud appeared in the sky over their heads.

"You never took responsibility for your actions, Desmond. I don't believe you set out to kill Sarah that night, but you did. You let your temper get the best of you. In that moment, after promising Sarah a life of freedom, you punished her for rejecting you." Addy's gaze flitted around the trailhead and up toward the storm cloud. "'Sheltered and safe from sorrow.'"

She shook her head in disappointment. "That's what you promised Sarah that night by the Don Vale House. You swore you'd lift the veil of sorrow that had fallen over her life. You must have meant it because you had those words etched into her gravestone later. And yet, that promise was a lie, written to make you feel better. Sarah wasn't sheltered, she wasn't safe, and she remains full of sorrow. You did that, Desmond, when you pushed her into the Don River, then walked away."

Susannah's head dipped and she closed her eyes. "I feel sick," she said, her face pinched. "No, disgusted. I feel disgusted...with myself."

"Hang in there, Suz." Edwina squeezed her hand.

"Is that what you feel, Desmond?" Addy demanded. "Disgusted with yourself? You should. Sarah was clear with you that night. She felt for you and tried to be kind but you kept pushing. Governed only by fury, you murdered her."

"Noooooo!" The reply shook the nearby trees like a breeze.

Every hair on Will's body bristled. His skin crawled.

There was a shuffling noise on the gravel a few feet away from where they stood. Will turned in that direction, his spine tight with apprehension, but there was nothing there. Nothing visible, anyway.

"If you had really loved Sarah," said Adelaide, "you would have accepted her decision to stand by Aiden, even if you disagreed with her."

"Still love her." Desmond's words were carried on a sigh. "Still mourn her."

"Oh, yeah," Addy drawled. "Well, talk is cheap, bucko. You know what they say about actions speaking louder than words."

The water of the Don River churned behind them. Will had grown up steps away from the urban waterway and had never seen it like this, other than in extreme weather.

Something hid in its depths.

Edwina spoke in low, cautious tones. "Addy, I feel another presence."

"I know." Adelaide rolled her shoulders. "Sarah's coming."

All of a sudden, Desmond appeared outside their circle. Will was amazed as he took in the spirit man's appearance. Desmond manifested as a young man, probably the age he'd been when Sarah died. He wore a sack suit, a pocket watch and a worn cap. He really did resemble Will with his short sandy hair and bright eyes. He was tall and thin but strongly built, with calloused hands.

Desmond slowly angled his head toward the water, his mouth going slack in terror. "I didn't mean to do it."

Addy stopped addressing the spirit man. She aimed her gaze toward the river, and the rest of them followed suit.

From out of the rushing waters, Sarah arose. She walked toward the riverbank, her steps sure and deliberate, no longer held back by the current. Her gown was soaked and her hair hung like damp lengths of rope. She was pale and sickly. Although her eyes were as murky as the water Robert Taylor polluted, they saw everything, and they definitely noticed Desmond. As she climbed up out of the water, parting the shrubbery with her thin fingers, she offered him a smile.

Will had never seen such a sight and he knew he never wanted to see it again.

"I didn't mean it, Sarah," pleaded Desmond. "I loved you. I still do."

Sarah put a finger to her lips and walked toward him. "Sshhh. It's all right."

Desmond began to shake, but he seemed frozen to his spot and unable to move.

Sarah stood directly in front of him. Water dripped from the edges of her skirt and her hair. She was horrifying to behold, and yet Will had never seen anything quite so sad. "You shouldn't have done it, Desmond. You shouldn't have pushed me."

"I'm sorry, Sarah," said Desmond, defeated. "Truly."

"You let them believe I had fallen in, that I'd taken my own life. But I didn't. And when my battered body drifted to shore many days later, you acted the part of the grieving brother. You lived with your lies for decades and when you finally passed from one life into another, you chose to cower in the dark again instead of facing me. No more." She reached for his hand, her eyes lit with an inner fire. "Come, dear brother, to the river!"

Edwina leaned over toward Adelaide. "Should we, um, maybe do something?"

"There's nothing to do." Addy just shook her head. "Desmond and Robert decided Sarah was disposable. She wasn't, and if she needs this to move forward, so be it."

Pulling on his sleeve, Sarah dragged Desmond toward the river's edge. Whereas in life he was the dominant force, Sarah now had the upper hand. No matter how he struggled, he couldn't impede her progress. When they got to the point where the ground dropped off, she angled him with his back to the water.

"Sarah, please."

Sarah didn't reply. She simply put her hands on his shoulders and shoved.

Desmond cried out, but as he fell, he disappeared and so did the sound of his voice. Will had a vision of Desmond falling, falling, falling, as if the river had bottomed out. Even though he figured the image would haunt his dreams for years to come, he allowed himself a sigh of relief.

Sarah had gotten her justice. It was over.

However, she slowly turned around and pinned her gaze on Will. She walked toward him, just as she had with Desmond. "Come home, my love."

Will shot a glance toward Adelaide. "Uh, Addy?"

Adelaide's breath hitched. She clearly hadn't anticipated this either.

Susannah and Edwina moved closer to Will, ready to defend him, although after seeing what Sarah could do, he didn't hold out a lot of hope. The famished look in Sarah's eyes was the scariest thing he'd ever seen.

"Sarah," Adelaide said, her voice shaky, "Look at me."

But Sarah would only look at Will.

"You don't want Will," Addy continued. "It's Aiden that you want, Sarah. It's Aiden that you love."

Sarah reached out a hand toward him. "How could you leave me all alone, darlin'? Please come home with me. We'll be happy again."

Will's head began to pound again, harder than any of the previous times. His brain rocked inside his skull. He wouldn't be able to fight her, not like this.

Suddenly, a terrible coughing noise erupted around them. One glance from Adelaide told Will what it was.

Maria.

"Maria, go to Will. I'll be fine," said Adelaide.

The coughing stopped. Two warm hands pressed on his shoulders. A beautiful floral scent surrounded him, but it was unlike any flower he'd ever encountered. Maria's fingers grazed his cheek. Miraculously, his headache faded.

Addy caught his eye. "I've got you."

She broke their circle and stood apart. Raising her hands to the sky, she called out in a loud voice, "Aiden Byrne, husband of Sarah, I'm talking to you! If any part of you still remains in this place, make yourself known!"

"Are you sure he's even here, Addy?" Susannah asked.

"If he is, this should be the best place to find him." She called out again. "Aiden, your wife needs you. Sarah has been alone for far too long. She misses you." She glanced at Sarah, who was still focused on Will. "Aiden, please. If you're here, I need you to take control of my body. I invite you to use my voice to talk to Sarah. You're the only one she'll listen to. Please, come into me now!" Addy threw her head back and closed her eyes.

Will lurched into action, but Maria held him back. Horrified, he turned to her sisters. "What the hell is she doing?"

"It's okay. She's just inviting a dead man to occupy her body for a little while. She's done this before." Edwina's calming tone was clearly meant to placate him, but judging from the way she kept darting glances toward Addy, she wasn't feeling too great about it either.

"Normally," Susannah said, "she gives us a bit of a heads-up that she's going to resort to this sort of thing, but I don't think she had this planned."

Will put a hand out toward her. "Addy, please don't do this for me. Please." If she'd done this before, did that mean she would just bounce back afterward? Or would Aiden Byrne linger in some way? Either way, he wasn't willing to take that chance.

Even as Adelaide pleaded with Aiden to take notice, Sarah reached Will. As much as he wanted to look away, he couldn't. Her eyes held him captive and the more she looked at him, the less he wanted to look away.

She extended her hand toward his face and he held his breath.

Maria released one of his shoulders and he felt a whoosh on that side, as if she were holding Sarah at bay. Sure enough, Sarah was forced back a few steps.

In the meantime, Adelaide swayed in her spot. Her voice had gotten weaker. "Please, Aiden. We need you. Sarah needs you."

There was a vague roaring sound somewhere in the distance. The cloud that had gathered above them earlier seemed to spin above Addy's head. When she threw her head back this time, she opened her mouth and a mist seeped in.

Will watched in horror. Even Sarah's unsettling concentration was broken. She turned toward Addy.

Adelaide's posture changed and she stood straight, so straight she almost appeared taller. The hollows in her face shifted, giving a new sharpness to her cheekbones. Confusion was written on her brow as she glanced around the area, but as her gaze settled on Will, on Sarah, her face took on an aspect of woe. When she spoke, a man's voice emerged, a deep one with an Irish accent. "Sarah? Is it you?"

The dead woman turned. "Aiden?"

The pressure in Will's head lessened right away, but Maria kept a grip on him. In all honesty, he was glad to have her support. Without it, he probably would have collapsed.

Sarah moved toward Addy. If she saw anyone other than her husband, she didn't show it. Rapt, she reached out to touch his hair, his cheek, his lips. "You're really here?"

"I am, and I'm so sorry, my love. I was lost for so long. I didn't know how to find you." Through Adelaide, Aiden caressed his wife's arm. "I was stuck, a prisoner of the Don Vale House. I didn't know how to leave."

A small building appeared at the edge of the river. Semi-transparent, it had windows that glowed from preternatural candles. Inside, spirits caroused. The sound of distant cheers issued from a half-open door.

"Holy shit," Edwina uttered.

Astounded, Will could only shake his head. The tavern appeared as it had in his history books. The plank road was there, the hitching post, with the Necropolis dominating the landscape in the distance. He'd never seen anything like it.

Aiden ran a hand over Sarah's gaunt face and dirty hair, his mouth lined in sadness. "Oh, what my brother did to you. What I did to you. I'm sorry, Sarah. I was weak. I didn't know how to be strong for you, for our family. I was a dead man long before they put me in the ground. Can you forgive me?"

"There's nothing to forgive."

Maybe it was Addy doing something behind the scenes, or maybe the universe had decided the couple had suffered enough. Whatever it was, Aiden stepped forward into Sarah's arms, and out of Adelaide's body.

Maria must have flown to her because Will no longer felt the pressure of her hands on his shoulders. He hurried over to Addy as well, supporting her in his arms.

"Are you okay?" he whispered.

Her appearance restored, she clutched his arm. "Yeah."

Aiden held Sarah, and as they murmured secrets and apologies to one another, her appearance began to transform as well. The river water and leaves fell away from her clothes. Her hair took on a healthy luster. Pink roses ornamented her cheeks and her teeth became whiter than they may even have been in life. And those terrible eyes, so full of sorrow, brightened. The murky film disappeared, leaving sparkling orbs behind. Anything that smacked of death simply fell away.

Forgiven, his own burden gone, Aiden kissed Sarah.

For the first time in many weeks, Will was free.

Sarah approached him, sheepish. "I'm sorry. I just wanted my Aiden back. I thought, I hoped, to find him in you."

"It's all right. I'll make sure your story isn't forgotten."

She turned to Addy. "I can go now?"

"Yes." Addy smiled. "It's long overdue."

Aiden held out his hand for his wife. "Let's go home, love." She gripped his hand, and they disappeared. Within seconds, so did the Don Vale House, taking all its haunted patrons with it. The dark cloud above them dispersed, leaving in its place hundreds of twinkling stars.

"Funny," Will said. "You never see stars like that downtown, but they're sparkling tonight."

Adelaide simply smiled and held him.

As they collected their things, and walked away from the trail, Will leaned over. "I met Maria."

"So, I hear," Addy said. "She's been Team Will from the start, you know."

"Really?" Content, he draped an arm around her shoulder. "Sounds like we're all going to get along just fine."

Chapter Twenty-Five

"I see you hogging the guacamole, Simon." Noah gave his brother-in-law the evil eye. With the tip of his finger, he tugged on the small bowl of guac.

"Who, me?" His face practically cherubic, Simon tugged back. "I have no idea what you're talking about."

"Now, now, boys," Edwina warned. "I'm sure we all remember the great guacamole wars of last summer. Let's not do this again. There's enough here for everyone."

Simon turned his baby blues upon his lady love. He even batted his eyelashes at her. "But my darling, don't you want this for me?"

Adelaide laughed. If Simon thought that tactic was going to work, he might need to return to the drawing board.

Then again, Edwina was mush whenever he flashed his headlights at her. She called it 'the power of periwinkle blue.'

Funny. Adelaide was partial to amber eyes nowadays, especially the pair owned by the man sitting next to her.

Will moved a stray hair away from her forehead. "I don't remember Simon and Noah being so territorial with the food at our last dinner."

"It's the guac," Adelaide explained. "Susannah makes it so it's addictive. Make sure you get some."

As Will picked up a nacho chip and prepared to dip it in the guacamole, Simon and Noah both gave him a look but it was all in good fun. Adelaide was thrilled to see the group had accepted Will as one of their own. They'd had drinks a couple of times since sending Sarah and Aiden into the light. The three men got along really well, and Simon and Noah had already made plans to include Will for one of their guys' nights out, a regular event that Adelaide liked to think of as a support group for men who loved Darke sisters.

Tonight, they sat around Susannah and Noah's downtown-condo living room, sprawled on the various chairs and couches, munching on appetizers before dinner. Will had planted himself in an oversized chair and Adelaide sat in front of him, wedged between his legs. With his body heat behind her, she felt cozy, especially with him stroking the length of her arm or leaning forward to kiss her.

Susannah grabbed another bag of nacho chips and refilled the bowl. "Will, are you excited for the museum opening tomorrow?"

"Yeah. Nervous, but excited. It feels right. I appreciate you all coming to the event."

"We wouldn't miss it," Edwina said.

Adelaide shot her sisters a grateful smile. They'd been so supportive of her relationship with Will and it meant a lot because she knew they were protective of her. They always had been and, on some level, they probably always would be. She knew she'd always feel that way about them as well. The Darke sisters might all have accepted love into their lives and moved on to do new and exciting things, but they would always be tight. Addy knew she only had to reach out and Susannah and Edwina would drop everything to come to her.

But now she had Will too and the novelty was still causing her head to spin. It wasn't all that long ago that Adelaide had thought love would never be possible for her, or at least, that she'd struggle to find someone who accepted her.

Will not only accepted her, he championed her. She was always thrilled to wake up next to him and there was nothing better than falling asleep in his arms.

"Addy, you look like you need a top-up on your margarita." Noah filled her glass with the lime concoction.

She took a sip. "You're officially my favorite brother-in-law."

"Hey!" Simon pouted.

Addy winked. "You know I'm kidding, Simon."

Simon pretended to wipe his tears. "I don't appreciate you messing with my fragile feelings. You know, Will, it's not too late for you to reconsider this arrangement. These Darke women can be cold."

Will slid his arm around Adelaide's waist, pulling her tight against him. "I'll take my chances."

"We're very happy for you two," Susannah said. "Will had to pass a rigorous series of tests to date our younger sister, you know."

"Yup," Edwina said. "We had to make sure he was good enough for our baby girl."

Adelaide groaned. "Oh my God, stop it. You're all being weird."

"Being weird is our specialty." Susannah grinned. "Anyway, I'm happy to report that Will passed all our tests with flying colors."

Simon arched an eyebrow. "Oh, yeah? What did I score on your tests?"

"The jury's still out on that one." Edwina stole a chip from Simon's plate.

Simon rolled his eyes but kissed Edwina on the tip of her nose.

Noah stood and grabbed a couple of the empty appetizer plates. "I don't know about you guys, but I'm ready for the main course. Simon, Will, want to help me bring the food in?"

Will gave Addy a squeeze and she let him up from the chair. The guys disappeared into the kitchen. The women collected their margarita glasses and headed to the dining room.

"Hey," Edwina said when they were alone. "I wanted to give you two an update. I'm thinking of putting my theater work on hold for a while."

"Really? I thought you loved working for the Shaw Festival," Adelaide said.

"I do, but I think I've done everything I can do in this role. Simon and I have been talking. Things have been going really well at the B&B and I like being there. He's considering buying another property, a fixer-upper. I think it would be fun to work on it with him, to help him run it. Of course, it'll be an old house." She smiled. "Probably haunted."

"You should do it," Susannah said. "And if you need a paranormal investigator, I know a couple."

"Maybe you could find a property that's absolutely teeming with ghosts," Adelaide suggested. "We could probably get a whole series worth of shows out of that!"

"I like how you think." Edwina held up her glass and they clinked them together. "More spooky adventures for the Darke sisters!"

Adelaide grinned. It was fun being a weird girl.

* * * *

Early the next evening, Adelaide and Will left the Cabbagetown Museum on a high. The opening event had been a success. After introducing the guests to the museum, Will had invited everyone to join them out back, where a tent had been set up. There had been beverages and snacks, and everyone had had fun mingling.

He'd told everyone about the history behind the Amelia Street house, including the story of Sarah and Aiden and the countless worker-class people who'd put their blood, sweat and tears into making Cabbagetown a thriving community.

The mayor had enthusiastically congratulated Will and his team on a job well done. There had been a terrific turnout, including folks from local schools and historical societies, members of the public and neighbors, as well as officials from various levels of government.

Just no ghosts, and no one was complaining about that.

Will had been nervous before the event but Adelaide had pulled him aside and had helped him defuse a panic attack.

"What would I do without you?" he'd said with a grateful embrace.

"You never have to worry about that."

Now, as they walked home hand in hand after the event, she marveled at the change in Will. He was certainly tired, but it was just a feeling of satisfied fatigue at the end of a busy period, nothing like what he had been experiencing while under Sarah's influence. The color had returned to his face. He no longer had dark circles under his eyes, and he'd been sleeping well.

"I'm very proud of you," she said, as they walked down Sumach Street.

"Thanks, Addy. I couldn't have done any of it without you, literally. Without your help, we probably wouldn't have been able to open."

"I'm just glad it all worked out for the best and that everyone is where they're supposed to be."

He was quiet for about a block. "Do you ever think about Desmond Byrne and Robert Taylor? About where they are?"

"Yeah, but I have faith that they'll cross over when it's their time. I don't believe in hell. I don't think they're being punished. I think they're just...finding perspective. Most of us hope to gain it when we're alive, but some of us find out later."

"Perspective, huh?" He moved behind her and put his hands on her shoulders. "Well, all I really want right now is to be able to soak in a tub with you. Maybe with another one of your grisly bath bombs."

She laughed. "They are not grisly. Besides, you knew what you were getting into when you asked me out."

"Yup, and I wouldn't change a thing." He turned her around and kissed her, softly, sweetly. "I love you, Addy."

"I love you too."

As they reached the intersection of Winchester and Sumach, Adelaide noticed a new sign in front of the old Taylor house. It said *Sold*.

Addy smiled. Cindy got her sale.

She stopped for a moment outside the house and glanced up toward the top window, looking for Lottie.

"Anything?" asked Will.

"Nope. It's just a house with a lot of history."

The door opened and a family walked out, accompanied by a guy in a suit. Probably another real estate agent. He shook the hands of the woman and the man, as well as the little girl standing next to them, and the family headed down the walkway.

"Excuse me," said Adelaide to the couple. "I don't mean to pry, but are you the new owners?"

"Yes!" The woman beamed. "I'm Harper. This is my husband, Josh, and our daughter, Avery."

Adelaide and Will introduced themselves. "Welcome to the neighborhood. You're going to love it here. It's a beautiful old house." She turned to Avery. "Have you seen the room at the top? It's perfect for a kid your age."

Avery jumped up and down. "That's going to be my room!" Humming, she skipped down the sidewalk.

"You've been inside?" Harper asked.

Adelaide's cheeks heated. "Yeah. I knew one of the families who lived here. They had a little girl too. I think you guys will be very happy."

"That's awesome," Josh said, chuckling. "To be honest, we're heard some stories that this place is haunted."

"Nah. I can assure you there aren't any ghosts in this house." Adelaide smiled, reaching for Will's hand. "That's just a story the neighborhood kids tell. I have a feeling you're going to be really happy here."

"Oh, yeah?" Josh asked. "Are you psychic or something?"

Addy met Will's gaze and they laughed. "You wouldn't believe me if I told you."

Want to see more from this author? Here's a taster for you to enjoy!

Handymen: A Good Man
Rosanna Leo

Excerpt

"I know, I know. I'm late." Michael Zorn tore into the *Handymen* production offices and seized the black coffee the production assistant, Franka, held out for him. "Is Lacey on the warpath yet?"

"Lacey's always on the warpath. Oh, and heads up—apparently our fearless director has info on some *exciting changes* and *new directions* for the show." An exaggerated eye roll accompanied Franka's air quotation marks.

"Crap." Michael took a gulp of coffee, scalding the back of his throat. He winced and swallowed some more. "I should have taken my clients out for a long, drawn-out lunch after our meeting."

"Now, now." Franka patted his cheek and ushered him toward the meeting room door. "You're the star of the show, big guy. Time to face the music."

Stifling a grumble, Michael opened the door. The whole team had gathered—everyone from the cameramen to the makeup ladies. He ignored the many looks and headed to his usual seat, the one next to his brothers and co-stars, Eli and Nick. Eli had the decency to cover his smile, but Nick just chuckled. *Spoiled brat.*

Lacey Styles, their director, had been in the middle of a speech, but had closed her mouth when Michael entered. She waited until he was seated comfortably. Well, as comfortable as he could get in the ridiculous designer chairs she'd insisted on buying for the office. They were so delicate they barely contained his bulk and creaked as he settled in.

As he'd grown accustomed to doing, Michael waited for the zing of electricity he used to feel in Lacey's presence. There had been a time when he couldn't wait to see her, when a glance from her would make the hairs on his arms stand at attention, to say nothing of various other body parts. However, as he sat across from her today, it was as one co-worker facing another. He wasn't even angry anymore. If anything, he felt sorry for her.

"Michael, how good of you to join us." She glanced at her watch. "A whole twenty minutes late."

"Yeah, sorry about that. I just came from another meeting. It ran over."

"Oh." She inclined her head. "I'm thankful you could squeeze us in. Considering this has been our regular meeting time every month for the past year, I can see how it might be hard to lose track."

"Perhaps you'd like to reprimand me later, you know, in private."

Louie, one of the camera guys, hooted from the back of the room.

"Knock it off, Louie," said Michael.

"I'm happy reprimanding you here," continued Lacey. "After all, you're the one who disrupted my meeting."

Michael bit back the comment on his tongue. Had he expected anything less from her? The woman had a flair for drama and sought it everywhere. It was only one of the reasons he'd called an end to their relationship.

"Lacey, when I accepted this job—"

"You mean when the Inspiration Network plucked you from obscurity and made you the star of your own home renovation TV show, fulfilling all your dreams?"

My dreams or hers? Some days, he wasn't sure.

"Hey," Nick piped up. "Michael's not the only star here, remember? Last I checked, the show was still called *Handymen*, emphasis on the *men*."

"I could never forget you, Nick. Or you, Eli." She smiled at each of them in turn, dropping the grin when she turned to Michael. "But my issue is with your big brother today. When I call a meeting, it's not for shits and giggles. We have important things to discuss and I need you to be here, Michael."

"I realize that and I'm here now. But as you may recall, my brothers and I still run our own contracting company. It's because of the reputation of our company that the Inspiration Network decided to *pluck* us. We have our own clients outside the show."

"You employ people to handle your contracting clients."

"It doesn't mean we don't stay in the loop. If a client wants my advice, he gets it. So now that we understand each other, how about catching me up to speed, rather than lecturing me?" He offered her his brightest smile, the one that told her in no uncertain terms he couldn't give a toss about her shits and giggles.

Lacey held his gaze for a moment, her blue eyes sparkling with frost. Lacey alternated between playing the cold Amazon queen in public and the wounded doe in private. God forbid she show some genuine vulnerability or a hint of concern for others. She might like to see others squirm, but he wasn't about to sit and swivel for her.

She straightened her pile of notes. "As I was about to say before you arrived, Michael, the network wants us to explore some new avenues. To be frank, they don't think we're sexy enough."

"Sexy?" Eli asked. "*Handymen* is all about helping people renovate their homes. There's nothing sexy about it."

Lacey's overly bubbly laugh grated on Michael's nerves. "Eli, in case you and your brothers have never looked in the mirror, you're a good-looking group of men. If you stopped to read any of the demographic reports I send you, you'd know most of our viewers are women. As much as they appreciate the show for its helpful do-it-yourself renovation hints, many of them watch because they're secretly hoping you guys might drop your tool belts. Have you seriously never checked out the social media pages? You all have groupies."

Nick's eyes widened with intrigue, proving Michael's theory about him and his brothers. Michael had inherited the take-charge attitude. Eli was the calming influence in their relationship. Nick, as younger brother, had long since landed the biggest ego of the three.

"Really? I need to go online more." Nick whipped out his cellphone and clicked the screen. "Where exactly does one find Twitter?"

Lacey clapped a hand over her mouth. "I swear you Zorns live under a pile of two-by-fours."

Michael glared at Nick. "Could you troll for groupies on your own time?" He returned his attention to Lacey, somehow even more annoyed than he had been ten seconds ago. "Define *sexy*."

"Well, for starters," she replied, reaching into a bag at the side of her chair, "they'd like the three of you to ditch the blue jeans and modest shirts and wear these under some coveralls." She pulled out white sleeveless tees emblazoned with the show's logo and held them up.

Michael's jaw dropped. Someone, in his wisdom, had also included little cartoon avatars of the brothers next to the logo. The tiny handymen each wielded a tool of the trade and had exaggerated muscles. Popeye on a spinach bender could not have looked more ridiculous.

Judging from the gasps next to him, Eli and Nick had also entered states of abject horror. The guffaws echoing around the room must have come from their burly crew members.

Michael crossed his arms. "I am *not* wearing a tank. Especially that one."

"You tell her, bro." Eli looked at the shirt the way he might look at a fresh wad of mucus on the sidewalk.

"I think they're cute," said Lacey. "Come on, guys. The women want close-ups of your guns. You have muscles. Most men would be happy to show them off."

"No offense, Lacey." Nick shook his head. "I'm all for sex appeal, but those shirts look like what fake contractors would wear in porn movies. Not that I've seen any."

"Out of the question." Michael sat up straighter. "Are we done here?"

"Not quite," said Lacey. "Look, I'll go back to Inspiration and let them know you're uncomfortable with the suggested wardrobe. As a compromise, however, I need more energy, more *oomph*. I'd like you to play a bit more on camera. The three of you come off stiff sometimes. Flirt a little."

"Flirt?" Michael rotated his shoulders, stretching out the tense muscles. "But most of the guests on the show are couples. I doubt the men want us flirting with their girlfriends. I sure as hell wouldn't."

"No one wants you to flirt with the women," she explained. "Flirt with the camera. You know. Little asides. Winks to the audience, that sort of thing. Act as if you're speaking directly to the female consumer. Engage her. Make that viewer feel as if she's the only woman in your life."

Eli put up his hand, like a kid in class. "You want us to *make love* to the camera?"

Louie made kissy noises at the back of the room, until Nick silenced him with a crumpled-up paper missile.

"This is insane," said Michael. "When we agreed to host this show, we did so because it would be a reflection of our contracting business. Professional, helpful and efficient. We didn't sign up for some weird TV version of a dating app."

"Look, Michael." Lacey lowered her voice, an attempt to placate him. "Just keep an open mind for now and trust I will do everything in my power to make you all look good. But in case you've forgotten, guys, our competition is not above a bit of gratuitous sex. We're dealing in fantasy here, and if we can't deliver it, someone else will. We can't forget about ratings. If you can help me achieve those ratings in some other way, I'd love to hear it." She paused, letting her words sink in. "Trust me. Have I steered you wrong yet?"

"No." Lacey had protected their interests for the past year, despite their personal problems. The brothers had agreed to do *Handymen* because they'd thought it would promote Zorn Contracting. Truth be told, business had boomed, so much so that they'd had to take on extra help. Still, none of the brothers had embarked on this venture to become Hollywood stars, or even Canadian TV stars. They simply wanted to promote good workmanship and help homeowners recognize the pitfalls of renovation. However, since the show had launched a couple of seasons ago, it had become popular. Apparently, just not popular enough.

"I don't want to let any cats out of the bag," said Lacey. "But I need everyone here to up their games. Important people are starting to watch this show. In fact, someone at the Create Network has even expressed interest."

This time, jaws dropped all around.

"*The* Create Network?" asked Michael.

"Yes."

For a moment, no one spoke. Even Michael had to admit he was impressed. If Create picked them up, the show would be broadcast almost everywhere. This was the sort of development for which the team had been hoping. A broader audience, greater resources and access to better supplies. It was a contractor's dream come true.

He'd be an idiot to say no. As long as the show didn't become tacky. Michael refused to lower his standards to appeal to the common denominator.

Nick was the first to pipe up. "Will Create make us wear tank tops?"

"They're not tanks. Look, forget the shirts for now." Lacey's eye twitched. "I want everyone here to think about how you can bring more excitement to the show, more emotion. I promise I won't ask anyone to do a strip tease. Now, is everyone set as far as the next taping? Our guests are Emily Daniels and Trent Andrews, the couple who want to renovate an old house in Little Italy so they can sell organic soup." Her lip twisted. "Apparently the world is in dire need of more watered-down food. Michael, is your team set for supplies?"

"Yeah. I've been in touch with Ms. Daniels by email several times. She's confirmed all her preferences. There have been no issues with sponsors. We've got all our appliances and hardware ready to go at the warehouse."

"Good. Thanks, everyone."

The crew members began to disperse.

When he stood, Lacey called him over. "Michael, do you have a minute?"

Here we go again. A dull pain flared at his temple. *Stress headache.* He'd been having them ever since the incident at the daycare last year. Lacey's antics only made them worse.

Nick leaned over. "She's totally going to ask you for a strip tease."

"Funny, little brother. Just remember, I know about all the skeletons in your closet too." When Michael winced, both of his brothers looked at him with concern.

"You need to go back to that doctor."

"Eli, I'm fine."

Nick joined in the clamor. "Why are you so stubborn?"

"Oh, because that's not a trait we all share?"

"Seriously, dude," said Nick. "It can't be good to bottle all that shit up. You don't want to drop dead of an aneurysm."

"Thank you for the comprehensive diagnosis, Doctor Zorn."

"Nick's right, in spite of his tragic bedside manner." Eli leveled a look at their younger brother. "You need to talk to someone about what happened. You sure as hell don't talk to us."

"I did talk to someone. It didn't help. Besides, there's nothing more to talk about. Don't you guys have something to do, other than nattering in my ear?"

Once Eli and Nick finally left the room, Michael reached in his jacket pocket and pulled out a bottle of acetaminophen tablets. So he got headaches here and there. Lots of people did. It didn't mean he was on his last legs. He popped a couple of pills and chased them down with a swig of coffee.

When everyone else had exited, Lacey glided over to where Michael was standing, her stiletto heels making no sound on the carpeted floor. She nodded at the pill bottle in his hand. "You've been popping a lot of those lately."

"Not you too. I have a headache, that's all."

"What happened to us, Michael?"

"Exactly what should have happened. We broke up."

"We didn't have to."

"Lacey, how many times do we need to discuss this? You slept with your ex, Alistair. That's sort of a deal breaker."

It wasn't often he allowed himself to dwell on the night he'd caught them, on the sight of their tangled legs and sweat-moistened skin. And when he did now, he barely even felt the acid sizzle in his gut as it had in the moment. Once the initial indignation had worn off, Michael had realized he was only pissed because it seemed like the appropriate reaction at finding another man's hairy ass in his bed.

He didn't really blame Lacey, although he questioned why she'd felt a need to go behind his back. He'd known deep down they weren't right for each other. She might like to put up a fuss, but she knew it too. They'd grown tired of each other so quickly that he hadn't even felt it coming on. Admittedly, the sex had been outrageous at first, but they'd been incompatible in every other way.

"I realize I made mistakes, but even before my ex dragged his carcass back on the scene, you and I had stopped sleeping together."

He wouldn't argue there. At the end of the day, their priorities were too different. Lacey loved gourmet restaurants, films with subtitles and boutique shopping.

Michael wasn't opposed to the finer things. In fact, if anyone tried to take away his favorite pair of work boots, there would be hell to pay. But, when all was said and done, there were just too many differences between him and Lacey.

They occupied different worlds. Now he just needed to work with her and keep his cool, something he didn't do too well.

After what had happened to Jane Ashton, he hadn't felt very calm or collected. He certainly hadn't been in the mood for romance. His failure with Lacey was just as much a case of bad timing as it was incompatibility. "We rushed into things. This whole experience just proves we were never right for each other."

"That's your opinion."

"Hell, yeah. Call me old-fashioned, but I don't think I'm cut out for the swinging lifestyle."

"I'm not a swinger, Michael. I had a…lapse in judgment."

"Among other things." The headache made Michael's tone gruffer.

"Look, no matter what you think of me, we still have to work together. That means you need to cut out the open animosity. You can't arrive late to my meetings and treat me with contempt. Whether you like me or not, we are part of the same team."

"You're right, but I agreed to do this show because it had integrity. Little by little, I see it changing. I don't want any part of that."

"Michael, I have your back, but I also need to uphold network decisions. Our show is doing well right now, but it can do better. You can't call it a day because the network vision doesn't match yours. Think of the crew. People's livelihoods are at stake."

"I don't want to disappoint anyone, but I've built my career providing a superior service. If the network wants this to become *Handymen, Kardashian Style*, they've got the wrong guy." He rubbed his temple.

"Just have faith in me, okay? We'll find a way to make it work, but surely you understand this isn't just about hammering nails into the wall. We need to tug at the viewers' heartstrings and share stories that will make them laugh and cry. We're not just fixing homes, we're changing lives." She dropped her gaze and her long dark lashes swept over the tops of her cheeks. "And for the record, I acknowledge sleeping with Alistair was the worst decision of my life. Let me show you how sorry I am. We could be good together again. You know we could."

"Don't."

"Oh, come on, Michael." She moved closer, crowding his space. Her strong perfume made his headache flare. "Don't tell me you're not even a little bit tempted."

Anyone else might be. Lacey Styles was a sought-after woman.

In truth, Lacey wasn't a bad person, and he knew she hadn't meant to hurt him, not really. If he went back to her, he'd only end up filling her days with frustration. Michael, at thirty-six years old, knew what he liked and knew he wasn't about to change. If a woman couldn't accept him and his slouchy, 'good old boy' ways, then she wasn't the woman for him.

He extricated himself from her still-roving hands. "Lacey, I—"

"You haven't forgiven me. I get it. You're still hurting."

"It's not that I haven't forgiven you. I'm just not interested anymore. I'm sorry. I need to know you understand what I'm saying. We can't have this conversation again. It's time to move on."

"Thank you, Michael. I think I've managed to absorb the message."

It had to be said. He moved to the door and held it open for her, but she dropped into one of the chairs. She turned her back to him and pretended to skim through her notes.

Michael hated breaking anyone's heart, but deep down, he didn't believe it would take Lacey long to get over him. Michael exited the room and let the door shut behind him. Hopefully he'd also closed the door on an awkward chapter in their lives.

About the Author

Rosanna Leo writes contemporary and paranormal romance. She is the First Place Winner of the 2018 Northern Hearts Contest (Contemporary Romance) for *A Good Man*.

From Toronto, Canada, Rosanna occupies a house in the suburbs with her husband and their two sons, and spends most of her time being tolerated by their cat Sweetie. When not writing, Rosanna works for her local library, where she is busy laying the groundwork to become a library ghost one day.

Rosanna loves to hear from readers. You can find her contact information, website details and author profile page at https://www.totallybound.com